For Peter, with love.

A Moment of Silence

ANNA DEAN

ISIS
LARGE PRINT
Oxford

First published in Great Britain 2008
by
Allison & Busby Limited

Published in Large Print 2008 by ISIS Publishing Ltd.,
7 Centremead, Osney Mead, Oxford OX2 0ES
by arrangement with
Allison & Busby Limited

British Library Cataloguing in Publication Data
Dean, Anna
A moment of silence. – Large print ed.
1. Upper class families – England – Fiction
2. Missing persons – Investigation – England –
Fiction
3. England – Social life and customs –
19th century – Fiction
4. Detective and mystery stories
5. Large type books
I. Title
823.9'2 [F]

ISBN 978–0–7531–8188–1 (hb)
ISBN 978–0–7531–8189–8 (pb)

Printed and bound in Great Britain by
T. J. International Ltd., Padstow, Cornwall

CHAPTER
ONE

Belsfield Hall, Monday 23rd September 1805

My dear Eliza,

I must begin another letter to you, although it is not six hours since I sent my last. I have some news to communicate which I think will surprise you not a little.

Miss Dido Kent hesitated, her pen suspended over the page. All her education and almost thirty years' experience of writing letters had not quite prepared her for this situation. As well as she could recall, the rules of etiquette said nothing about the correct way in which to convey the news that she now had to impart. However, her governess had once told her that the very best style of writing was that which gave information simply and clearly without any excess of sensibility.

She dipped her pen into the ink and continued.

There has been a woman found dead here — in the shrubbery — this evening.

She read what she had written, thought for a little while, then added:

It was the under-gardener who found her.

Her sister would wish to be reassured that it was not a member of the family, or one of their guests, who had made the horrible discovery.

Looking at the words gleaming blackly in the light of her candle, Dido thought for a moment how strange it was that something so extraordinary should be contained within the familiar, flowing pattern of the script, looking no more strange than a report upon the weather or an account of a sermon heard in church. Then she continued, her pen beginning to move more steadily as she found herself drawn away from the simple giving of information to that commentary upon men and women which seemed to come most naturally to her whenever she had a blank page before her.

No one knows who the dead woman can be. Sir Edgar and Lady Montague are quite sure that they know nothing of her. They are both, of course, deeply shocked. He, as you may imagine, is very much exercised over "what people will think," and how a dead woman in his shrubbery is likely to reflect upon "the honour of the family name". Altogether, I think it is the novelty of the event which distresses him more than anything else; if only his ancestors — those innumerable previous Sir Edgars who stare at one from dark portraits in every conceivable corner of this house — had suffered the shock before him, then dead women in shrubberies would be a family tradition and hold no horrors for him at all. Meanwhile, her ladyship sits upon her sofa and wrings her hands and declares that "one does not know what to think", hoping, I suppose, that someone will tell her what to think and so save her the trouble of forming an opinion of her own.

Her sister-in-law, Mrs Harris, is quite as animated upon the subject as my lady is languid and has been occupied with relating every shocking detail which she has been able to gather or can imagine — details which a woman of more sense would not give credit to, and one of more breeding would certainly not retail in the drawing room. Her husband, though one must believe he is a sensible man — or at least a clever one, or else how would he have made such a fortune in India? — instead of trying to check her, hangs upon her words and laughs over her extravagances as if they were the pinnacle of feminine wit and vivacity — a very disgusting display of conjugal affection which I think we might be spared from a husband and wife with more than twenty year's married life behind them — and two grown daughters into the bargain.

The daughters in question are, I believe, as undecided as her ladyship over "what one should think" and want to know whether interest, horror or indifference would be most becoming — or at least which Colonel Walborough would find most becoming. Although I think it might be a kindness to just mention to them that neither Miss Harris's pursed-lip silence, nor Miss Sophia's excessive sorrow over the death of "the poor, poor unfortunate woman," are likely to charm a sensible man.

The colonel himself seems to have expressed all that he feels upon the subject with a long, rather dull story which he told us at dinner about a similar incident that occurred when he was stationed in Bahama — at least I think it was Bahama. It was somewhere that has very hot weather and odd

3

diseases. The colonel has not quite that power of narration which chains the listener's attention. And then, when the story was done, Mr Tom Lomax must try to enliven our dessert by calling on Mr Harris to better it, since he was sure, from all he had heard from his numerous acquaintance in the place, that India was "as full of strange and shocking events as ever Bahama was." That sally did not amuse anyone, least of all Mr Harris, who seemed to be extremely discomposed by it; though I confess I liked it rather better than Mr Tom's next attempt at wit, which was to lament that his friend Richard was not at home to "see all this carry on, which by G _ _ is as good as play!" Which distressed poor Catherine terribly and I thought it quite unpardonable of him to draw attention to Mr Montague's absence in that way. I was glad when Mr William Lomax — his father — spoke the only bit of sense we had heard all evening, calling him to order and reminding him to show a little respect for the dead. By the by, I am excessively fond of Mr William Lomax; he is so kindly and so well made and he has a very fine profile. He has also the very great recommendation of being a widower. And, all in all, I am rather sorry that I gave up the business of falling in love some years ago.

Well, I have given you a picture of them all now — except those who, I make no doubt, you most wish to hear of. And I expect to be thoroughly called to order by you in your next letter for abusing my fellow creatures so dreadfully. Remember that I quite rely upon your strictures, for why else do I allow my pen to run on so cruelly, but that you may prove yourself my superior in candour and liberality as you are in everything else?

And as for our nearest relations, well, they are as you have probably imagined them. Margaret is almost as concerned for the health and welfare of the name of Montague as Sir Edgar can be, for, ever since Catherine's engagement to Mr Montague, she has considered the name as pretty much her own. And I daresay Francis feels the same; though I have not seen him. He left on business to town some hours before I arrived here. And dear Catherine? Well, to own the truth, she is too distressed over the business I explained in my last to notice much what happens around her. And yet, if this matter is not settled soon, I fear it will hurt her dreadfully.

You see, there is to be an inquest. It seems it cannot be avoided because of no one here even knowing who the dead woman is. Even the servants — and I have spoken to most of them myself — cannot guess who she might be. Though I suppose they may be lying.

She lifted her pen and smiled wryly at the last words, reflecting that she had not, as she wrote, thought to question the truth of the account which the baronet and his wife had given. She wondered whether to scratch the last words out, but decided that there was no need to spoil her neat white page, for Eliza would certainly see nothing amiss in what she had written. It was only her own strange mind which noticed such things. She continued.

So how she came to be in the shrubbery is almost as much of a mystery to us all as how she should be shot. For she was shot.

Another pause, for such details seemed indelicate. But Eliza would, quite naturally, wish to know, so: give the information simply and clearly and, of course, avoid excessive sensibility.

Well, it seems there was a great deal of shooting here today for the men from the house were out above three hours with their guns this morning. As is usual in these places, shooting is very much the order of the day and the gentlemen regard the birds as a kind of enemy army upon which they must wage a continual war. However, they are quite sure that there can have been no accident, for they were at the top of Cooper's Spinney and there is the hill and the Greek Temple and the ha-ha too between there and the shrubbery.

We understand that the body was not to be seen at nine o'clock this morning when two of the gardeners were on the very spot trimming the laurels, and no strangers are known to have come to the house. No one from the house set foot in the shrubbery all day. I do not believe that this is much of a walking household. The Misses Harris are too much engaged in being accomplished to take a great deal of exercise and their mother must save all her breath to gossip with. Catherine, as you know, lost her taste for gardens when she lost her taste for dirt. Lady Montague does, I understand, usually walk out in the shrubbery at about three, but today she was indisposed and spent the whole morning in her dressing room.

And, by the by, this isolation of her ladyship did arouse the delightful fancy in my mind that perhaps she had found from somewhere the energy to creep out into the shrubbery with one of her husband's shotguns and commit murder. However,

I was obliged to abandon this intriguing idea when I discovered that her maid was with her all the time and the footman visited her repeatedly to take, at different times, logs for her fire, a letter and chocolate.

So, the main point is that no one has been able to give any information about what happened. The constable was here above an hour and searched the shrubbery with enthusiasm; but, finding no murderer concealed among the laurels, he has gone away again declaring that it is a mighty strange business and he "never saw the like of it before, and that's a fact!"

And now Sir Edgar, who is the magistrate here, has told the coroner, Mr Fallows, that an inquest must be held — which will be of great interest to the whole neighbourhood, I don't doubt, for no one can remember when there was last an inquest held here. Poor Catherine. I would hope that such an event, terrible though it is, might at least serve to divert the gossips from her sad affair; but with the woman dying within the very grounds of this house, I fear it may only fix their minds upon her. And . . .

She stopped and this time decided that the smoothness of the page must be sacrificed. She scratched out the last word. Some things were best left unsaid and her fear that the idle chatter of the neighbourhood might connect this dreadful event with Catherine's disappointment was one of them.

She did not want to think that such a connection was possible.

She finished her letter with a hasty promise to write again as soon as there was more to tell, and blew out her candle — for she was a thrifty woman and wax candles were too costly to be wasted. Then she turned to the hearth where — even though this was the smallest and humblest of all the guest bedrooms in the house — there was a fire burning. It was but a small grate, and a small fire, giving little light and throwing long shadows from the old bed-curtains and turning the cloak and bonnet hanging on their peg behind the door into a hunched little fairy-story witch. But it was a fire nonetheless and a fire in a bedroom was a wonderful luxury. Dido held her hands to it gratefully as she turned matters over in her mind.

It was Catherine that she worried about. Which did not seem quite right with that unfortunate woman lying dead somewhere out in the stables. But, she reflected, it was really very hard to care for someone you did not know. One tried, of course — it was a Christian duty to show compassion for all God's creatures; but the truth was that a dead woman without a name was more a puzzle than a grief. And Catherine's anguish was much more immediate. After all, Catherine had asked for her help; she would not be here at all — she would have known nothing about the dead woman — if her niece had not asked for her.

Or "summoned" her, as she had said herself to Eliza when she first received the letter.

For an invitation to Sir Edgar Montague's country seat would most certainly not have found its way to Miss Dido Kent at Badleigh Cottage if the woman that Sir Edgar's only son was engaged to had not demanded her presence.

Catherine had told her father, "I want Aunt Dido." The invitation had been requested, and Francis had sent off an express informing his sister of the precise hour at which the carriage would be at the door to bring her here. No one, least of all Dido herself, had considered that she might refuse to come. For family was family, she loved her niece dearly and, besides, since Francis paid as large a share of her allowance as any of her other brothers, he considered, like the rest of them, that her time was entirely at his disposal when it came to illnesses, lyings in, funerals, house removals or, as in this case, wayward daughters.

Catherine has always been difficult, he had written, and now, when she is at last to make us proud of her, I would not have anything go wrong through one of her strange fits of temper. This morning she has done nothing but weep and shut herself away from us all. You must talk to her, Dido, and, if there is any danger at all of her breaking off this engagement, get her to see sense. Make her see how foolish she would be to give up such an alliance.

Alarmed for her niece's happiness, Dido had travelled in some uneasiness. It was a wretched journey and the final stage, enlivened as it had been by the company of Margaret, Catherine's stepmother, was the worst part of all. For in between a lecture on Sir Edgar's extreme wealth and a minute description of Belsfield and its grounds which encompassed almost the history of every window in the house and every tree in the parkland, Margaret repeated very determinedly, "She

9

must not give up this engagement. I tell you, she must not!"

But, on arriving at the Hall, Dido had quickly discovered that Catherine had no thoughts of ending her engagement. The difficulty lay in quite a different quarter.

"I think," Catherine had wailed tearfully within minutes of the two of them being alone together, "I think that he does not love me any longer."

And then, before the distressed Dido could say a word about the danger of holding a man to a promise when his affection was lost, the girl had contradicted herself.

"But he does love me," she sobbed. "I know he does. It is only . . ."

"Only what, my dear?"

"Only that he has taken a foolish idea into his head about it being better if we part."

"But why should he do that?"

"I don't know!" Catherine thrust out her bottom lip, reminding Dido irresistibly of the three-year-old Catherine who, on the death of her mother, had been entrusted to the inexpert care of her young aunts. She used to look very much like this whenever they had had to drag her from rolling about and making mud pies in the garden to be scrubbed and presented to company in the parlour.

"I don't know," repeated Catherine, her blue eyes shining through her tears and her curls trembling with every little sob. "That's what you have got to find out for me, Aunt." She mopped at her eyes and gave the smile which she had learnt could usually get her whatever she wanted. "You're so clever. I know you can do it."

The fire was burning low. Sighing deeply over the task she had been set, Dido bent to replenish the grate from the basket which was piled high with logs.

It was a curious fact that just at that moment Colonel Walborough, far away at the front of the house in the grandeur of the very best guest chamber, was reaching into *his* log basket and finding it empty. As he went shivering and cursing to his cold bed, the colonel would have been mortified to learn that the shabby little maiden aunt whom he had not thought worth talking to at dinner was comfortably toasting her toes before her fire, secure in the knowledge that there were two hot, flannel-wrapped bricks warming her small bed. But then, Colonel Walborough had had woodcock to kill today; he had not been able to spend any portion of *his* valuable time in talking to the housemaids, or administering cough mixture to the footman, or writing a letter for the kitchen maid to send to her brother in the army.

Dido had long ago learnt the trick of being comfortable in a great country house, and she usually enjoyed her visits to them very much indeed. But this time things looked bad and she doubted very much whether she would look back on her visit to Belsfield with much pleasure. For the story which half an hour's questioning had got from Catherine had an unpromising sound to it.

Things did not bode well for her niece's future happiness, even if — as she prayed would be the case — the late discovery in the shrubbery should prove to be quite unconcerned with her affairs.

CHAPTER
TWO

By Catherine's account, her troubles had begun at the ball three nights ago, the ball which had announced her engagement to the neighbourhood.

Before the ball there had been nothing to concern her? Dido had wanted to be clear about that.

No, there had been nothing . . . Well, almost nothing. Once or twice in the weeks before the ball, Mr Montague had been a little quiet, but he had said that it was nothing but the headache. She had had no reason to suppose he was unhappy in the engagement. And even at the ball . . . for most of the night he had seemed very well satisfied.

It had been a very grand affair and it ought to have been one of the happiest nights of Catherine's life. A memory to store up for the future; a triumph of successful love and beauty.

For Catherine would have been beautiful; she appeared to particular advantage in a ballroom. Her figure was light and graceful; her complexion was clear and delicate and, though sometimes thought lacking in colour, it had at least the advantage of not reddening in the heat of a country dance; and her hair, curling naturally, did not, like many fine coiffures, become lank and disordered as the evening wore on.

And her character, too, was as well suited to a ballroom as her person. In company, with a great many to please and be pleased, the sunniest aspects of her disposition were in full play and the little peevishness was hidden.

Dido could imagine her moving elegantly through Sir Edgar's state rooms, among his hothouse flowers and his well-bred guests, charming everyone; even Margaret, watching eagerly from her seat by the fire with the chaperones, had probably found remarkably little to criticise.

Of the young man on whose arm she would have leant, Dido had a less distinct vision, for she had never met Richard Montague. But the descriptions of Catherine's letters and the miniature portrait that she carried did something to supply what was lacking. She could picture a tall, black-haired man of just three and twenty, with rather fine brown eyes and a face that broke easily into a broad smile.

In short, she imagined him as that phenomenon which, at sixteen, Catherine had declared she did not believe in.

"I do not think," she had said solemnly once after a dance at Badleigh had proved a disappointment to her in some way which Dido could not now recall, "I do not think it is possible for a man to be handsome, agreeable *and* rich. I put it down as a kind of law of nature that he will always be lacking in one of those three cardinal virtues."

Indeed, for several years Eliza and Dido had feared that Catherine had no wish to discover such a paragon and intended to marry — as the phrase went — to disoblige her family. It was a fear that Margaret had certainly shared. And when Catherine — after only a two-week acquaintance — wrote to announce her partiality for Mr Richard Montague, the only son of a baronet, she had acknowledged that her stepmother's approval did rather tell against him.

However, she had continued, I do not think I could give him up now, even for the very great pleasure of offending Mama.

Dido's greatest concern had been for the suddenness of the attachment, but Eliza had foreseen trouble in its inequality. She had shaken her head sadly over that letter. "I fear it will be rather a matter of *him* giving up *her*," she had said. "She is in a fair way to get her poor heart broke."

And Francis himself had admitted that his daughter fell short of any equitable claim to the match by at least ten thousand pounds and a knighthood in the family as near as, say, an uncle.

But, to the surprise of them all, Mr Montague had very soon not only asked Catherine to marry him, but had also gained his father's consent to the marriage with remarkable ease.

It had taken four closely written pages to express all the young lady's delight to her aunts.

He is very kind, she had written — no doubt like many a young lady in love before her — and gentle and it is quite remarkable how we agree upon everything. It is impossible that we should ever quarrel. Indeed we have decided between us that we never shall.

She had found perfection!

And the ball had been her moment of public triumph. For three hours or more it had been blissfully happy. Catherine knew she was in good-looks, Mr Montague was charming and affectionate, and she felt that she had the approval of the entire company.

It was after midnight that the change happened.

In the ballroom the set had shortened a little, but very few guests had yet left. The company in the card room was animated and, under Lady Montague's influence, everyone was playing high. The fiddlers were still hard at work and the french doors were open on to the terrace, letting in the air of a remarkably mild September night and the scent of the last over-blown roses. Catherine had been dancing with Mr Tom Lomax. She did not like Mr Lomax, but, she said, dancing with him had been a necessary attention on two counts: firstly because he was Mr Montague's particular friend, and secondly because he was only the son of Sir Edgar's man of business, and so was blessed with Margaret's disapproval.

As her dance with him ended, Mr Montague came to her.

"I have you again," he whispered as the musicians started a new tune and the set reformed. "I believe even your esteemed stepmother would agree that it would be quite proper for us to dance together again now."

She laughed and leant on his arm as he led her to the dance. Her feet were hot and tired, but her head was light with dancing and night air and the smell of roses — and love. She gazed at him across the set, charmed even by the hair falling down into his eyes, the cravat slightly unravelling.

And it was then, before they started to dance, while they were still working their way up the set, that it happened.

A man appeared at his shoulder . . .

"Appeared? Appeared from where?" Dido asked quickly.

"I don't know exactly," said Catherine. "From among the lookers-on, I suppose. There was still a little crowd of people standing by, watching the dancing."

"And who was this man? Did you know him?"

"No. He was a stranger to me. I had not been introduced to him. I do not even remember seeing him before during the evening — but there were a great many people, you know. I may not have noticed him."

And yet he was a rather noticeable man. Catherine described him as being red-haired and strikingly tall; but with a thin face and a "business" look about him.

"And what, pray, is a 'business look'?" Dido enquired.

"Oh, Aunt, don't be tiresome. You know what I mean. He did not look quite a gentleman of property. He had that worried, fagged look of a professional man:

a clergyman perhaps, or a lawyer — maybe even a medical man."

"A professional man? Like your father? Or have you got too grand since your engagement to remember that?"

Catherine coloured and looked conscious; but she only said rather crossly, "Do you wish me to tell you the story or not?"

"Yes, yes, please continue."

"Well, this man came to Mr Montague and it was as if . . . as if he had thrust a knife into him. He staggered — almost fell. And when he turned back to me, the look on his face was like death."

"My dear, you are sounding like a character in one of Mrs Radcliffe's books. You have read a great deal too many 'gothic' novels."

"And if I have, Aunt, it is because you lent me the volumes!"

"Well, well," said Dido, "just carry on with your story and tell me what happened as simply as possible. This man came and spoke to Mr Montague as he was standing in the dance?"

"Yes . . . No, no, he did not speak. That was the strangest thing. He touched Richard's shoulder and Richard turned to him — and smiled. But the man did not say anything. I was watching his face all the time. He looked into Richard's face but he said nothing."

"Did he perhaps show him something?"

"Maybe . . . But I think not. If he did show something, he must have put it into his pocket very quickly when Richard staggered backwards, because I remember I saw the man's hands very clearly then and they were empty."

"How very strange. And did Mr Montague speak?"

"No — at least I don't think he did. His back was turned to me, but I think I would have heard if he'd spoken — even through the music. You do, don't you? I mean you can hear a voice you love when any other would be lost to you." Fresh tears welled in Catherine's eyes and hung gleaming on her lashes.

Dido's mind was working quickly. "Let me be clear about this," she said. "It was not simply the sight of the man that shocked Mr Montague?"

"No. When he first saw him he seemed surprised — but pleasantly surprised. As if he had not expected the man to be there, but was pleased to see him nonetheless. It was only afterwards, when they had stood together for a moment, that Richard became distressed."

"I see. Go on," said Dido patting her hand. "What happened next?"

"It was all so quick. The man walked away — I think he did, at least. I didn't see because Richard seized my hand and pulled me out of the set. We went onto the terrace and he told me . . . He told me everything was over between us."

Dido pictured the scene. The two of them out in the mild night, the music of the dance they had just abandoned still playing in the room behind them. There had been candles out on the terrace that night; she had seen the pools of wax they had left on the stone balustrade between the urns of roses. She imagined their light playing across the young man's troubled face as he said . . .

"What exactly did he say?"

It was some minutes before Catherine was collected enough to reply. "He said . . . He said that he and I must part because . . . because he was ruined."

"That was all he said?"

"He barely stayed two minutes with me. He said he must go at once to his father. 'I must talk to him,' he said, 'and he will not like what he hears.' He said . . ." Little frown lines gathered over Catherine's eyes as she struggled to remember the words. "He said, 'It is impossible that he and I can remain friends after tonight.'"

"And then he left you?"

"Yes. I waited above an hour on the terrace, thinking . . . hoping he would return. But he did not, and in the morning I learnt that he was gone from the house."

"Without speaking to you again?"

Catherine nodded. "He left this," she said in a flat, dull voice, holding out a folded note. "Tom Lomax gave it to me at breakfast."

Dido opened it and read, in a hasty masculine scrawl:

My dearest Catherine,

As I told you last night, we must part and it grieves me that I can give you no more reasons than I did then. But you must understand that I have broken completely with my father and I have nothing, nothing at all, to offer you. I am a poor man, Catherine. It is right, therefore, that I release you from our engagement. I shall say nothing of the matter so that you may make it known to the world that you have ended the engagement. This is all that I can do for you — except to give you this advice, which I beg you to heed.

Cast me off publicly as soon as you may and leave my father's house. I would not, for the world, have you tainted with the shame that is soon to fall on the family of Montague.

God bless you and keep you,

Richard

She stared in confusion at the letter. "Catherine, this puts you in a very delicate situation. What have you done? Have you spoken to Sir Edgar? Does your father know what has happened?"

"My father knows nothing," Catherine answered quickly. "And you must not breathe a word to him — or to Margaret! You must promise me you will not. I have spoken to Sir Edgar and he ... he surprised me."

"Why? How did he surprise you?"

"He was very calm. He does not seem to be angry with Mr Montague at all. He says the whole thing is a silly misunderstanding and it is best to say nothing about it and it will all blow over. He has put out a story that he has sent Richard to town on business — which seems strange to everyone so soon after the engagement and of course it gets stranger every day that he does not return. I know people are saying that we have quarrelled. But what can I do?"

"You have no idea of where Mr Montague might have gone? Some place that he is partial to, perhaps. Or somewhere that he visits often."

Catherine thought and shook her head.

"And you do not mean to take his advice?" Dido continued gently. "You are not going to end the engagement?"

"No!" Catherine's nether lip jutted dangerously. "How can I give him up when I don't know what has happened?"

"But, my dear, supposing there is, in the end, a rupture with Sir Edgar and Mr Montague loses his fortune."

Catherine glowered at her aunt defiantly and Dido said nothing more on that subject. In point of fact, Catherine was most unlikely to suffer poverty happily; but she was in love and naturally felt equal to any sacrifice.

"Well," Dido said cautiously, "supposing . . . just supposing Mr Montague had done something which, well, shall we say, lowered your opinion of him . . . Something which showed him to be unworthy of your love."

Catherine glowered harder.

"My dear, we must consider that possibility. After all, he seemed to fear his father's disapproval. What was it he said? 'It is impossible that we can be friends after tonight.' And he writes in his note of shame coming upon the family."

The tears had dried on Catherine's cheeks; her little chin lifted proudly. "I will not believe any such thing until it is proved against him."

22

"And probably not even then."

Catherine chose not to hear that remark. "I certainly will not end my engagement until I understand exactly what has happened," she said firmly.

"My dear, your loyalty is very noble, very romantic. If I was reading about it in a novel I should applaud it with all my heart, but —"

"I must know why Richard changed so suddenly," Catherine interrupted. "I must know who this stranger was and why he had such power over him. You must find out for me, Aunt."

"Must I?" Dido echoed irritably.

But, in her heart, she knew that she must indeed. She must find out for her own peace of mind, and because it seemed the only hope for Catherine.

But what could have happened? How could this stranger, with no word spoken, change Mr Montague's — and Catherine's — life? Why had the young man become convinced, in that one moment of silence, that he must break with his father and end his engagement? It made no sense at all.

That task had seemed hard enough. But, since this evening's grim news had broken upon the household, Dido had come to see that she had another as well. Now she must not only discover the cause of Mr Montague's strange behaviour, she must also prove, to her own satisfaction at least, that what had happened between the young lovers had nothing to do with the terrible discovery in the shrubbery.

And Dido's last thought as she settled to sleep that night was of how short a time Catherine had been acquainted with Mr Montague and how much there must be that she did not know about him and his family.

CHAPTER
THREE

Dido and Sir Edgar were the first to make their appearance in the breakfast room the next morning and, on discovering that it was so, Dido felt a strong inclination to walk back out of the door — in spite of the tempting smell of chops and eggs and toasted bread. There was something alarming in the sight of Sir Edgar rising ceremoniously from his seat at the head of a table gleaming with silver and white linen to enquire whether she had passed a comfortable night.

He was a rather well-looking old gentleman of only average height; but there was such an excess of dignity in his silver-grey hair and lined face that he seemed large. And, as he made his bow, Dido was struck by his manner. There was a ponderous air about him; as if his land, his money and his importance weighed him down and made him do everything slowly.

"It is very kind of you, Miss Kent," he said gravely, "to come to your niece at this troubled time. I am sure you are a great comfort to her."

She made as slight a reply as she could for her treacherous fancy was now busily remarking on the similarity that there was between the man before her and the lines of framed Sir Edgars in the gallery upstairs. The resemblance was so striking that she was looking for paint-cracks in his face and, in her imagination, replacing his modern dress with a doublet and ruff. All of which rather distracted her from his words.

"I believe you are aware," he was saying — and all the while watching her closely, "I believe your niece has informed you of Richard's . . ." He hesitated and seemed to force himself to continue. "That is, I am sure your niece has told you about the manner of my son's departure?"

Dido acknowledged that she had.

"Yes." He was silent for so long that she began to think that he had done with the subject. But then, with a heavy shake of his head, he continued. "It is quite natural, of course, that Miss Catherine should seek a sympathetic confidante. Quite understandable. But I hope, Miss Kent, that you will agree with me that it is a very delicate business and not a matter for general discussion."

"Oh, no, Sir Edgar. I understand," she said virtuously. "I have spoken to no one about it." (What she had *written* was, of course, quite a different matter.)

"Ah, good!" He turned away to the window, at which mist was pressing so closely that it was scarcely possible to see beyond the first gravel walk and some stone urns that flanked the steps leading down to the lawns. "I hope you will enjoy your stay here," he continued smoothly. "I hope that the weather will improve and it will be possible for you to enjoy our countryside."

26

"Thank you. You are very kind." And then, with her heart beating with trepidation at her own daring, she returned to the former subject. "Do you know, Sir Edgar, why Mr Montague felt he must leave — or where he may have gone to?"

There was a long silence in the elegant room. The chops hissed softly in their heated dish; footsteps sounded across an upper landing and, out in the misty garden, a wheelbarrow squeaked and rattled.

"Well now, as to that . . ." said Sir Edgar at last. He stopped and watched a dispirited peacock as it picked its way fastidiously across the wet gravel. "The reason . . . It is nothing of great consequence, Miss Kent. A family matter which can easily be smoothed over. And the less said about it, the sooner it will be forgotten. And as to *where* he might have gone. Well, it is my belief — and it may be as well, Miss Kent, if you say nothing of this to your niece — I think it very likely that he . . . that Richard may have gone to town to consult with a physician."

"A physician?"

"Yes. You were perhaps unaware that . . ." Again there was hesitation and a forcing of himself to go on. "That the poor boy does not always enjoy the best of health."

"Catherine mentioned to me that he is liable to headaches."

"Yes. Quite so," he replied. Then, turning to the door with palpable relief, "Ah, Colonel Walborough! Good morning. I hope you passed a tolerable night."

Dido was left to her own thoughts. And chief amongst those thoughts was that Sir Edgar was far from easy in talking about his son. There was something in his manner as he spoke of him: a hesitation, almost a reluctance — as if he disliked naming or acknowledging him.

"Oh dear! Rose, are you unwell?" The clear voice echoed across the gloomy back yard, making itself heard above the sounds of rattling pots in the kitchen and the rhythmic squeaking of the pump in the wash-house.

The kitchen maid wiped her mouth on a corner of her apron and reflected that only a lady would ask you such a question when you were so "unwell" the remains of your breakfast were there for the whole world to see, spread all over the cobbles. But, seeing that it was that nice Miss Kent, she managed not only to give a civil, "Sorry, miss," but even picked up a bucket of fresh water and sluiced away the mess.

"You had better sit down for a moment." Dido seated herself on a low wall, beckoned the girl to sit beside her and studied her face in the dim light that found its way down between the high brick walls.

She was a well-grown, sturdy girl of fifteen or sixteen with a complexion that was usually highly coloured, but at the moment was drained to a mauvish grey. There were dark shadows like bruises beneath her eyes.

"Have you eaten something that has disagreed with you?"

"No, no, it ain't that, miss. I've just been . . . doing a nasty job."

"Oh?" Dido tilted her little head questioningly, then — apparently — received inspiration. "Oh, you mean that poor woman they found in the shrubbery yesterday?"

Rose nodded. "They sent old Molly Sharpe from the village to . . . well, to do what had to be done before they could take her away to be buried. But she ain't so strong as she used to be and she said she needed someone to help — with the lifting and such. So, of course, it had to be me, didn't it?"

"Dear, dear, how perfectly dreadful for you." Dido felt in her pocket. "There now, have a peppermint; it will help stop the sickness."

"Thank you, miss." Rose took the sweet and sucked gratefully.

Dido's little round face puckered thoughtfully beneath the edge of her white cap. "You say the woman has been taken away to be buried?"

"Why, yes, miss."

"But I understood — that is Sir Edgar spoke yesterday as if she would be taken to the inquest."

"But Mr Fallows came this morning to look at her again and when he'd done he said they should bury her." Rose sucked harder on her peppermint. "She wasn't fit to be seen."

"But now they will not be able to discover who she was."

"Nor would they by looking at her, miss. Her face . . ." Rose put her hand firmly over her mouth and prayed that her breakfast was all gone and nothing remained with which she might disgrace herself before the lady.

"I see," said Dido. "I had not understood that she was injured in the head." It was a detail which even the hardy Mrs Harris had failed to discover. But, she thought, it was a shame that Mr Fallows should order immediate burial; there was surely a great deal of information which a body might reveal . . . If only one could get at it.

"Was there anything you wanted here, miss?" asked Rose. "Only I'd better be getting on. There's all the breakfast dishes to be washed and cook'll be shouting for me."

"No, no, you just sit down until you feel a bit better." Dido gave a conspiratorial smile. "You have had a shock, my dear, and you need to go about things a little slowly this morning — otherwise I don't expect you will be able to tell cook and all the others everything they want to know."

"Everything they want to know," the girl repeated with a confused look.

"Yes, everything they want to know about the dead woman. I expect everyone is wondering about her and, after all, you have actually *seen* her."

"Oh yes, yes, I suppose I have."

"And — with you being so upset and everything — I don't suppose you will be able to remember much at all unless people are kind to you."

Understanding dawned and Rose gave a lopsided grin that lit up her grey face. "No, no maybe I won't.

But . . ." The grin dissolved. "But the truth is, miss," she said sadly, "I don't think I've got much to tell, what with her face being all . . ."

"Oh, I am sure you have plenty to tell," said Dido bracingly. "Let me see, what might they want to know? Well, what sort of woman do you suppose she was?"

"I'm sure I don't know, miss."

"Was she a lady?"

"Oh no!" came the immediate reply. "Not with hands like that!"

"What were her hands like?"

Rose dropped her eyes. "Red, working hands, miss."

Dido followed the girl's eyes, which were fixed on her own hands, clasped in her sacking apron: red, cracked and scarred with chilblains. "This woman had chilblains on her hands?" she suggested.

"Yes," said Rose. Then she stopped herself. "At least she had old ones. Healed mostly. No new ones."

"Now, it was very clever indeed of you to notice that. Very clever indeed. It tells you a lot about her, you see."

"Does it, miss?"

"Why, yes. It means she was a working woman, you see; but one that had perhaps gone up in the world a bit just lately. Got a better job perhaps."

"Yes, yes, I suppose it does," said Rose, much encouraged.

"And what of her dress?"

"Covered in blood it was." Her hand flew back to her mouth.

Dido quickly produced another peppermint; Rose took it and sucked noisily.

"Apart from that," said Dido gently when the crisis seemed to have passed, "was it a nice dress?"

Rose nodded thoughtfully. "Yes, yes, it was, now you ask. A very nice dimity it was, with a pretty blue stripe."

"New?"

Rose was thinking hard now. "Yes, I think it was new."

"The dress has made you think of something?"

"Yes. It was when I said that then about it being blue-striped dimity. It made me think because I'd never seen anything like it before and I remember Jenny — that's one of the housemaids here — I remember her saying she'd seen some lovely blue dimity new in from London in a draper's shop last month when she had her day off."

"That's very interesting, Rose. Do you remember what shop it was?"

"Oh, I wouldn't know the name of the shop, miss; that was way over by Hopton Cresswell, I should say, because that's where Jenny's people live."

"Well, well, you have got a lot to tell them all! You can even make a guess that the unfortunate woman lived somewhere near Hopton Cresswell. And I suppose you know roughly how old she was."

"Oh no, miss! Because her face —"

"Yes, yes. I know you could not see her face. But what was her hair like?"

"Fair, miss," said Rose, frowning to remember. "Long and yellow and it didn't curl over much."

"Was it thick?"

"Yes, quite thick."

32

"Were there any grey hairs mixed in with the fair ones?"

"Oh no."

"Well then, she was rather young. On the right side of thirty, I would think."

"Oh yes, miss, yes I suppose she was."

"And was she fat or thin?"

"Neither really, miss."

"A good figure then?"

"Yes. Yes, I suppose so."

"There now," said Dido, getting to her feet, "I should think all that is worth a nice little sit down in the housekeeper's room at least — and perhaps a dish of tea too. Remember, don't tell them anything unless they are kind to you."

"No, miss, thank you, I won't." Rose smiled happily, picked up her skirts and started off across the wet cobbles to the kitchen door. But then she stopped and turned back, biting her lip thoughtfully.

"Have you remembered something else, Rose?"

"Yes, miss, it's that dress I keep thinking about. Funny, it was. But I don't seem to be so good at making out what things mean like you are."

"What was funny about the dress?"

"It was made really odd. Too much stuff in it. Lots of little tucks, and stuff all folded into the seams. I ain't never seen a dress like it. Do you think that's interesting at all? Does it mean something like those other things?" She peered hopefully at Dido's frowning face. "Well, miss? What do you think?"

"Oh? Oh no. No, I doubt it is important. I expect it just means that she was a bad dressmaker and a little bit wasteful. And," she added brightly, "we should not speak ill of the dead, should we? No, I would not bother to tell anyone about that. You have plenty to tell without that. Remember now, a nice rest by the fire and a drink of tea."

Dido smiled encouragingly and clattered away across the cobbles in her pattens. She went out of the yard, skirted the red-brick wall of the kitchen garden, and came, by a side gate, into the park.

She had left the house with the intention of inspecting the place where the woman had been found and it was only the sight of a covered cart from the village bearing its sad burden away from the stables that had prompted her to make a detour into the kitchen yard, in the hope of learning something there.

But now her mind was full and she walked on in some agitation across the park until she came to a little rise in the ground which afforded a particularly good view of the house and estate. Here there stood the broad stump of a walnut tree — one of the ones which Margaret had pointed out to her in their drive through the park yesterday as having been felled in the "Great Storm". It must have been a remarkably fine tree, for even its broken remains had a kind of melancholy dignity. There was an ornate bench of green wrought iron standing close beside it and Dido sat herself down upon it to think.

Before her the yellowing autumn grass stretched away under a heavy grey sky, each blade thickly beaded with dew. The great trees of the park stood out black against white mist and the squat tower of the family chapel rose up above a dark bank of yews. On her right, a well-trodden path led off along the edge of the ha-ha that bounded the shrubbery, and beyond the shrubbery rose lawns and fountains and all the columned grandeur of the house-front. It was a beautiful, tranquil scene which spoke not only of the master's wealth, but also of his care that everything around him should be well kept and present a picture of perfection.

Thoughts of guilt and murder seemed out of place amid such tranquillity.

That the dead woman had been young was very bad news indeed. Respectable spinster though she was, Dido understood the ways of the world quite well enough to see that a woman of that class was much more likely to be . . . acquainted with the son of Sir Edgar Montague if she was young and . . . not ill-looking. That she should have been rather well dressed and that she should seem to have lately given over menial work was worse still. That telling phrase "a kept woman" would insinuate itself into Dido's mind in spite of all that she could do to keep it out.

She gazed at a beautiful, intricate mass of spiders' webs that hung between the iron curls of the bench and she recalled Mr Montague's words: "I must speak with my father." "He will not like what he hears." "It is impossible that he and I can remain friends after tonight."

The words of a young man whose secret *amour* had been discovered?

But no, Dido would not, could not think that. After all, a woman was dead. This was not simply a matter of a gentleman's youthful indiscretion (and again the vicarage-raised Dido proved herself more worldly-wise than most people would have suspected) such as had been passed over and covered up in many respectable families. This was a case of murder. By allowing herself to consider that Mr Montague's strange behaviour and the woman's death were connected, she seemed to be delivering up Catherine's beloved, not simply to moral stricture, but to the very hands of the hangman.

Except, she thought guiltily, I am not delivering him up. I am protecting him.

Her last words to Rose had come unbidden to her tongue, surprising her with their fluency and calculation. For she had believed that her role at Belsfield was to uncover the truth, not to obscure it. But she had moved instinctively to conceal the last fact that Rose had unknowingly revealed to her.

The dead woman's dress had been a puzzle to the scullery maid, coming, as she no doubt did, from a family where women's clothes were coarse and loose and probably passed around among them as needs changed. But there were others among the servants who would have known precisely what the meaning was of those tucks and folds in the blue dimity gown. The ladies' maids could certainly have enlightened her.

Dido had herself constructed dresses for her sisters-in-law in just the same way. One did it when the dress would have to be let out as the months progressed — and the time of confinement grew closer.

Dido gazed out across the park and wondered whether anyone else had discovered this truth. Perhaps not, for it did not seem as if the young woman's figure had been betraying her yet. Perhaps she was the only one to know that the dead woman had been expecting a child.

CHAPTER
FOUR

. . . I have told no one about the baby, Eliza. By which, of course, I mean that I have told no one but you. I hope you will excuse these long letters full of my own concerns; but it is such a relief to tell someone what is in my mind and I hesitate to confide in Catherine when everything is suspicion and uncertainty, for I do not wish her to be hurt more than she must be.

Exactly how much she must be hurt is not easy to judge. I am almost certain that it must all end in a broken engagement, no matter what I discover, for that is the course of action which Mr Montague himself desires. Her acquaintance with the young man has been brief and I trust the suffering of her heart will be in proportion. But how much the scandal will injure her reputation is much harder to determine.

Well, the next thing I want to tell you about is the shrubbery.

I went there yesterday, after I had spoken to Rose, and I found it to be as well cared for as everything else about this place. The laurels are as neatly clipped as Sir Edgar's own side-whiskers. No great branches to collect the rain and be shaken over unsuspecting heads as we used to do when we were children. Here it is all very orderly: gravel paths raked quite clean of weeds, a murmuring of doves and a rich smell of damp earth and leaf-mould. Anyone knowing nothing of what had happened there could pass through without suspecting anything.

However, my eyes were awake to suspicion, so I noticed that beside the summerhouse — which, by the by, is called the hermitage; I do not quite know why, except that Belsfield is rather too grand to have something as commonplace as a summerhouse, which every farmer may have these days — well, by the summerhouse, I noticed that there was a patch of gravel which was particularly well raked, and rather wetter than any of the rest. It looked very much as if it had been washed clean. And then, when I stooped down and looked closer, I saw that the water that had been thrown down had washed traces of a red crust onto the large white stones that border the path.

This was, undoubtedly, the place where the woman lay.

Eliza, knowing that, there was something indescribably disquieting about the very ordinariness of the place. I was not quite frightened, but it was oppressive to stand upon that spot and think that this picturesque little grey building, these banks of laurel gleaming with damp, were the last sights upon which a fellow creature's eyes had rested.

Well, just beside the wet gravel was the door to the hermitage. I tried the lock, though of course I had not much hope of gaining an entrance. For you know how it is in these grand places: all the keys are jealously guarded by the gardeners and only they are able to go about wherever they like. But, to my very great surprise, the door swung open — letting out a faint smell of damp and dead leaves. There was not much light inside because the shutters were closed, but it was possible to see that usual collection of stools and basketwork chairs that fill such places, a stand with three umbrellas in it, and two forgotten sunhats lying on a small table. The floor was covered in dust and dry, brown leaves.

Nothing of interest, I thought, and I was about to close the door when my eyes became sufficiently accustomed to the dim light to make out footprints in the dust. I looked closer. Yes, some time recently someone — or maybe two people — had come into the summerhouse. I followed the track of the feet and saw that two chairs had been turned slightly towards one another. On the back of one of the chairs a cushion had been balanced and bore still the impression of a resting head.

Well now, Eliza, I did a very clever thing. I sat down in that chair and I tried to rest my own head against the cushion. But I found that it was impossible for me to do so and I was able to calculate that the person who had placed it must be almost a foot taller than I am. Was not that remarkably well done of me?

Indeed, I begin to think that, terrible though this whole business is, it has at least the advantage of allowing full play to my genius, which I have long considered wasted in the contriving of new gowns and roast mutton dinners out of a small income; and if there was such a profession as Solver of Mysteries, I think I should do as well in it as any man. Perhaps I should set myself up in town with a brass plate upon my door: "D Kent. Detector of Crimes and Discoverer of Secrets." Do you not think I should do good business?

But, rather than cry my own praises, I shall tell you instead of everything that I have been clever enough to deduce.

First of all, there is the question of when this murder took place. Well, about that there can be little doubt; we are all quite certain that it must have occurred while the men were out shooting. It must have happened then, otherwise the single shot would have been heard and remarked upon, if not by people up at the house, then certainly by the men working in the garden.

So much is certain.

But, Eliza, this has brought me to a shocking conclusion. You see, after most exhaustive enquiries among the servants — and I might add that there is a veritable army of men employed here in maintaining that exquisite order that Sir Edgar demands in his park and pleasure grounds — none of these men are able to recall seeing a stranger here during that time. So, you see, it seems most likely — though I find this hard to countenance, and nobody else in the household will even acknowledge it to be possible — that it was a man from the house who did the terrible deed. Of course there are the beaters and the servants to consider; but they would have had no weapon. Eliza, <u>it was only the gentlemen who were carrying guns</u>.

It is a shocking conclusion, is it not? But I think it must be braved. What was it that Edward used to say when he was preparing for his debates at Cambridge? "Logic is a matter for the head and it is best not to let the heart have anything to do with it."

And I sincerely hope that Edward would have approved of the logic I applied yesterday in my study of the shrubbery.

After I had closed the door of the hermitage, I followed the gravel path beside its wall. This brought me to the edge of the shrubbery and the ha-ha that divides it from the park. I stopped here and looked about me.

The first thing I noticed was that it would indeed have been impossible for the woman to have been killed by a shot fired from the park side of the ha-ha because the summerhouse itself stands in the way. The fatal shot must have been fired from within the shrubbery.

But, as I looked across into the park, I also saw that the little wooded hill known as Cooper's Spinney, which is the place where the gentlemen were shooting that day, begins barely two hundred yards away.

Here the parkland ends with a romantic little Greek ruin, which, it seems, Sir Edgar built last summer. It is rather pretty with its white, fresh-looking walls and fallen columns, though it probably has as much of Greece about it as the stable block; for Sir Edgar has never visited Europe, since England has, as I heard him telling the colonel at dinner yesterday, "always been enough" for him. Anyway, this ruin marks the end of the parkland and beyond it is the rougher ground where the game birds thrive.

Now, looking at the spinney, I thought that one of the men might, just possibly, have been able to slip away while the guns and the beaters were all intent upon the sport and, if luck was with him, his absence might not have been noted. I looked carefully at the distance between the spinney and the shrubbery and I am sure that a man running could have covered the ground in a minute — or maybe two.

And could he have crossed the ha-ha?

Well, yes, I think that he might. It is formed of only a moderate ditch — just deep enough to prevent the fence it contains from interrupting the view from the pleasure grounds — and the fence itself is not high. It does not need to be, for Sir Edgar's park has no deer in it to come marauding in the gardens; there are only sheep and cattle, neither of which are remarkable for their prowess in jumping. Yes, I think a man in shooting dress might scramble down into the ditch and climb the fence without too much difficulty.

In fact, I can say more than that, Eliza. I can say that I am almost <u>sure</u> that someone did just that.

You see, I went and stood beside the ha-ha at the point nearest the hermitage. The point at which it would have been most convenient to cross. And there, sure enough, in the soft mud of the bank, were furrows gouged as if by the skidding heels of boots. And there were marks on the other side too coming down from the park. Someone had crossed there — recently.

So, the question filling my head now is: were all the men of the house out that day? Must they all be equally under suspicion? I must ask Catherine about it.

Which reminds me that I have promised to go with Catherine upon her morning calls; I am to meet her in the morning room at eleven o'clock and it is already just a quarter before the hour. I cannot write much more, but there are yet one or two points that I wish to mention.

First, there is this, rather happier, thought: whoever else might have been a member of that shooting party. Mr Montague was certainly not in it, because he had left Belsfield two days before. So he cannot have been the man who crossed the ha-ha with a gun in his hands, can he?

He cannot have been here on that day . . .

I have been thinking it over carefully. My information on this matter all comes from dear Mrs Harris and I am almost certain that she said the gatekeeper had been questioned very particularly and that she had said she admitted no <u>strangers</u>

that day. A suspicion arises in my mind — this solving of mysteries is very apt to make one suspicious. Is it possible that, either by chance or design, the gatekeeper omitted to mention admitting Mr Montague because he was not a stranger?

I must make my own enquiries about that too.

And now the clock has struck the hour and Catherine will be becoming very impatient; but there is one more thing that I must tell you before I close and it concerns Colonel Walborough.

He is a very strange man. He is large and corpulent and has what I make no doubt our mother would have called a "bilious look". Moreover, he has very large, flat feet and walking does not seem to be easy for him — though I suppose he must be rather more nimble on horseback or he would never have won the high reputation that he has in his profession.

Well, as I was returning from the shrubbery yesterday, I saw a very strange sight. I had just crossed the lawns and come onto the drive in front of the house at a place where it is bounded on either side by a succession of large, high yew bushes. I was amazed to see Colonel Walborough making his way along the drive and, as he passed each bush, peering around it — and into it.

He looked so strange, Eliza! He was perspiring with the effort and he looked rather as a man does at a ball when he has been, by the tyranny of good manners, trapped into a dance against his will.

"Are you looking for something, Colonel?" I asked.

"Ah!" He came to a standstill on the gravel. "Good morning, Miss . . . er, yes, good morning to "ee."

"Can I help you?" I said. "Have you perhaps lost something?"

"Oh, no. No, I thank 'ee, but no."

The colonel, I should say, has a rather strange way of speaking, which it is difficult to do justice to on paper; it is rather like a gallant young fellow of fifty years ago. It suggests to me that he has perhaps not always lived in the best society and has learnt his manners by reading the wrong sort of novels.

He smiled at me and gave an exaggerated bow. "I was just looking for that boy," he said, "that footman. The young one, you know."

"Jack?" I said. "I believe all the footmen are in the butler's pantry cleaning silver at this time in the morning."

"Ah, good. Thank 'ee."

I must have looked as puzzled as I felt because after a moment he added, as if in explanation, "Logs. Logs you know, Miss . . . er . . ."

"Logs?" I said.

"Yes, logs," he said. "Gad! My basket is always empty, don't you know, and I believe it's that young rascal's duty to fill it."

"Oh, I see," I said.

And then he made another ill-judged bow and wandered off. But, Eliza, I noticed that he was not walking towards the house. And I do not believe that it was Jack he had been searching for at all. His manner of peering around and into the bushes suggested a search for something that had been deliberately hidden.

Unless, of course, young Jack has taken to playing hide-and-seek with his master's guests . . .

CHAPTER
FIVE

Catherine was not in the morning room when Dido went there. Miss Harris was there with her paints and her drawing board and some hothouse fruits arranged upon a table — and Mr Tom Lomax was at her side, trying very hard to be gallant. As Dido entered he was entreating the lady to paint his likeness and obligingly turning his, undoubtedly handsome, face from side to side so that she might judge for herself from which angle he might be best portrayed.

"I have told you, Mr Lomax," she said, primming her lips over her slightly prominent teeth, "that I do not take likenesses. I know nothing of the art. It is landscape and still life which are my passion."

"But I will be still," he said. "I will be as these oranges and pineapples and you know it does not matter to me one bit whether the likeness is good or bad, for I only care that you will have to look at me a long while. And I really do not see why this pineapple should be honoured with your attention when it has done nothing but sit upon its dish while I have been labouring this last half hour to entertain you."

Miss Amelia shook her head helplessly.

"Come now," said Tom, stretching his long body in the chair. "Could you not paint a picture of me?" He picked up a cushion, balanced it upon the back of his chair and threw his head back on it.

Dido studied his pose for several minutes — then crept away unseen.

"I think," she said when she had found Catherine in the drawing room, "that Mr Tom Lomax is being very attentive to Miss Harris."

"Oh, as to that," said Catherine carelessly, "I am sure he would happily catch her and her twenty thousand — or her sister for that matter. Indeed, Tom Lomax probably wishes he was a Mohammedan so he could have both girls and all forty thousand pounds. But he is wasting his time, for there is not the least chance of their papa agreeing."

"You do not think so?" said Dido cautiously. "You do not think that . . . well, it might be important to him to keep secret from Mr Harris anything that might be to his disadvantage. Twenty thousand pounds is a great deal of money. A man might go to some lengths to secure it . . ." she mused. "He might, I mean, go to some lengths to silence anyone who could speak against him and to . . . well, to appear respectable."

"My dear aunt, I have no idea what you are talking about. But I assure you that under no circumstances would Mr Harris consider Tom as a husband for one of his daughters. Tom is penniless, you know. It is well known that he is over his ears in gaming debts, which his father has refused to pay."

"Mmm, but he is a good-looking fellow."

"Is he? Yes, I suppose he is. And what do you mean by saying that so earnestly?"

"Just that it is not unknown for a young lady to marry without her papa's consent. Mr Harris had perhaps better take a little care. And Colonel Walborough too, if, as one must suspect, he has an interest in the matter. A man of forty — and that, I think, is being kind to the colonel — had better take a little care if he finds himself opposed to a handsome fellow of five and twenty."

"No, I am sure you need not worry on his account, Aunt. The Harris girls may not be very clever, but neither of them would be so foolish as to give up the colonel and his four thousand a year for Tom Lomax. The colonel may take his pick; he only needs to decide which inflames his passions most: paintings of pineapples, or indifferent concertos." She cast a meaningful look in the direction of the piano stool, which was occupied by Miss Sophia Harris: a short, fussy-looking girl who wore her hair looped about her ears in a way that put Dido in mind of a spaniel.

"Do not be ungrateful," said Dido. "The music may not be quite polished, but it has the recommendation of allowing us to talk unheard." And she looked beyond the instrument to the other end of the long room where a fire was burning and working candles had been lit against the darkness of the day. There, in the circle of warm light, sat the other three ladies, working — nominally at least — upon their embroidery. In fact, Mrs Harris was chiefly employed in relating a long narrative of her own affairs, while Margaret yawned and Lady Montague played with the rings on her fingers with a look of such extreme ennui upon her face that not even the dreadful music and the tedium of Mrs Harris's conversation could account for.

Dido was arrested by the lady's look and began to study her with interest. The profile thrown back wearily against the brocade of the sofa was remarkably beautiful. But her expression, her pose, her whole air seemed to suggest that the morning — the day — or perhaps even the whole life — was a blank.

"How do you like your new mother-in-law?" she asked Catherine after a moment or two.

Catherine shrugged. "Well enough," she said calmly. Then a dimple flashed in her cheek. "But then you know, Aunt, I am quite liberal in my notions."

"Oh? And what does that mean?" asked Dido. She knew that dimple well; it meant mischief.

"I had better not tell you, Aunt. You would find it too shocking."

"I shall do my best to bear it philosophically, my dear. Please tell me."

"Well," whispered Catherine leaning close, even though Miss Sophia's music was now making up in volume what it lacked in fluency, "they say that her ladyship has a lover."

"Oh yes? Who says it?"

"People in the village, you know. I understand it is very generally believed among the tradesmen and shopkeepers."

"I daresay," said Dido sharply, "that there are a great many things believed by the tradesmen of Belston, which you and I would do well to give no heed to."

"Ah," whispered Catherine. "But I have my own grounds for suspecting her. In fact, if you were not being so ill-tempered, I could tell you who the gentleman might be!"

"I have no need to improve my temper, my dear," said Dido calmly, "because I know that you are quite incapable of not telling me what you suspect."

"And I daresay you will give me no peace until I do explain. So I shall tell you: I think it is Mr William Lomax."

"What nonsense!" cried Dido indignantly. Unluckily there was a slight pause in the music just then and her exclamation made everyone turn in her direction.

Catherine giggled.

"And what grounds do you have for making such a preposterous claim?" whispered Dido when Miss Sophia had resumed her playing.

"Well, twice since I have been staying here, she has driven away in his carriage. She *says* that it is to deal with business."

"But you do not believe that it is business she goes about?"

"My dear aunt, what business has a married woman to deal with? And besides, even if she had, my lady is the last woman in the world to be conscientious about it."

"Mmm," mused Dido. "I wonder." She studied the elegant, fashionably dressed figure and the pale face against the dark green brocade. The features were as small and delicate as a girl's and the lines about the mouth and eyes had more of discontent than age in them. She must have married — and borne her son — very young, for she could not now be very much past forty, and she was perhaps twenty years her husband's junior.

And Mr Lomax, though he might have a slightly grave air and what Catherine would, no doubt, call a "business look", was a fine figure of a man and had, moreover, a kindly manner and a pleasing consideration of other people's feelings that must be preferred by any woman of taste to Sir Edgar's excessive self-importance and that devotion to ancestry which made him seem as much a part of history as the dark old portraits that hung upon his walls . . .

Oh dear, thought Dido when her musings had reached this point, that is the very worst of gossip: it has a way of being more believable than discretion.

She was going to pursue the subject, but just then the music began to falter a little. "Catherine," she continued hurriedly, "before Miss Sophia exhausts her repertoire, there are other things I need to ask you."

"Then ask, my dear aunt. I am quite at your service."

"Well, first of all: who exactly was in that shooting party the day before yesterday?"

"All the men from the house. Sir Edgar, Mr Harris, Colonel Walborough, Tom Lomax and his father. Though I do not believe Mr William Lomax was shooting that day. He rarely does; but he walked out with the others and remained out with them all morning."

"And at what time did they return?"

"At about one o'clock."

"I see." Dido considered in silence for some moments.

"Excuse me," said Catherine abruptly, "I will go and order the carriage." She got to her feet and hurried away before Dido could stop her. And the reason for her hasty departure was plain: Margaret had detached herself from the group by the fire and was sailing down the room towards them.

Dido would just then have dearly loved to have an hour to herself in which to think over all that she had seen and heard. But instead of being left to the luxury of solitary reflection, she found herself instead condemned to a tête-á-tête with her least favourite sister-in-law, a situation which she knew was not likely to promote amiable feelings on either side.

"Well?" demanded Margaret, lowering herself into the chair Catherine had vacated — and setting it creaking under her. "What do you think now of this strange affair of Catherine's? Can you find out whether she has heard from the young man, or when she expects him to come back?"

"I suppose," said Dido guardedly, "that only Sir Edgar can tell us when his son will have completed his business and be at liberty to return."

"Oh, don't you give me those excuses! Anyone can see that there has been a falling out and that Sir Edgar, like the gentleman that he is, is covering up for them."

"Really, Margaret, since you understand it all so well yourself, I wonder that you need to ask my opinion."

"Hmph!" said Margaret sourly. "I hope, Dido, that you are not encouraging Catherine in anything foolish. You must see that she is not likely to get another offer as good as this."

"I would never encourage Catherine in anything that was likely to injure her happiness."

Margaret was driven to be more explicit. "You must know that it is very important to me that this marriage takes place. For the boys' sake."

"Oh?" said Dido with mock innocence. "The boys? What boys?" She knew the answer, of course, but she could not help but be irritated when Margaret spoke of her little sons as if they were the only boys in the world.

Margaret coloured and retaliated sharply. "You know what I mean, Dido. Girls who are too choosy over getting a husband have a way of turning into old maids. And I would not have Catherine being a burden on *her* brothers."

Dido winced.

"Aunt Dido, you look out of sorts," said Catherine as the carriage started off up the drive. "Have you been quarrelling with Mama again?"

"No, she has been quarrelling with me."

"That is what you always say."

Dido chose not to answer that. "My dear," she said instead, "would you be so kind as to ask the coachman to stop at the gatehouse? I would like to just put a question or two to the gatekeeper."

"Annie Holmes? But you will get no sense from her. She is a very stupid woman."

"Nevertheless, I should like to speak to her."

Stepping down from the carriage a few moments later, Dido was pleased to find that Catherine was not following her, for she was not sure that she wanted her niece to know the direction that her enquiries were taking.

She stood under the stone arch, where the air was chill with the scent of moss and damp, and waited as the carriage was let through the gates. The gatekeeper herself was rather a surprise to Dido, for she was neither the injured soldier nor the favoured pensioner of the family for whom such a post is usually reserved, but a rather pretty young widow who drew the bolts and swung open the gates with neat, economical movements that were particularly pleasing to watch. On the step of the little lodge house stood a solemn-faced child with large brown eyes. She was perhaps four years old and she was holding a rather fine china doll by its neck.

Dido smiled kindly at the girl and made a polite enquiry about the name of the doll, but the attention threw her into a fit of shyness and she fled to hide behind her mother's skirts.

"I'm sorry, miss," said Mrs Holmes with a bob. "She's usually got enough to say for herself!" Then, as the carriage rolled through the gates, she raised her voice above the echoing noise of it. "Is there anything I can do for you?"

Dido, conscious that Catherine was waiting for her, lost no time in making her enquiry about Mr Montague: had he returned to Belsfield during the last three days? As she spoke she thought that there was a fleeting look of anxiety on the pretty face. There was certainly a flush of colour. Mrs Holmes put a hand to a dimple in her chin, then tucked up a bright brown curl that had escaped from her cap.

"Why no, miss, I haven't seen Mr Montague since he left on the morning after the ball."

"I see. And at what time did he leave?"

"About nine o'clock, miss."

"In his curricle?"

"No, miss. On horseback."

"And could he have returned without your knowing about it?"

She frowned. "On foot he could, miss. He could have come in by the side gate over there." And she pointed in the direction of the chapel in its cluster of yews. "But if he came on horseback, or in a carriage, he would have to come by this gate and I'd have been sure to see him."

"Thank you." Dido began to follow the carriage through the gate, but slowly, with a feeling that there was more to discover here, if she only knew the right questions to ask. Why did she suspect that the woman knew more about Mr Montague's departure than she was telling? She stole another look at her: despite her blushes there was a kind of assurance about her. It was not quite insolence, no, you could not call it that, but there was a calm fearlessness in her address which sat strangely upon a servant.

Dido was level with the high red wheels of the carriage now and was about to mount the step when a different thought came to her. She spun round on the gravel.

"Mrs Holmes," she called. "May I ask one more question?"

Annie Holmes turned back. There was no mistaking the reluctance on her face now. Her lips were pressed tight together. "Yes, miss?"

"On the night of the ball, you opened the gates to all the guests, did you not?"

"Yes, I did."

"Do you remember a man who came here that night? A tall, soberly dressed man with red hair."

There was relief on the gatekeeper's face now; she half smiled. "Would that be the gentleman who came very late, miss?"

"Yes, I think perhaps he did arrive late. Do you remember what kind of a carriage he came in?"

"Oh yes, miss, I remember." Mrs Holmes smiled comfortably and reached down to take her daughter's hand. "It was a hack chaise. The old hack chaise from the Feathers."

"I see. And the Feathers is the inn here in Belston village, is it?"

"Oh no, miss. The Feathers is over at Hopton Cresswell."

CHAPTER
SIX

And Hopton Cresswell was six miles away. Six miles of very indifferent road. It took Dido almost an hour to complete the journey — which was just as Catherine had foretold.

"And what am I to do while you go there?" she cried when Dido told her that she wished to drive on to Hopton Cresswell — alone.

"You can make your calls in Belston."

"But, Aunt, I am not intimate with anyone in the village," cried Catherine, with outraged propriety. "It would be most ill-mannered for me to pay any visit of longer than a quarter of an hour — or twenty minutes at the very most."

"Then I suppose you must pay a great many calls — and walk very slowly between them," said Dido heartlessly. "For I must go to Hopton Cresswell and there is no knowing when I might have the use of the carriage again."

Fortunately, Catherine saw the importance of discovering more about Richard's visitor and agreed, in the end, to the arrangement with so little complaint that Dido was in hopes of only being reminded of the great kindness four or five times a day for the next week or so.

Of Hopton Cresswell's other claim upon her interest — the suspicion that the dead woman had lived there — she said nothing to her niece. The gatekeeper's words had shocked her — providing, as they did, the first hint of a connection between the murder and Mr Montague's sudden departure and, as she travelled along the narrow lanes beyond Belston, she had ample time to worry over it.

Was it possible that the young man's disappearance and the murder were part of the same mystery? The thought could not be avoided.

It would all have been so much easier, she reflected, if she knew Richard Montague. Then she might know — or at least be able to guess — what he might be guilty of. But she had never set eyes on the young man and the accounts that others gave did very little to delineate his character.

What kind of a young man was he? Was it possible — was it conceivable that he had known the woman in the shrubbery? That he had taken her life? Catherine's testimony, being that of a lover, was not to be relied upon, of course. But yesterday Dido had tried to discover what she could about him, starting first with the one who might be supposed to know him best — his mother.

When the ladies retired from the dining room after dinner, Lady Montague had immediately engrossed herself in an intricate game of Patience, which she spread out on an inlaid table by the fire. The Misses Harris, tireless in their pursuit of accomplishments, had taken themselves respectively to their instrument and drawing board, so Dido had had only to signal to Catherine with a little motion of her head to intercept the garrulous Mrs Harris, before she herself stepped over to her ladyship's side and began her enquiries.

It had been heavy work, standing there, almost overwhelmed by the rose-water scent of the lady and with the heat of the fire beating upon her cheek.

Her ladyship was, of course, properly charmed at the approaching marriage. Delighted with the prospect of having Catherine for a daughter. And as for Richard himself, yes, he was a sweet boy. And she believed he had done very well at the university. Or rather well, at least; for young men did not generally like to apply themselves, did they?

Dido had suggested that, at three and twenty, he was rather young to marry.

Her ladyship pulled the lace of her long, full sleeve down over her wrist and twisted a ring about on her finger. "Yes," she owned, "I was a little surprised when I was told that it was all settled. But Sir Edgar says that an inclination to marry early is no bad thing in a young man."

"Did you expect that it would be some years before Mr Montague settled?"

"Oh, no . . ."

For a moment her ladyship looked so very vacant, with a kind of milky staring in her pretty green eyes, that Dido suspected her natural languor might be receiving a little artificial aid. Laudanum perhaps? She had known several Ladies to make rather free with the stuff.

She repeated her question.

"Oh no," said her ladyship vaguely, "I do not know that I expected anything, but Sir Edgar thinks the boy should marry. Sir Edgar thinks that it might serve to fix him at Belsfield and make him attend to the business of the estate. That it will prevent him from always wandering off to town — or wherever it is that he goes."

As she spoke her ladyship turned up a card — one which seemed to necessitate a rearrangement of all the others on the table. She bent over the table, rapidly making her calculations and placing each card into its new position with a neat little snap.

It became impossible for Dido to draw her attention away from the increasingly complex patterns of her Patience. Reluctantly she turned away and abandoned herself to the unwelcome confidences of Mrs Harris.

Mrs Harris was a large woman with extravagant greying curls and plump red arms below the fashionable short sleeves of her gown. She very neatly manoeuvred across the drawing room and trapped Dido upon a corner sofa where she talked unceasingly of how the world despised her because she had once been nurse to the first Mrs Harris, until tea and the gentlemen arrived to distract her from her grievances — and to give Dido an opportunity for a change of companion.

She watched with interest as the men disposed themselves about the room. Colonel Walborough going to Miss Harris's side and Mr Tom Lomax, on seeing that, taking up his station at the instrument with Miss Sophia. Sir Edgar, she noticed was a very dutiful husband, going immediately to his wife to enquire how she felt and had she taken her physic? Though the lady was so far from appreciating his exemplary behaviour that she turned her face away and pulled the rings about on her fingers, hardly giving him two words in reply.

Dido continued her enquiries into Richard Montague's character.

Miss Harris clearly felt that the most remarkable thing about her cousin was that he was, "Handsome. Oh, very handsome indeed. He has beautiful eyes and he moves extremely well."

This seemed to exhaust the ideas of Miss Harris. But Dido was almost sure that as she spoke she cast a significant look in her sister's direction. Immediately, Miss Sophia left the instrument and came to add the highly original information that "*Dear* Richard" was "*sweet.*" And that he was "*really* the most *delightful* man." And "you can have *no idea* how *very agreeable.*"

Miss Sophia was much given to emphasis. If her conversation had been a letter, more than half the words would have been underlined. And when Dido ventured to press her further on the subject of her cousin's character, she showed an alarming propensity for the strangest, most rambling of anecdotes. Dear Richard, had, she cried, been so *terribly sweet* about the rats. Miss Sophia had been *enchanted* by the rats.

Dido was at a loss to know what to say to such an extraordinary declaration. But — and this time she was quite sure that she was not imagining it — there was a nod of encouragement from her sister and Miss Sophia continued.

You see, all the gentlemen had gone ratting in the great barn, oh, two or three days before the ball. There had been a great many rats, you see. And they were to be chased somehow with the dogs — though quite how, Miss Sophia did not know because she could not *bear* the thought of it. So she had been at her instrument all the morning, because there was nothing like music to put *anything* unpleasant *quite* out of her head. Well, when the gentlemen came in to dinner they were all *extremely* vexed with Richard for not playing his part properly. And Tom Lomax swore a *great many* oaths. For she made no doubt Mr Tom had bet *a great deal of money* on his own dogs killing more rats than anyone else's. Well, of course she knew *nothing* about the business of ratting, so she could not say quite what had happened, but it seemed that Richard was to have let the dogs go on a word or a signal or something; but he had not done so. Well, he *said* it was because he had not heard the signal. But she was *quite certain* that that was not the case because he was *so very very distressed* about it.

In short it was quite plain — at least to Miss Sophia's penetrating understanding — that Richard had been overwhelmed by compassion for the rats. She could tell that he was too soft-hearted, much too kind to let the dogs kill the rats. He had let them escape on purpose.

And that was so like *dear, dear* Richard. He was so very, very *sweet.*

All this was run through with breathless enthusiasm while Miss Harris gravely nodded approval.

"He is a dear boy." This was the remark of Sophia's mother, who had followed Dido and now sat herself down beside her. "And what is more, he is a true gentleman. Richard has real good manners; the kind of manners which put everyone at their ease. He does not go out of his way to make other people feel inferior."

Fearing a renewal of Mrs Harris's grievances, Dido took the opportunity of a slight fit of coughing on that lady's part to escape to the table where Margaret was (with considerable pride) doing the honours of the tea and coffee tray, which her ladyship was too indolent to perform herself.

She judged this to be a good opportunity of questioning Margaret on the subject of her future son-in-law's character, since her duties prevented her from answering at any great length.

Between her pouring and her gracious smiling, Margaret gave Dido to understand that Mr Montague was a very pleasant young man. And that "that silly girl" wasn't likely to find a better one.

Dido took her teacup and stirred thoughtfully. "You think that he and Catherine are well matched?" she asked. "You are sure they will be happy together?"

"Oh yes," came Margaret's reply in a voice fit to sour the cream in the jug she was holding. "Very well suited indeed. She has the upper hand of him already. He will do just what she tells him and that suits Miss Catherine very well indeed — spoilt madam that she is!"

The subject of whether Catherine was spoilt or not was an old argument between the sisters-in-law and Dido was about to retort with spirit when she became aware that Mr William Lomax had paused beside her in his way to returning his cup.

"I beg your pardon," he said in his pleasant, gentle voice. "You are enquiring about Mr Richard Montague?"

Dido replied that she was and, Mr Harris just then appearing in quest of coffee, they were able to step away from Margaret's little domain.

"It is very natural that you should wish to know about Mr Richard Montague and I am sorry that your meeting with him has been postponed," he said gravely. "I am sure he is as anxious to meet you as you are to meet him." Dido smiled at this kindly fiction. "But my dear Miss Kent, you may put your mind at rest. He is a very pleasant young man and I don't doubt he will make your niece very happy indeed."

Dido looked into the grey, penetrating eyes. "I confess I cannot help but worry," she said.

"Of course not. Standing almost as a mother to Miss Kent as I understand you did for several years. And now she is engaged to a young man who you have never met. It is only natural that you should be concerned. But I don't doubt that when you become acquainted with Mr Richard Montague you will be as happy in the prospect of the union as all their friends are." He glanced quickly at Margaret, but he was too well bred to mention the ungracious words he had overheard. "And I am sure too," he said in a lower voice, "that the marriage will not divide you from your niece. It will, no doubt, give her great pleasure to have a home of her own to which she can invite you."

This conversation, though it undoubtedly formed the pleasantest part of Dido's evening, did little to advance her enquiries, for she was left thinking less about Mr Montague than about Mr Lomax — how long he had been a widower; whether he had been too much attached to his first wife to marry again; and what a great pity it was that such a pleasant man should remain single.

From these reveries she was roused by Mr Harris, who came to her and said abruptly, "You want to know about Mr Montague?"

"Yes," she said in some surprise.

"Well, I shall tell you. He is not like his friend." He nodded in the direction of the pianoforte where Sophia Harris had now reseated herself — and where Tom Lomax was ceremoniously arranging music on the stand while he smiled and whispered to her.

Mr Harris's weather-beaten face was tinged crimson with disapproval. "Miss Kent," he said, "Montague is a steady, decent young man. He tells the truth and he has a sense of duty: a sense of what is proper. In short, my dear, if you imagine a gentleman as different from Tom Lomax as he possibly can be, then you will have a pretty good picture of Mr Montague."

And with that he walked off.

Considering the results of the evening's work now as the carriage rattled into the yard of the Feathers, Dido could not help but feel that she had learnt more about the people to whom she had applied for information than she had about Mr Montague himself.

Hopton Cresswell was a pleasant village. It had a church with a lych-gate and a green with a broad, yellow-leaved chestnut tree and a fine gaggle of geese, who stretched their necks in a loud chorus of disapproval as the carriage rattled past. The Feathers itself was an old-fashioned house with a creaking sign, twisted chimneys and leaded casement windows — and a bustling yard, which suited Dido's purposes very well indeed.

In just crossing the cobbles to the inn door of blackened oak, she fell easily into conversation with an elderly ostler and progressed very naturally from a discussion of his business ("Running about so fast, miss, I reckon I'll meet myself coming back soon") to some enquiries about the size and nature of the village ("Pretty big, miss, but all scattered about, if you know what I mean. We don't like to live in each other's pockets in Hopton Cresswell") to a few compliments about the prettiness of the place and enquiries as to whether they saw many strangers at the inn.

"Not so many, miss. We're a bit out of the way for folk driving down to Lyme and the other seaside places."

"I see. In that case, you may be able to help me." She took refuge on the inn's doorstep as a boy led past a skittish horse. She smiled her conspiratorial smile at the ostler — a wiry, tough-looking man who was not much taller than she was — and pitched her voice to carry over the clatter of hooves and hobnails which echoed off the walls. "There is a man who I think may have stayed here," she said. "He is an acquaintance of my niece and I ought to remember his name, but it has quite escaped my memory and I do not wish to appear rude when we meet again . . ."

"What sort of a gent is he?"

"A very tall gentleman, with red hair."

"Ah, would that be Mr Pollard? A thin gent with very fine white hands? A university man from Oxford?"

"Yes, indeed, that is the man!"

"Ah yes, miss, I know him. But he didn't stay here."

"Oh? But I understood him to say that he had hired your chaise."

"Ah, he did, miss. But he didn't take a bed here. He was Mr Blacklock's visitor. Stayed with him two or three days and left on the London coach the day before yesterday."

"I see. And Mr Blacklock is . . .?"

But unfortunately the door of the inn was now opened by a maid with a very long face and the kind of nervous bobbing curtsy that made Dido feel seasick. The ostler was obliged to return to his business and Dido had to begin her pleasantries all over again. However, by the time she was seated by a coal fire in a dark, low-beamed parlour and had been supplied with tea and muffin, she felt herself to be sufficiently well acquainted with the bobbing maid to venture upon a question or two.

"Mr Blacklock? Oh, he's out at Tudor House. That's three miles up the Great Cresswell road, miss."

"And what sort of a gentleman is he?"

"Well, now." The girl considered and Dido suspected that she had been fortunate enough to touch upon a favourite subject of gossip. "Well, I wouldn't know, miss," she said with relish, "because you see, I *never have seen him*." She nodded meaningfully. "He never comes into the village."

"Oh? Is he a very old gentleman?"

"Old? No, miss, I don't think he's so very old. But some kind of an invalid, I think."

"And has no one in the village ever seen him?"

"Well now." The girl took a step closer, and a slight flush of excitement crept up her thin face. "Mrs Potter's Kate — she's seen him. She goes up regular with the milk and eggs. Sometimes, she says, he's sitting out in the garden when it's fine."

"I see. But he never leaves the grounds of the house?"

"Ah now, as to that, miss, I don't know."

"But you say he's never seen."

"No, miss," said the girl with the air of one revealing a great and significant truth to an unpromising pupil, "not in the village he isn't. But there's a carriage comes to the house from time to time and it's my belief — and Mrs Potter's too — that Mr Blacklock sometimes goes away in it." She nodded significantly and dropped another curtsy.

"How interesting! Now, why do you and Mrs Potter think that?"

"Because of the way his servants carry on, miss. Young Kate says some days when she goes up there, there's a rare old carry-on — the boot-boy and the gardener kicking a ball about on the drive and the maid standing by laughing and shouting. Now that'd not be happening if their master was at home, would it?"

"Well, if Mr Blacklock is an invalid, perhaps they feel secure that he will not come out and see them."

"Maybe, miss. But he'd *hear* them, wouldn't he? No, you mark my words, they'd only carry on like that if the house was empty." Her voice suggested that this was a matter only a fellow servant could understand.

"I see. How very, very interesting."

The girl smiled, bobbed about like a cork in a storm, and then seemed to decide to tell all. She glanced about the empty parlour and lowered her voice. "It's my belief, miss," she said in a rush, "it's my belief — and Mrs Potter's too — that he might be a-spying for the French."

"Indeed!" whispered Dido in return. "And, I wonder . . . I don't suppose you can remember what sort of carriage it is — this one that comes to Mr Blacklock's house sometimes."

"Why yes, miss, I can. It's a small post-chaise with yellow wheels."

"Do you know whose carriage it is?"

The girl shook her head. "It doesn't belong to anyone about here, miss, that I do know."

"Well, thank you," said Dido setting down her cup and recalling poor Catherine paying her visits in Belston. "I have enjoyed our chat very much indeed. Now, perhaps you could direct me to the draper's shop."

Fortunately, the shop was barely fifty yards from the inn. And before she had even climbed the three brick steps and set the merry little bell jangling on its wire behind the door, Dido knew that she had found the right establishment. For there in the small bow window, between a remarkably ugly puce bonnet and an olive green shawl, was a large roll of blue dimity dress material.

The inside of the little shop smelt of leather and newly cut cloth and it was packed from floor to ceiling with everything that the folk of Hopton Cresswell might wish to wear: from cards of ribbon to shelves full of pattens, bonnets on wire stands and parcels of gloves wrapped in brown paper, tied with hairy string and bearing labels like *men's beavers* and *York tan*.

Behind the counter, squeezed into the smallest of possible spaces under the crowding shelves, was an elderly woman who wore an old, well-mended lace cap and an air of faded gentility. She was not, unfortunately, inclined to chat. All Dido's attempts at conversation met with short discouraging replies. And, as she took the blue cloth from the window and laid it on the counter, she scowled darkly at it as if she held a grudge against it.

70

Dido pulled off a glove and felt the quality of the stuff as her mother had long ago taught her to do. It surprised her. In the window it had looked like good cloth; close to it was coarser than she had expected. Almost — but not quite — what her mother would have dismissed as "maid's stuff". And, she thought, as she pretended to consider buying, there was something else that was strange. The housemaid from Belsfield had seen this cloth in the window last month, so it had been on offer for at least so long. But the roll was still fat — no more than one dress length could have been cut from it.

"I do not quite know," she said doubtingly, rubbing a corner of the blue cotton between her finger and thumb. "It is not such good quality as I thought."

"It is but three shillings a yard," said the woman with a deep sigh. "If you wish, I can show you some better stuff."

"No, wait a moment." Dido laid a hand across the roll to prevent it being removed. There was something in the woman's manner which suggested that she had heard the same complaint many times before. So this was perhaps why she disliked the blue cloth. It was too poor for gentry: too good for servants. Unsaleable.

And yet it was not quite unsaleable: one length had been sold. Yes, one length had certainly been sold. Looking closely at the end, she could see where the shears had slashed through; a long blue thread came loose upon her finger. But to whom had that length been sold?

Since the shopkeeper was clearly no gossip, strategy alone would get her the information she required.

"I wonder . . ." she began thoughtfully. "A friend who is unwell has asked me to look about for stuff for the Christmas dole in her household. Now I wonder . . ." turning the end of the blue cloth over in her hand, "I wonder whether this might do for the upper servants . . ."

The elderly woman's manner changed rapidly at the prospect of selling a great deal of an unpopular commodity.

"Why yes, madam, it might do very well." For a moment her look of pale refinement was swallowed up in eager calculation. "And if your friend was to buy, say, more than twenty yards of the stuff, I might be able to see my way to only charging her two and six a yard."

"Oh, that is kind! Now let me see. What kind of woman might this stuff be suited to?" She thought of those hands with the healed chilblains. A working woman who had achieved a better post? "It might perhaps do for the cook," she mused. "And then there is the upper housemaid." As she named each post doubtfully she studied the shopkeeper's face hoping for a response or a word of encouragement; but she received nothing but a small nod. She began to wonder how large she could make her friend's imaginary establishment.

"And maybe it would do for the housekeeper."

That brought an encouraging little smile.

"Mmm, now I wonder about the housekeeper," pursued Dido — and she was beginning to rather enjoy

72

her own inventiveness. "She really is a most superior woman, you see, and she has been in my friend's employ for nearly twenty years. I would not wish to offend her."

"Oh, I don't think she would be offended, madam. I think she'd be pleased to get this dimity."

"Do you truly think so?"

"Oh yes, I'm sure she would. You see, Miss Wallis — that's Mr Blacklock's housekeeper — she bought some for herself just a few weeks ago. And very pleased she was with it, I assure you."

CHAPTER
SEVEN

. . . And so, you see, Eliza, I am now convinced that the dead woman was actually housekeeper in the house where Mr Montague's mysterious visitor stayed. This brings Mr Montague dangerously close to the murder and I must own that I rather wish I had not discovered it. It has already lost me Catherine's favour; she has hardly spoken to me since I told her about it. Of course, it was raining heavily when I reached Belston again, and she assures me that her yellow bonnet is now quite ruined because I was so late in returning with the carriage. But I think that my worst offence lies in mistaking her instructions. When she said that I must find out what was happening here, she did not, of course, mean that I must find out just anything, but that I must discover things that pleased her.

How foolish of me to misunderstand.

However, as somebody says somewhere in Shakespeare — and I believe it is in connection with a murder — "what is done cannot be undone." And I certainly cannot undo my morning's work, nor cease to know what I know. I believe that all I can do now is to carry on my enquiries and discover what I may. Though I shall try not to tell Catherine any more until I am quite certain of what has happened here. Perhaps it will all yet work out well and I will discover a solution that Madam

Catherine approves. And if not — well, I shall at least have the comfort of knowing that I have saved her from an unfortunate alliance — and, though she may hate me for the rest of her life, she will no doubt recover from the loss of the young man within a few months.

For what, after all, is this "love", Eliza, which can be supposed to arise from such very slight acquaintance and which is often described as being felt before two words have been exchanged with the object? Any girl is authorised to say she "loves" a man she has danced a few dances with and sat beside during a half-dozen dinners. I doubt whether Catherine has ever conversed with Mr Montague upon a serious subject . . .

But this is quite by the by and I must be wearying you with my strange ideas — and with telling over all the events of my day. But truly I feel that I must tell it all, for I do not know what is of importance and what is not. It is getting late now and if I do not finish soon the bricks in my bed will be cold. Rose has brought me three bricks tonight and I expect to be very snug indeed. It seems that she has had an extremely pleasant day, sitting in the housekeeper's room and telling her story.

But, before I close, I shall lay before you all the little unconnected questions which keep returning to my mind, in the hope that if I communicate them to you, they will not trouble me so much as to keep me from sleeping. Here they are:

Firstly (and maybe this is not such a very little question), there is the matter which has long puzzled us, and which has particularly troubled me since I have become better acquainted with Belsfield and its ways: why has such a man as Sir Edgar — one who sets more store upon dignity and ancestry than anything else — promoted the match between his son and Catherine — a girl of small fortune and no alliance at all?

Second: why does it pain Sir Edgar to talk about his son?

Third: why did Annie Holmes look so uncomfortable when I asked her if she had seen Mr Montague?

Fourth: why has Annie Holmes' daughter got such a costly doll?

Fifth: why does Lady Montague seem so languid and yet play such difficult games of Patience? One can, after all, play simple undemanding forms of Patience. When Catherine said this morning that her ladyship was the last woman in the world to be conscientious about business, it occurred to me that she was wrong — that my lady might indeed be very conscientious about something that interested her. And yet she chooses to be so very supine that one almost forgets she is there.

Sixth: is Mr Tom Lomax up to no good?

Seventh: what do the constant looks passing between the Misses Harris signify? They make me uneasy and make me suppose that they have some secret and are determined to play a part or ensure that they tell a story correctly.

And lastly: what exactly was the colonel looking for in the garden yesterday morning?

If you have any answers to offer to these questions, then I hope you will write to me straight away; but I suspect that you will think me ridiculous for worrying over trifles. I cannot help myself though, Eliza, for I believe that the very air of this place breathes suspicion. It seems to be a house of secrets and I see mystery and intrigue wherever I turn.

*   *   *

It rained very heavily during that night, but the morning showed a blue and white sky with raindrops gleaming on the storm-battered roses of the terrace and puddles shining in the worn hollows of the lawn steps.

All the gentlemen were gone to the inquest and the ladies were left with nothing to do but to settle the verdict among themselves without the inconvenience of considering any evidence. By about three o'clock Dido had become weary of their speculations, which ranged freely over burglars and gypsies and highwaymen without any regard for what was probable, or even possible, and she announced her intention of walking into Belston village.

"You will be ankle-deep in mud," cried Catherine.

"I shall wear my pattens and my old pelisse."

Catherine looked pained and lowered her voice to a hissing whisper. "Aunt Dido, no one but maids and farmers' wives wear pattens now!" She glanced quickly around the comfortable room and its elegant inhabitants. "Do you mean to shame me in front of everyone?"

"No, my dear," said Dido calmly, "I only mean to stop my shoes being spoilt by the dirt."

"Well, I tell you honestly that in that shabby pelisse and pattens, you will look like a servant."

"If that is so, you will not wish to accompany me?"

For answer Catherine turned away and picked up some needlework. (Which Dido considered to be a mark of how deep her displeasure was; for it must be an extreme emotion which could make Catherine willingly open her work-box and sew.)

Unfortunately for Dido, who had been counting upon a solitary walk, Mrs Harris did not shrink from the shame of being seen in company with a woman wearing pattens. She had a bit of ribbon she wanted to match at the milliner's and she was sure that an airing would "set her up nicely."

"For, would you believe, I have not stirred from the house these last two days, Miss Kent," she said comfortably as they walked up the drive, "and to own the truth, my dear, it doesn't suit my digestion to be always sitting down. Doesn't suit it at all."

Dido was saved from any further details of Mrs Harris's digestion by the servant's dinner bell, which rang out from the little tower above the stables just then, and when speech was again possible she began to remark with energy upon the pleasantness of the afternoon. But Mrs Harris was one of those women to whom the notion of friendliness is quite inseparable from confidences and who are determined to demonstrate their regard by sharing the most intimate details of their lives. She was, with the best will in the world, forever boring and embarrassing her most favoured companions and, since she had taken rather a fancy to Dido, it was not long before praise of the day had proceeded to her hope that her eldest daughter would be able to walk out with the colonel later in the afternoon, and that led very naturally to her other hopes upon the colonel.

"Just between ourselves, my dear, I think Amelia will be disappointed if he does not come to the point during this visit. Poor girl, she will be three and twenty next month."

"The gentleman does seem to be very attentive . . ."

"Oh, my dear, he is! He is very attentive and quite struck with Melia, I am sure. Though I confess I am rather surprised it is her and not Sophie. For he has been very attentive to her too and, of course, he shares her passion for music. But then, there is no understanding love, is there, Miss Kent?" she said with an arch smile.

Dido agreed that there was not.

"Well, I don't mind telling you, that I shall be heartily glad to see either one of them settled with the colonel, for I don't know quite why it is, but there seems to be a little difficulty. Not that there is any shortage of beaux — but somehow it seems so difficult to make them come to the point. I don't know why it should be. They are dear girls and so very accomplished and, bless them, they try as hard as any mother could wish. And they are certainly pretty . . . Well they are, are they not, Miss Kent? I don't think a mother's pride is blinding me, is it?"

"Oh no," said Dido civilly. "They are pretty girls." And that, she reflected was not quite a lie. The Misses Harris were, as the saying went, "pretty enough". Certainly they were more than pretty enough for girls who had twenty thousand pounds apiece. Pretty enough, under those circumstances, to bring any reasonable man "to the point". Or so one would have supposed. It crossed her mind that "the little difficulty" might lie with the mother — her manner perhaps? Or

79

her low origins? But gentlemen were not usually so fastidious — not when twenty thousand pounds was at stake.

"And it is such a compliment to the girls," continued Mrs Harris. "Such a compliment that the colonel should have seemed to quite make up his mind to have one of them as soon as he met with them here two weeks ago. For you must understand, my dear, that the colonel does not generally fall in love. He is well known for not doing so. Indeed, I once overheard the gentlemen talking about him — you know how gentlemen talk in those unreserved moments when they think that there are no ladies present — well, from what I overheard they were all quite sure that Colonel Walborough would never marry. That he had no wish to do so at all and was quite set against the idea. And bless me! I remember clearly how Mr H struck the table — as he does when he is very sure of something — and he cried, 'No, no, Walborough is not interested in the ladies. His interests take quite a different direction.' And all the gentlemen laughed and laughed! Which I thought was strange, for I do not see why it should amuse them so much that the man should be too devoted to his career and like his own company too well to marry. But there is no accounting for gentlemen's jokes, is there, Miss Kent?"

"No, indeed, there is not," agreed Dido, who was more concerned with the colonel's recent change of heart than impenetrable masculine humour. "It is quite remarkable, is it not," she said, "that he should now have decided to marry after all?"

"Oh yes, my dear, it is," exclaimed Mrs Harris, her pink cheeks glowing in triumph. "And so romantic, don't you think? Why, I heard him telling Melia that he had waited because he had not yet seen the woman he could be happy with — which I thought was very charming. Though, now I think of it, it was Sophie he said that to, because it was before he had settled on Melia, you see. 'Well,' he said, 'I should have married years ago if I had been so fortunate as to make the acquaintance of the *right* lady.' Which was very pretty."

"Very pretty indeed! I congratulate you; he must be very much in love."

"And a very comfortable establishment it will be for Melia. For I don't mind telling you, Miss Kent, though I wouldn't mention it in general, that the colonel is rather richer than most people suppose. That is to say that he has *prospects*. For besides his four thousand a year, there is his uncle's estate in Suffolk which he is almost sure to get for there is no one else the old man can leave it to."

"Indeed? I am very glad to hear it for Miss Harris's sake."

"Oh yes." Mrs Harris lowered her voice to a suitably respectful whisper. "Five thousand a year," she mouthed. "Mr H reckons that the Hunston estate clears five thousand a year after land tax, and a very pretty house it is too . . ."

Mrs Harris talked on happily, but Dido gave her as little attention as she safely could. Her mind was full of suspicions. For, lacking the mother's partiality, she could not help but wonder why the colonel should have decided so suddenly to break through his resolution of not marrying. And why should he have fixed upon the Harris girls, whose charms were, it had to be admitted, nothing out of the ordinary?

Dido did not accompany Mrs Harris to the milliner's, she went instead in search of the village's apothecary. She had need of some aromatic vinegar and was also anxious to get a new cough mixture made for Jack, the footman.

She found the place about halfway along the muddy street. It was a small dark shop sunk five steps below the level of the street, with the name of *Bartley* just visible in faded black letters above the door. The many shelves and drawers of dark old wood that were ranged behind the counter, together with the bottles and jars and boxes of pills displayed in the small window, made it seem very gloomy indeed. There was a smell of herbs and aniseed and horse liniment. Dido did not like the place. It was her experience that dark apothecary shops dealt too much in patent medicines of dubious character and too little in good old-fashioned stuff.

Nor was she pleased to see that the apothecary himself was absent. Behind the counter there was only his assistant — an extremely thin youth with a bad complexion and an apron which had perhaps, long ago, been white. He was talking to a gentleman — in fact he was talking to Mr Tom Lomax. As soon as she recognised him, Dido stepped back into the shadows, though she hardly knew why.

Tom was impatiently tapping a silver-headed cane against the counter and demanding a supply of horse pills. But there seemed to be a difficulty.

The shop-boy was red in the face and rubbing his hands together with discomfort. "I'm sorry," he kept saying. "I'm sorry, Mr Lomax. You know I would if I could. Truly I would. But Mr Bartley was very definite. He said I wasn't to let you have anything at all. Not till your account was settled. It seems he has spoken to your father . . ."

"My father," began Tom hotly, "is an interfering old . . ." He recollected himself and said, with an effort at calmness, "It is all nothing but a misunderstanding. A temporary lack of funds. It will all soon be put straight."

"I'm very glad to hear it, Mr Lomax."

"In fact, Robert . . ." Tom clasped his hands over the head of his cane and leant across the counter familiarly. "In fact, I don't mind telling an old friend like you that I shall soon be coming into a fortune of twenty thousand pounds. It is all quite settled."

Robert grinned proudly and rubbed his hands harder than ever, looking as if he did not quite know what to do about being so honoured with a gentleman's confidence — and being called a friend into the bargain.

"So if you could see your way to just letting me have a dozen of the pills . . ." said Tom.

And then it was all, Well, Mr Bartley did say . . . But then, sir, with you coming into money . . . And it's always a pleasure to do a favour for a friend . . .

83

And the upshot of it all was that a few minutes later Tom walked out of the shop with a package of horse pills whistling cheerfully to himself. Dido quickly turned her face away as he passed and he saw only an insignificant female in pattens and a shabby pelisse. A creature not worth a second glance.

And, much to her mortification, it seemed as if the shop assistant received a similarly unfavourable impression, for no sooner was she alone with him than he began with, "Are you the maid from the hall? Mr Bartley has my lady's stuff ready," and produced a package wrapped in brown paper.

Chagrined at having Catherine's unkind remark confirmed, and still occupied with what she had overheard, Dido spared herself the pain of an explanation and, for the next ten minutes — as she gave detailed instructions for the making of her cough medicine — the boy fumed inwardly against the arrogance and self-important airs of great ladies' maids.

However, as she stepped out into the sunny street carrying her two parcels, Dido found that she was not sorry the mistake had been made; indeed she was very much tempted to take advantage of it.

She hesitated and looked up and down the street; Mrs Harris was not to be seen. There was a small boy eyeing gingerbread in the little bow window of the baker's shop and a stray dog lapping rainwater from a dirty puddle. Two housewives with laden shopping baskets hurried by deep in conversation. She caught the words "murder" and "inquest" and "Sir Edgar" as they passed. Then she was alone again with the dog and the child. No one was watching her.

Should she look at the package she had been given? She was almost certain that her ladyship's languor was aided by laudanum. One quick look in this parcel might confirm that suspicion. Of course she should not do it. But it was for Catherine's peace of mind that she was acting. She had to find out all that she could. It was all done in a very good cause.

As usual, her curiosity triumphed over her manners.

Very quickly — before her conscience could argue against her — Dido unpicked the knots in the string and pulled the paper away to reveal the bottle inside. She read the label.

And then, thinking that she must have been mistaken, she read it again.

"My dear Miss Kent! Are you unwell?" Mrs Harris was at her side now, looking concerned. "You are very pale."

"Oh no, no, I am quite well, thank you. Just a little tired perhaps." Dido hastily pulled the paper back about the package and did her very best to smile; but the shock she had received had been so great that the rutted street and the little black and white shopfronts, and even Mrs Harris's plump pink cheeks, were all swimming together in a kind of mist.

"I think we had better go home." Mrs Harris linked arms very kindly and set off on the road to Belsfield. Dido was glad of her support — and glad, too, to find that she had heard enough gossip in the milliner's shop to keep her occupied all the way in retailing it, without expecting many answers from her companion.

"For it seems the inquest is over and still no one knows who that poor woman was. And there's no one missing from the village that it might be. Though Judith Jenkinson, the milliner, was almost certain it was Clara from the Crown because no one had seen her for almost a week, and everyone in Belston has been quite sure that she'll come to a bad end these last two years; but then she came home safe and well this morning and it seems there's a young sailor at the bottom of that little mystery.

"So you see, my dear, the verdict the jury gave was that the poor woman was killed wrongly . . . or unlawfully . . . or something of that sort because Judith Jenkinson says it can't be murder on account of them not knowing whether it was planned beforehand or whether someone just took it into his head to shoot her all at once — because then it would be only homicide — so Judith says. Which seems very strange to me for the poor soul is just as dead whether the fellow was thinking about it before or not . . ."

Dido let her run on unchecked while she struggled for comprehension of what she had seen inside the parcel. Never had she expected to see such stuff sent to a respectable woman. What use could a prosperous married woman have for it? Indeed, a gentlewoman ought not even to know what it was . . .

She paused there, recollecting that she herself had recognised it.

86

In fact, she remembered seeing such medicine twice before — on charitable visits to the homes of the poor and despairing, but . . .

"So, there you are, my dear, what do you say to that?"

Mrs Harris was looking at her, her little dark eyes sparkling. Dido was obliged to ask her to repeat herself.

"What do you say to Sir Edgar's generosity?"

"His generosity?"

"Why yes, my dear. Did you not hear me saying? You see, there being no kin to come forward and prosecute the case, Sir Edgar has taken all the trouble upon himself — and he has offered a reward. Two hundred guineas," she mouthed with a significant nod.

"Oh! Indeed, yes, that is very generous."

"It is, and I am glad to say that everyone in the village seems to agree that it is. Everyone is full of praise for Sir Edgar. Which is just as it should be and, just between ourselves, my dear, it does not happen often enough. People are too much inclined to speak against the poor man, in my opinion. For they say he is proud and his tenants call him hard, which I do not believe is true . . ."

Dido could not attend any longer. Her own thoughts made her deaf. She was certain . . . yes, she was quite certain that this was the same stuff she had seen in those wretched, overcrowded cottages. And she knew how it had been used. She was not deceived by the benign-sounding message on the label: *Guaranteed to speedily relieve all female irregularities.* She knew that the irregularities it cured were the sort which would, in the natural course of events, result in the birth of a child.

And why would her ladyship use such stuff — in defiance of the laws of God and man — unless the gossip about her was true?

Dido remembered now that that gossip had seemed to have its origin among the tradesmen of the village. Perhaps the supplying of medicine like this had begun it.

She thought again of that pale face lolling against the green brocade: its beauty and, above all, its discontent. Yes, she thought, my lady might be capable of an indiscretion.

But could Mr Lomax be her fellow sinner? Dido found that notion much harder to countenance.

CHAPTER
EIGHT

The party presently collected at Belsfield was much inclined to play at cards; it was perhaps her ladyship's influence. Every evening ended with the tables being set and, while Lady Montague was careful to gather about her whist table the most serious-minded and the best players — her husband, Mr Harris and Margaret — the cheerful Mrs Harris was left to preside over a round game where the slight demands of play allowed for a great deal of flirtation and gossip.

There was only one exception to this general passion for cards and that was Mr William Lomax. When the tables were brought forward, he would excuse himself and retire to the fireside with a book.

Having observed this, on the evening after her walk to Belston, Dido pleaded a slight headache and moved away from Mrs Harris's table as the first cards were being dealt. She had no particular aim in view, other than to try what a little conversation with the gentleman might produce. She could hardly make direct enquires; she could not ask whether he was my lady's lover. But, she thought, she would see where their talk might lead.

"You do not play at Speculation this evening?" Mr Lomax enquired, politely laying his book aside as she took a seat near the fire.

"No," she said with a smile, "the speculation is a little too wild for me today."

"Ah yes!" he replied with instant comprehension.

At the table behind them Mrs Harris, who, it seemed, was a great advocate of divination, was strenuously maintaining her conviction that a fashionable practitioner of that science from Bath should be employed to discover the name of the dead woman. Meanwhile, her youngest daughter was expounding her own ideas of how that *poor, unfortunate* creature had come to be in Sir Edgar's shrubbery. Dido did not quite comprehend the details of Miss Sophia's theory, but the general idea seemed to be of a highwayman choosing — for some unspecified reason — to hide the body of his victim in the baronet's pleasure grounds, and the story made up for what it lacked in sober reasoning with a great deal of riding about in the dark and shooting with pistols.

"And yet," said Mr Lomax after listening for a moment or two, "it is a subject which must arouse speculation in us all. The discovery cannot be easily explained."

"No, it cannot," Dido agreed. "But that does not authorise us to invent brigands and strangers blundering about, miraculously unobserved by the household."

"Maybe," he said with a smile. "But," he continued, looking at her very earnestly indeed, "my dear Miss

90

Kent, if we do not include strangers — and strangers with evil intentions — in our explanations, does that not lead us to a very distressing, and I might say, even more unlikely conclusion?"

Dido coloured and did not quite know how to reply. The steady regard of his grey eyes was disquieting and she found it necessary to lower her own gaze. They were both silent for a while. At Mrs Harris's table gossip had given way to play and Miss Sophia was now in eager negotiation for a queen with Tom Lomax — who was allowing himself to be cheated shamelessly. At the other table a sedate silence prevailed, broken only by a little satisfied snap as her ladyship laid down a trump card.

"Miss Kent," pursued Mr Lomax at last, "if we do not include strangers in our accounts, does not that lead us to conclude that an inmate of this house committed the terrible deed?"

Dido was discomfited; it was extremely unpleasant to admit to such suspicions — and yet she was determined not to lose the opportunity for the conversation at which she had aimed when she left the card table.

She spread her hands and gave a self-deprecating smile. "You must forgive me, Mr Lomax. I am only a woman and I know little of how to reason — or how to draw conclusions from facts. Yet I must confess that, terrible though such a prospect may be, it seems to me to be the least unlikely."

"Does it indeed!" He left his seat and moved to one closer to her. "And, may I ask," he continued in a lowered voice, "why you should think such a thing?"

"Well . . ." It was, she found, rather difficult to think clearly when he was so close and watching her so very intently. "Well, if the guilt does not lie within the house, then we must suppose that someone — some stranger — entered these grounds carrying either a dead woman, or else a shotgun. And this, Mr Lomax, could not have occurred under cover of darkness, for the body was not in the shrubbery at nine o'clock and yet it was there at dusk. So it must have arrived there in broad daylight."

"I see." He thought for a moment, resting his chin on his interwoven fingers. "Well, I grant you that the carrying of a body unobserved seems extremely unlikely. But is a gun so very improbable?"

"What?" cried Dido raising her brows. "On the property of such a sportsman as Sir Edgar? A stranger walk across the park and into the very gardens with a gun upon his arm? Mr Lomax, I doubt whether the most adventurous poacher in Belston has ever achieved such a thing undetected on a moonless night in the most distant copse upon the estate!"

He smiled. "Well, well, you argue very convincingly." He was silent for some moments, tapping his foot upon the carpet and watching her with a kindly expression. "But I think that this conviction gives you no pleasure."

"Naturally it does not."

"Then perhaps you will allow me to put your mind at rest, by showing to you that, though the intrusion of a stranger might seem improbable, the deplorable alternative is even less likely; that it is, in fact, impossible. Miss Kent, I assure you that the woman could not have been murdered by any one of us."

"I shall be very glad to hear your proof."

"Very well then, I shall do my best to persuade you." He leant forward intently and, speaking in a quiet tone that was easily covered by the laughter and chatter from the nearby card table, he began. "I think we are agreed that the murder must have taken place between ten o'clock and one — while we were all shooting over in the spinney. Do you allow that to be true?"

"Oh yes," said Dido. "It must have been then, otherwise the shot would certainly have been heard and remarked upon."

"So, we have to consider how everyone was employed during that time."

"Yes, I agree."

He smiled courteously. "It is not, of course," he said, "permissible to suspect ladies of murder. But even if it were, we would not, in this case, have to do so. For during that time all the ladies were together in the house — except for yourself, Miss Kent who, I believe, did not arrive until . . .?"

"About four o'clock."

"Exactly. So the ladies can all vouch for each other. And so, I find, can the gentlemen — for we talked it all over after the ladies retired from the dining room yesterday, you see. As it happens, we were split into two parties that day. Tom and Harris went down on the south side of the hill while Sir Edgar and the colonel were shooting more to the east — and I was with them."

"And the two parties were not in sight of one another?"

"You are a keen questioner, Miss Kent! No, the two parties were not in sight of each other. But, and this is my main point, every man is sure that he did not lose sight of the rest of his party all morning. Tom and Harris are sure that they were together all the time and I will personally swear upon my honour that neither the colonel nor Sir Edgar left the spinney." He paused and then leant a little closer in order to add, "And, since I must not suppose that *I* am not included in your suspicions, I will add that both Colonel Walborough and Sir Edgar are willing to take on oath that I did not run away to commit murder either."

"I am very glad to hear that you can prove your innocence, Mr Lomax," she said with a smile. And it was true; it would be awful to have to suspect such a charming man of murder.

Of course, nothing that he said actually removed the suspicion of adultery; but his open, pleasant manner of talking made it very hard to believe that he could have any guilty secret to hide.

... and all of this — this elegant proof that none of the gentlemen from the house could have carried out the crime — ought to be very consoling, Eliza, as I am sure Mr Lomax intended it to be. And yet, I confess that I cannot be at ease about it. I keep remembering those boot-marks in the ha-ha and the chairs that had been so recently occupied. I cannot rid myself of the conviction that someone left the shooting party for a meeting in the hermitage. And it must have been a secret assignation, for why else would anyone use such a place on a cold day in September? Furthermore, I am almost convinced that that person was Mr Tom Lomax. Though this is founded on no more than his liking for sitting with a cushion behind his head and my own prejudice which makes me feel that if any of Belsfield's inmates must be proved guilty of murder and surrendered to the punishment of the law, I would give up Mr Tom with an easier mind than any other. Supposing, Eliza, that he had seduced poor Miss Wallis, got her with child and then abandoned her in order to make his fortune by marrying one of the Harris girls. And she had pursued him, threatening exposure . . .

But Mr Lomax says that his son did not leave the spinney that morning. If what he told me holds true, then a stranger must have been responsible. It is certainly the only explanation which has been put forward by anyone in this house — and no one from the village has yet been so impertinent as to connect the Belsfield family with the crime.

Sir Edgar's offered reward has already produced some fruit and there have, I understand, been a great many reports of a company of gypsies who were encamped in the vicinity a week ago, and a young sailor boy who was seen loitering near the village. However, the gypsies, we now understand, were more than ten miles away on the Bristol road when the murder occurred. And, as for the sailor boy, well, I rather think that Miss Clara-at-the-Crown can account for him.

Then there are the servants here in the house. Mrs Harris, I should say, rather favours the under-butler for a murderer. It seems she is an advocate not only of divination but also the science of physiognomy, and she assures us all that the under-butler has the chin and the eyebrows of a villain. But, for my own part, I cannot conceive how a servant — no matter what the appearance of his chin and eyebrows — could carry a shotgun about the grounds unchallenged, even if he was able to obtain one.

And I cannot escape from the possibility that Mr Montague returned home unseen — or else seen only by Mrs Holmes, who has been bribed into silence. I cannot help but think that the gatekeeper and her child have a remarkably <u>prosperous</u> look . . .

In short, I am so surrounded by unanswered questions that I do not know where to turn next. There is only one thing I am quite determined upon and that is pouring away that terrible medicine of Lady Montague's. No doubt she will soon procure a replacement, but at least I will share no guilt in the business.

The next morning, having sent her letter to the post and disposed of the patent medicine, Dido set out with her cough mixture in search of Jack, the footman. Another chat with one of the servants might prove useful and she could, she thought, at least discover whether the colonel had indeed sought him out to complain about the logs.

However, on the stairs she met Lady Montague, who upon seeing the medicine bottle in her hand said, "Ah, Miss Kent, I believe you may have been given a package for me yesterday — by mistake — by the apothecary."

"Oh!" Dido started guiltily, then decided that a bold attack might serve her best. "Yes, My Lady, I was." She looked directly into the clear green eyes. "But I am afraid I got the package mixed up with my own and opened it by mistake." Fear stirred deep in the eyes but the beautiful face remained impassive. "I found that my mistake was not the only one," continued Dido smoothly. "Instead of your physic, the apothecary — or his boy — had sent some patent rubbish."

"Indeed? How provoking!"

"Naturally, I poured the stuff away."

"Naturally."

"I did not want anyone to see it and be shocked."

"No, of course not."

"If anyone found out about it I thought it might be an embarrassment to Your Ladyship."

Her ladyship merely nodded and turned to continue on her way up the stairs. Dido moved very slightly into her way. "I could not help wondering, though," she said boldly, "how such a mistake came to be made."

The hard green eyes swept over her in chilling contempt. "I really have no idea, Miss Kent. I cannot be expected to explain a tradesman's blunder." And the lady brushed past her up the stairs.

That, thought Dido, certainly put me down. And perhaps I deserved it, she admitted after a few moments. She found she could not resent her ladyship's sharpness; in fact, she rather preferred it to the usual insipidity.

She continued thoughtfully on her way and found Jack stacking logs onto the roaring fire in the hall. Another footman — a rather older fellow with a knowing face — was leaning upon the mantel and talking urgently. "You had better do it," he was saying.

Jack bent over the fire and pushed another log into place; his reply was half lost in the crackle of flames, but Dido thought she caught the word "wrong".

The older boy laughed. "What's so wrong about it? And the colonel will pay you well; they say he always does. I tell you, Jack, if it was me . . ."

Unfortunately, he looked round then and saw Dido standing at the foot of the stairs. He stood up smartly, pulled his livery jacket straight and hurried off towards the offices.

Jack also straightened himself and gratefully accepted the medicine. Unlike her ladyship he was willing, indeed anxious, to talk. "There was something, miss, I wanted to ask you, if you don't mind," he began as soon as he had finished thanking her.

He was a slight young man with a pale complexion and very thick black hair, and had such a sickly air as made her wonder how he was able to discharge his duties. At present he seemed very worried. His speech was punctuated by a great many brief, nervous smiles that displayed white, almost too perfect teeth.

"No, I do not mind. What was it you wished to ask me, Jack?"

"Well, I hoped, miss," he said, dusting fragments of bark and moss off his hands and cuffs, "I hoped you could tell me what to do about . . . something."

"I shall certainly do my best to advise you. Does it perhaps concern Colonel Walborough? I believe I heard your companion mention his name just now."

"Oh no, miss!" he said quickly. "It is nothing to do with the colonel. It's about . . ." A look of panic crossed his face as he wondered how he should refer to a murdered corpse in the presence of a lady. "Well, it's about what Mr Downe found in the shrubbery. They say . . . I mean Mr Carter — that's the butler — he's saying if you know anything about that business you've got to speak up. And if you don't you might lose your place."

"Mr Carter is quite right, Jack. If you know anything, you must speak out."

"But you see, miss, I don't know who I'm supposed to speak to."

"If you told Mr Carter, perhaps?"

"But that don't seem right, miss. You see, its something . . ." He wiped his hand nervously across his mouth and looked about him. "It's something about one of the gentlemen, miss."

"I see. Then perhaps you had better speak directly to Sir Edgar. That might be more discreet."

"If that's what you think is right, miss," he said, but his face had gone paler than ever at the suggestion.

"Are you are afraid of speaking to him?"

"Well, miss . . ." the boy began. But just then there was the sound of heavy footsteps upon the stair. She turned and saw Colonel Walborough descending in his slow, flat-footed gait.

"Thank you again for the cough stuff, miss," said Jack hurriedly and, before she could stop him, he was gone.

The colonel reached the foot of the stairs and, leaning heavily upon the newel post, looked about the hall suspiciously.

"Good morning, Miss . . . er . . . Were you talking to young Jack just now?"

"Yes," she replied. "Did you succeed yesterday in getting your log basket replenished?"

"What? Oh, no. I could not find the young rascal."

"I am sorry to hear it."

She turned towards the drawing room and it seemed as if the colonel would accompany her, but just at that moment the pianoforte began to be played, and played in such a stumbling manner as clearly announced Miss Sophia to be the musician. The colonel winced and hurried away to the billiard room.

Dido was much inclined to follow his example and flee from the noise too, but unfortunately it was raining and there was nowhere to which a lady might fairly retreat. There was nothing for it but to take her place in the drawing room and, under cover of some slight employment, let her mind range over the many mysteries that seemed to surround her.

It was a long, wretched day. Margaret teased and insulted her; Catherine continued to sulk despite Dido's attempts to be reconciled; her ladyship fidgeted interminably with her rings and Mrs Harris talked. And even when she was free to think, her own meditations produced nothing new and seemed only to confuse her more.

CHAPTER
NINE

Dido awoke the next morning to brighter thoughts and the happy recollection that the discovery of a murderer was not, after all, her principal task. Her first duty was to find the reason for Mr Montague's sudden departure from his father's house. It would perhaps be best to set aside considerations of how the killing could have been accomplished and which gentleman it was of whom young Jack had something to report. Her first care must be for Catherine and the state of her engagement. She would visit Annie Holmes again — for she seemed to know something of Mr Montague which she was not telling.

However, her resolution of visiting the lodge house was no sooner taken than she discovered that the rain was still falling heavily and she was confined for another three long hours to the drawing room, where Margaret wore her patience with questions about Catherine's affairs which she could not answer, and Miss Sophia played upon the pianoforte without mercy.

At one time Mr Harris came to sit with the ladies and alarmed Dido with one of his abrupt questions.

"She plays well, does she not, Miss Kent?" he said, taking a seat beside her and nodding in the direction of his youngest daughter. "She has talent, has she not?"

She was at a loss for an answer, for it was impossible to tell from the gentleman's tone whether he judged the music to be good or bad himself. After a moment's struggle she replied, "She appears to have a great deal of taste, Mr Harris."

In Dido's experience the word "taste" was so ill-defined — it was so frequently laid claim to by women who could not distinguish one note from another — that it might be safely applied to the least competent of performers.

"Ah, yes, taste," said Mr Harris and he listened in silence for a while.

Dido studied him curiously. He was lean, with a face so lined and suntanned it was almost leathery, and he had the worn, fagged look common in men who have spent a long time in a hot climate. There was, altogether, something hard and unyielding in his appearance that reminded her of what her brother Charles had once said about "fellows who make great fortunes out in India." It was, Charles maintained, possible for such men to remain honest — but only just, and any kind of softer feelings were not to be expected of them.

And yet, despite his appearance — and his fortune — Mr Harris seemed to be a devoted husband and a kindly father. He was now watching his daughter with a troubled expression.

"Perhaps I lack taste myself," he said at last. "For sometimes Sophia's playing seems delightful and sometimes . . ." He shrugged and took his leave of her.

She sat smiling for some time over his words for they presented an amusing picture of the battle between affection and sense; that constant denying of truth which can form a part of love.

And that brought her to a more sombre consideration of Catherine's behaviour. For never had she seen a stronger inclination to hide from unpleasant thoughts about the beloved; never had she encountered such determination to believe the best, contrary to all evidence.

Yesterday she had affronted Catherine badly when she had tried again to persuade her to end her engagement.

"It is, after all, what he wishes you to do," she had argued. And then, when that proved fruitless, she had tried, as delicately as possible, to suggest the most likely circumstance, which had, days ago, suggested itself: that Mr Montague had formed a dishonourable attachment in the past which could no longer be hidden and which had lost him his father's favour. Of her other, darker, thoughts, which connected Mr Montague's strange behaviour with the death of the young woman, she dared not speak; though she could not doubt that her niece suspected them.

"But his father has not disowned him," Catherine argued stubbornly. "He is not even angry with him."

"Perhaps," said Dido, voicing another idea which had been forming in her head for some time, "perhaps Sir

Edgar is not yet aware of all the truth. Yes, I know that Mr Montague *said* he was going to tell him everything on the night of the ball, but perhaps, when it came to the point, his courage failed him."

"No, it did not," cried Catherine. "Mr Montague is no coward. If a thing had to be said then he would have said it. Besides, he had no such shameful secret to reveal. I am sure he had not."

"My dear, how can you be sure?"

"Because . . ." Catherine stopped herself. There was just a touch of colour in her cheeks, which in another girl would have been scarcely noticeable but which in Catherine was as telling as a blush. "I just know," she said. "I cannot explain it."

"But how can you be certain? You have been acquainted with Mr Montague for so short a time. You scarcely know him."

"I do know him. I love him."

"I make no doubt you love him, Catherine. But what did love ever have to do with knowing? We hear every day of people falling in love at first sight . . ."

"Oh, spare me the lecture, please!" cried Catherine, jumping to her feet. "You know nothing of love. You have never loved a man. You are too cold and satirical."

You have never loved a man . . .

Was that true? Dido wondered now, as she sat in the stuffy drawing room, gazing out of the rain-washed window at dripping rose bushes and puddled paths. Was this the reason why she was so impatient with Catherine's determination to think the best of her lover?

It was, of course, a great failure in a woman's life — to never have achieved even a doomed and unsuccessful love. But she was not quite sure whether she had failed or not.

When she was young there had been moments, of course. But those moments had never amounted to much more than a little fever of admiration — a little flutter and agitation in a ballroom — so slight a feeling that the cautious Dido had never considered it a secure foundation for a lifetime of living together. And then, sooner or later, she had always made an odd remark, or laughed at the wrong moment, and the young men became alarmed or angry — and the flutter and the agitation all turned into irritation.

Dido could laugh and gossip about love as well as any woman but, deep down, she suspected that she had not the knack of falling into it.

Well, she told herself bracingly, if she had never experienced such an elevating passion, neither had she been afflicted by the foolishness that so often accompanied it. *She* would never be so stupid as to deliberately blind herself to any man's guilt.

This reassuring thought, together with the ceasing of the rain, did a great deal to raise her spirits and she resolutely escaped for her walk, despite Margaret's chiding and her ladyship's languid protests that she would find it "too dirty for anything".

Outside, she was further cheered by the fresh smell of wet leaves and the singing of a blackbird — and by meeting William Lomax who was just alighting from his carriage in the drive.

He, too, feared that she would have rather a wet walk.

"But, Mr Lomax," she said, laughing, "a wet walk is much to be preferred to being confined any longer in the drawing room."

"Ah," he replied with a kindly smile and immediate sympathy. "Too much Speculation?"

"Oh no. After two days of rain, we are all grown too irritable to even speculate."

"And you will soon be reduced to Snap?"

"Quite so!"

"Then I sincerely hope that your walk will refresh you." He bowed and walked into the house.

Dido continued happily on her way, noticing as she did so that his carriage was a small post-chaise with yellow wheels. But then, she thought, what of that? There must be hundreds of such carriages in the world.

"I thought you would come back," said Annie Holmes bluntly.

"And why did you think that?"

"Because you thought I was lying when I said I'd not seen Mr Montague since the day after the ball."

"And were you lying?"

The woman smiled, as if she was amused to have her honesty met with equal honesty. "No," she said quietly. "I was not lying."

Well, perhaps you were and perhaps you weren't, thought Dido, but you are certainly hiding something. You know something about Mr Montague. But how to find it out?

Mrs Holmes was remarkably sure of herself. She did not behave like a servant. She was a pretty little woman with a dimpled chin and, sitting now beside the hearth in the little kitchen-parlour of the gatehouse with her hands demurely clasped in the lap of her black dress, she had rather the air of a gentlewoman receiving a morning call. And her home did seem remarkably comfortable. The firelight was dancing on two copper pans above the hearth and on the polished wood of a good, solid table and chest; there was a cream jug on the window sill filled with sprays of red leaves. And Dido noticed that the candle in its pewter stand upon the mantelshelf was made of wax, not cheap tallow.

The little girl was sitting beside her mother — and trying to make the china doll eat bread and milk from her bowl.

"Mr Montague has, I believe, gone to town on business of his father's?" said Dido cautiously.

"Yes, miss, that is what I heard."

"Do you know — did he happen to mention that morning — what that business might be?"

"No, he did not." But as she said that she turned away and began to chide the child for spilling milk on her pinafore. "Eat it up now, Susan. It's for you, not the dolly."

"Did he say anything else to you?" persisted Dido.

There was a sigh. "He said that he expected to be gone a long while and . . ."

"And?"

Another sigh, then Mrs Holmes turned away from the child and her bright blue eyes met Dido's gaze. "He said that . . . there was trouble between him and his father."

"I see." Dido held her eyes. Colour was creeping up her cheeks. "And did it surprise you, Mrs Holmes, that Mr Montague should confide in you in that way?"

There was silence for a moment, broken only by the ringing of Susan's spoon in her bowl and the bubbling of the black kettle on the hearth.

"No, miss," came the reply at last, spoken very quietly. "No, it did not surprise me. I have known Mr Montague all his life and he has always been a good friend to me." There was a pause. "And I hope that, in my way, I have been a friend to him."

"A friend to whom he can speak without reserve?"

"Yes, miss. We were children together here at Belsfield, you see, because my father used to be Sir Edgar's head gardener. And Mr Montague was always a kind-hearted boy."

Dido smiled. "I understand," she said. Then after a moment's thought she added, "Since you are so well acquainted with Mr Montague, I wonder if you would be so kind as to tell me a little about him. What kind of a young man is he? You see," she added confidingly, "I have not yet had the pleasure of meeting him and it seems as if my visit may end before he returns. And since my favourite niece is engaged to him . . . I would particularly like to be able to tell my sister a little about the young man. She worries so about Catherine!"

Annie's blue eyes were wary; her fingers wove together tightly in her lap. "I would have thought, miss, you could learn more from his ma and pa."

"But someone of nearly the same age . . . Someone who has grown up beside him . . ."

"I'm sorry, miss," came the firm reply. "It's not my place to speak about him."

"Ah well," said Dido, drawing her pelisse around her as if preparing to leave, "it is a shame. I had so wanted to have something *good* to write in my letter to my sister, something to mitigate the very unpleasant impression she has at present of the young man."

That shot hit home. "And why," asked Mrs Holmes sharply, "would your sister think badly of him?"

"Well, because of the way he has behaved, of course. He has been so very thoughtless. Leaving my niece alone on the very day after their engagement is announced — and staying away without any word sent of when he is to come home."

"But that was his pa's doing. He sent him away."

"Yes, but —"

"Truly, miss, if Sir Edgar said go, then Rich — Mr Montague, he'd go. And ask no questions about it. He'd do anything to please his pa. That always was his way."

Ah! thought Dido, at last I am hearing something to the point about young Richard. "Do you mean that Mr Montague is afraid of his father?" she asked.

Annie looked confused. "Not exactly afraid," she said quickly. "He's just always wanted to make Sir Edgar proud of him, that's all. And he never could quite manage it. Never. Not clever enough with his books. Not brave enough about riding his pony. It was always the same. I've always thought it was because —" She recollected herself and stopped.

"What is it that you think?"

"No, miss," said Mrs Holmes with a shake of the head that dislodged a bright curl from her cap. "It's not for me to talk about it. That was hardly fair just now; you tricked me into speaking out. But I hope you will be good enough not to tell anyone what I've said."

"Of course I will not. Anything you say is quite between ourselves." She waited, hoping that this would be enough encouragement to make her go on. But the young woman was in control of herself now and resolutely held her peace, her eyes cast down upon her clasped hands. "I believe you were going to tell me why it was so hard for Mr Montague to please his father."

Mrs Holmes' cheeks burnt red and she shook her head again. "No, miss, I can't say. In every family there are secrets, things no one talks about."

Such an opening! Such an invitation for further questions! But looking at the head bowed in the firelight, Dido recollected that, for all her strange, dainty ways, Annie Holmes was a servant and a dependent of the Montague family. It would be unpardonable to force a confidence from her. Reluctantly, she stood up to go.

Mrs Holmes followed her to the door, but at the moment of parting, as they stood together upon the step, blinking in the sudden light of the sun, she turned up a troubled face and said suddenly and all in a rush, "Miss, I'd be as glad as you to know what the trouble is with R — Mr Montague and I'm truly sorry I can't say more — it wouldn't be right. But I will say this — it's not so difficult to figure out why Sir Edgar has always been hard on him, miss. If you were to go up into the gallery at the great house and just look about you, I think you might begin to understand it."

And then she made her bob and closed the door before Dido could recover from her surprise and ask another question.

Dido walked slowly down the wet drive towards the house. The sun was beginning to break through in bright, sharp rays and blackbirds were busy in the laurels, shaking down little showers of water from the overburdened leaves. She had a great deal to think about: that comfortable little parlour, Mrs Holmes' assured manner, her way of speaking of Mr Montague . . . But she had liked the woman. There had seemed to be an appealing honesty about her . . . No, not honesty exactly, rather a desire to be honest. She had wanted to say more than she dared.

And what was it that she was supposed to discover in the gallery? What was there besides all those old Sir Edgars peering out of their dingy brown paint?

But at least she felt nearer to understanding Mr Montague himself. A nervous young man, lacking in confidence and standing in awe of his father. Perhaps Margaret was right and Catherine's affection for him was founded on the certainty that he would be easily managed.

She had now reached the steps that led to the front door and there was Catherine herself running down to meet her with a look of great excitement on her face. Clearly something so momentous had occurred as to make her forget, for a while at least, her great displeasure with her aunt.

"Aunt Dido," she cried, "I have been looking everywhere for you. Where have you been?"

"Just talking to the gatekeeper."

Catherine frowned. "I don't admire your taste in company! But listen, Sir Edgar has just told me the strangest thing! One of the footmen has told him that he heard a man talking in the shrubbery on Monday — at about twelve o'clock — which is about the time when they think that woman was killed."

"Indeed? That is very interesting."

"It seems the footman had been sent out with a message for the gardener and he went down onto the lower lawn looking for him. And he heard a voice talking quietly within the shrubbery. He could not see, of course, because the hedge was in the way. But he heard the voice clearly and he is sure it was —"

"Mr Tom Lomax."

Catherine stared. "Aunt! How could you possibly know that? For I had it from Sir Edgar not five minutes ago and he had but that moment finished speaking to the boy."

"Oh," said Dido lightly. "It was just a moment of premonition. I have them sometimes."

"Do you?" said Catherine eyeing her with a mixture of disbelief and amazement. "I have never heard of them before."

CHAPTER
TEN

. . . Well, Eliza, you will remember that I always did rather favour Mr Tom for a murderer. I am not certain what Mrs Harris would say about his eyebrows and his chin but there is certainly that in his smile which makes <u>me</u> think him insincere and quite capable not only of betraying a woman but of disposing of her ruthlessly if she threatened his plans for a comfortable future . . .

But I hardly know what I write. Of course, in sober truth, it would be shocking to discover that one was sharing a house with such a villain. And my best comfort is that if the guilt does indeed lie in that quarter then it is no business of mine; for it would seem to be quite unconcerned with Catherine's affair and the woman's living in the same house as the one that Mr Montague's visitor stayed in is no more than a strange coincidence. It is not for me to consider how the deed might have been accomplished or how Tom contrived to leave the shooting party unobserved, any more than it is my business to dwell upon what will become of him now.

So I am instead employing my mind with the riddle Mrs Holmes has set for me. I am at present in the gallery, sitting with my writing desk upon the window seat, and hoping that this long stretch of beautifully polished floorboards, these squares of light thrown in by the late afternoon sun and these ranks of long-dead Montagues in their gilded frames, may somehow suggest a solution to my struggling brain. I regret to inform you that there has, so far, been no startling burst of understanding. But it is a pleasant place to sit, except for the sensation of being very much watched. My framed companions have, in general, a rather forbidding look. It is strange to consider that these sombre ladies in their stiff bodices and farthingales were the giggling young misses of their day — and that these frowning fellows with padded breeches and pointed beards were, no doubt, the gallant young men about whom they giggled.

I have found a portrait of Sir Edgar — the present Sir Edgar — painted, I rather think, to mark his coming of age. There are no lines upon his face, but he seems to have changed in little else — at one and twenty he had already that same air of importance and extreme weightiness. There is also a picture of his father at a similar age and wearing a similar expression of self-importance beneath his periwig. And one of his father. And so on along a whole line of Sir Edgars, darkening with age down the gallery and wearing more and more preposterous outfits. Which all makes me think that the painting of such pictures upon reaching manhood is a tradition in the family and I am rather surprised to discover that there was no portrait of Mr Montague done two years ago when he was one and twenty. Indeed, now that I consider the matter, I realise that the only picture I have seen of him is that miniature he gave to Catherine and which she carries in her great-grandmother's silver locket.

Which, I suppose, might be a proof of his father's disfavour, but does not supply the explanation of it which

Mrs Holmes seemed to promise. And, in short, I am at a loss . . .

Dido paused, realising that she was no longer alone in the gallery. A figure was walking towards her from the head of the stairs.

"Good afternoon, Lady Montague," she said, politely putting aside her writing desk and standing up. "I have been enjoying your remarkably fine collection of paintings."

The lady stopped abruptly at the sound of her voice and pulled her shawl about her arms. "Oh," she said and looked about at the walls as if she had never noticed the portraits hanging there before. "Yes, they are very pretty, are they not?" She smiled vaguely. "Sir Edgar says there is not another collection to compare with it in the land."

Dido regarded the lady sidelong. The sunlight pouring through the high window showed that her cheeks were flushed and her eyes red — maybe she was distressed — or maybe she had been drinking wine. One damp little curl clung to her brow. She looked brittle and frail in the bright light; but their late encounter over the medicine had made Dido wary of her. However, she thought that maybe she would just try to probe a little . . . Just a question or two . . .

"I have been looking for one picture in particular," she began.

"Oh," said the lady languidly, "I daresay there are a great many that are worth your attention, Miss Kent. That man sitting on his horse there." She gestured wearily. "I believe he is generally reckoned to be very well done. And this lady with pearls in her hair was painted by an artist who is famous — but I am afraid I do not recollect his name." She half turned as if she would walk away.

"Yes," persisted Dido, "but there seems to be just one portrait missing. I have not been able to find any representation of your son."

There was a long pause. The sun from the window shone in on Dido's back; she began to feel hot and uncomfortable. The lady lowered her head and pursed her lips. "You are quite mistaken, Miss Kent," she said quietly at last. "There is not one painting missing from this gallery."

"Is there not?"

"No, there are about four thousand missing."

"Four thousand?" cried Dido, thoroughly confused and discomfited. "I am afraid I do not quite understand."

My lady raised her eyes and there was in them the same impenetrable coldness as Dido had seen there before. "Do you not?" she said placidly. "And yet it is quite simple. My husband's ancestor, the first Sir Edgar, was given his estates and title by Queen Elizabeth in 1582. Since then, Miss Kent, there have been *twelve generations* of Montagues."

She stopped as if her explanation were complete, but Dido continued to stare blankly. Her ladyship smiled mockingly. "My dear Miss Kent, have you never considered that everyone has two parents, four grandparents, eight great-grandparents, and so on."

116

Dido, who hated even the simplest sums, had indeed never considered such a calculation before and, now that it was forced upon her, her head began to ache with the extraordinary arithmetic it involved. "If you continue the reckoning over twelve generations," said her ladyship, "I believe you will find that the number of ancestors that should be represented here is exactly four thousand and ninety six." She raised her hand in the same weary gesture. "But here there are only a few Sir Edgars and their wives." Her eyes swept over Dido in chilling triumph. She turned to go. "I say again, Miss Kent, that there is *not* only one portrait missing from this gallery."

Left alone in the sunny gallery with the solemnly watching ancestors, Dido was torn between amazement that her ladyship should have accomplished such strange computations, chagrin at the way in which she had been distracted from her own enquiries and admiration for the way in which that distraction had been accomplished.

And the end of it all was a growing certainty that her ladyship's languid manner was only put on to shield herself — though precisely what she wished to shield herself from was much harder to determine.

It was about an hour later, as she was in her room, pondering upon my lady's strange behaviour and getting ready for a walk in the grounds, that Dido's attention was claimed by a commotion that was carrying on in the lower part of the house. There was a great deal of running upon the stairs, doors opening and banging closed again, chattering voices raised almost to a shout and then suddenly silenced.

She opened her door and walked to the head of the stairs. The disturbance seemed to be in the entrance hall and upon the main staircase. She started down the steps towards it — and almost immediately ran against Mrs Harris: her pink and white face very flushed and her grey-brown hair falling down out of her cap. It was a fortunate encounter. Dido could not have met with anyone with more to say about recent events — or one who was more likely to tell what she knew.

For the long and the short of it was that Sir Edgar was shut up with Mr Tom Lomax in the library and it seemed likely that the constable was to come and bear him off to the goal. Mr Tom Lomax! Who would have thought it? Mr Tom who seemed such a pleasant lively young man — though a little bit too free, perhaps, in the way he spoke; but he was very young and you had to pardon him for that and, to be sure, you wouldn't want to see him hanged for it, would you? Though, by the by, Mr Harris had never thought very highly of the young man, which was probably on account of the acquaintances he kept. People out in India that he had known, and Mr Harris had known too and had no great opinion of them. But still! Murder!

Dido ventured to hope that it was not quite certain that Mr Lomax must be hanged.

But, bless her soul! It seemed as if he would be. Because she had it on very good authority from her own maid who had spoken to the cook who was the sister of the under-gardener, that the footman — or the gardener's boy — or someone — had actually heard Tom Lomax in the shrubbery — murdering the young woman! Actually heard him!

Dido suggested that it was perhaps not quite murder which the boy had heard.

But it was. Shouting and shooting and the woman crying out pitifully. He heard it all. And now there was Mr Tom in the library and without a doubt he'd be dragged off to the assizes before he could look about him. And the Lord only knew what the poor dear girls would say about it. They were so sensitive and tender-hearted. It was a shocking thing for them to have to hear.

And with this Mrs Harris hurried away to find "the poor dear girls" so that no one else might have the pleasure of shocking them.

Left on her own, Dido made her way slowly to the main staircase and down into the hall — which seemed to be tranquil and deserted now. The great clock ticked ponderously in its corner, the black and white tiles shone in testimony of the housemaids' labours, a fire of logs blazed cheerfully in the high basket grate and on the rug before it Sir Edgar's favourite spaniel dozed, her paws and nose twitching as she sought out woodcock in her dreams. Opposite the stairs was the door to the library and it was, as she had expected, closed. She hesitated for a moment; reluctant to go away, yet not wanting to be suspected of eavesdropping. And as she stood with her hand upon the newel post, she saw that, after all, the place was not quite deserted.

A small movement drew her eye to a chair by the fire, a big, old-fashioned chair with a hood to it that all but concealed its occupant. She stepped forward and saw that Mr Harris was sitting there — in a state of great distress.

He was leaning forward with his hands planted upon his knees and his weather-beaten face had turned to a dangerous purple colour. His mouth was moving frantically, but no sound was coming out of it. He seemed to be experiencing some kind of seizure.

"Mr Harris, are you unwell?" She hurried to his side. "Shall I ring the bell? Shall I send for your man?"

"No." He made a great effort to control himself. "No, no, I am quite well, thank you, my dear. Just a little overcome, just for a moment."

"Let me call for help . . . a glass of wine perhaps."

"No," he said more firmly. "No, there is no need at all to distress yourself, Miss Kent. I am only resting for a moment." He got to his feet. "There is something I must do. A duty. Not pleasant, but it must be done."

And with that he put back his portly shoulders, crossed the hall, knocked upon the library door and entered without waiting for an answer from within.

As the door closed behind him, Dido sank thoughtfully into the hooded chair. Now, what, she wondered, was Mr Harris's business with Sir Edgar and Tom Lomax? Something unpleasant.

There were, she thought, two possibilities. Firstly there was the business of how Tom could have been in the shrubbery when everyone had been led to believe that he had not left the spinney. She recollected that, according to Mr Lomax's account, only Mr Harris had been able to vouch for Tom's remaining with the shooting party. Was Mr Harris now having to admit that he had not told the truth about that?

And secondly, if Mrs Harris was to be believed, there were acquaintances her husband had in common with Tom. Was it possible that, through them, he knew of something to Tom's disadvantage? Something which he now felt it was his duty to communicate to Sir Edgar?

Dido sank back as far as she could to hide herself in the hooded chair and resolved to wait until the men left the library. Despite what she had just written to Eliza, she could not be uncurious on this subject. Nor could she quite believe that it had no bearing upon the trouble between Catherine and Mr Montague.

She would wait until the gentlemen emerged. Then she might be able to judge from their behaviour something of what had passed between them.

But concealment proved difficult for, no sooner had she settled into the chair than the dog woke and came to sit beside her, with a hot, friendly paw placed upon her lap. Catherine, coming down the stairs a moment later, saw immediately that there was someone sitting in the chair. And, rather unfortunately, Catherine seemed to be in a very good temper. She was all smiles and friendliness.

"Oh, there you are, Aunt Dido!" she cried peering around the hood. "I have been looking everywhere for you!"

"Well, now that you know that I am safe, you may leave me in peace to think, may you not? And you can take this dog away with you."

"There is no need to be so peevish," said Catherine, dropping into a chair on the opposite side of the hearth. "It is very ungrateful of you, when I have been all morning spreading your fame as a future-gazer. Mrs Harris is particularly pleased with the notion and now she is telling everyone how clever my old aunt is."

"I am not anybody's *old* aunt, Catherine." Dido pushed the dog's paw from her lap, but it was speedily replaced.

"No, perhaps you are not so very old. But you are odd; I am sure people here were beginning to notice your strange ways. But now, you see, it does not matter how odd you seem, because you have remarkable talents and remarkable talents excuse all manner of oddness."

"I see. If I can predict the future then I am allowed to be poor. I can wear pattens and have a shabby pelisse."

"Yes."

"And this is why you are friends with me again! I am not at all sure that I welcome such popularity, Catherine."

"Upon my word! You are quite determined to quarrel with me this morning."

122

"On the contrary, I do not wish to quarrel with anyone. I wish rather to be left alone."

"But I need to talk to you," persisted Catherine.

"What do you wish to talk about?"

"Well, I have been thinking over what you asked me when you first came to Belsfield. Where might Richard have gone? Do you remember?"

"Yes," said Dido, wondering what might follow. "I remember. Have you thought of where he might be?"

"Yes, I think perhaps I have. Of course everyone believes he has gone to town. But I do not think so. Richard does not like town, you see. When he goes away — as he does when he feels unwell — he likes to be quiet. Somewhere in the countryside. But I could think of no particular place. Nowhere that he had mentioned as somewhere he liked. And then I remembered!"

"Remembered what exactly?"

"Lyme!"

"Lyme?"

"Yes. Once, when he was a little boy of about six years old, he was sent to a tutor at Lyme. He had been ill with scarlet fever and he was sent to Lyme to recover. To a house overlooking the sea. He told me about it. He said it is a beautiful place and the summer he spent there was the happiest summer of his life."

"I see. And you think perhaps . . .?"

"No, no I don't think at all, Aunt! I am sure. Absolutely sure. Richard is at Lyme."

"I do not see how you can be sure."

"But I am. I know Richard, you see. You would not understand . . ."

"No, of course I would not, because I have never loved a man."

Catherine looked a little ashamed. "I did not mean to hurt your feelings, Aunt Dido."

"It is of no consequence. But I think your idea is worth considering . . ."

"We must do a great deal more than consider it. We must go to Lyme."

"Must we indeed? And how are we to accomplish that? It is more than twenty miles off."

"Nothing could be easier. Sir Edgar has said he wishes you to see the countryside, has he not?"

"Yes . . ."

"And of course you would wish to see Lyme. Everyone goes to Lyme. It shall be a regular exploring party."

"I am not sure I wish to go exploring just now."

But Catherine would not be denied and a moment later she was off to "talk to Mama about it."

Dido sighed. She really was a very wilful, difficult girl!

Which was, of course, just what Margaret was forever saying and what Dido and Eliza regularly denied. Margaret maintained that it was those three formative years spent with her aunts that had done the damage; she believed — and frequently said — that by the time she had taken control of Catherine at six years old, she had been spoilt beyond hope of correction.

124

Maybe she had been spoilt, just a little, the sisters would sometimes admit to each other. But not so very much. And who could help indulging a little lost child who used to open her eyes every morning to ask, "Has Mama returned yet?" It was certainly more than they had been capable of.

But today Dido was ready to admit — to herself at least — that it might have been better if the girl had not learnt so early the pleasure of getting her own way; nor formed such a determination to believe only what she wished to believe.

All she could hope was that Catherine's exploring party would not take them from Belsfield while there were still questions to be answered there.

It was beginning to seem that the interview in the library had been going on a very long time and Dido was becoming very impatient to know whether a charge of murder had been brought against Tom and whether Mr Harris's information had told heavily against him. The clock ticked on beside her and she became drowsy. She was dimly aware of someone playing the pianoforte in the drawing room and she was wondering who the musician could be since the performance was much too assured and accomplished to be Miss Sophia's, when the door opened at last and the three men came out of the library.

The dog at last dropped its paw from her lap and crept away to hide behind the chair.

She peered eagerly around the great wooden hood, but, to her surprise, only one of the three was looking at all distressed — and that one was Mr Harris. His colour had improved a little, but he still looked seriously discomposed. Sir Edgar, on the other hand, was smiling benignly. And, as for Tom Lomax, he strode out into the hall looking very pleased with himself indeed.

CHAPTER
ELEVEN

"Sir Edgar, might I speak with you a moment?" Dido made her way across the hall as Mr Harris hurried off up the stairs and Tom lounged away towards the billiard room.

Sir Edgar stopped and eyed her gravely. She rather fancied that there was disapproval in his look. "Good morning, Miss Kent. How may I help you?"

"I was," she said with a look of innocence, "I was just wondering whether my young friend Jack had spoken to you. He told me yesterday that he had a rather delicate matter on his mind. I recommended that he should speak with you."

"Ah! He mentioned the matter to *you*, did he, Miss Kent?" There was no mistaking the note of dignified disapproval now: the slight, the very slight, emphasis upon the pronoun, which was intended to remind her of what a humble position she occupied in the great commonwealth of his house.

"He did not give any details, of course," Dido assured him.

"I am glad to hear it. I would not recommend that you trouble yourself over the business."

"So," said Dido, rather wondering at her own audacity, "his information was of no use to you?"

Sir Edgar sighed. "Well, I would not say that it was of no use. I know now that the young woman was killed after five and twenty past twelve. It seems Mr Tom Lomax was in the shrubbery at that time and saw nothing."

"So it is true? He was in the shrubbery?"

"Miss Kent, I beg you will not trouble yourself over this matter."

"I am sorry, Sir Edgar, but it does seem so very odd that he should not have mentioned this circumstance before."

Sir Edgar looked so angry for a moment that Dido quaked. But then, all of a sudden, he seemed to relent. He gave his benign smile. "Ah," he said, "but Mr Lomax was there upon a private matter — an affair of the heart — you see, Miss Kent. Something he preferred to keep silent about. It seems he and Mr Harris came down together from the spinney to the hermitage. On a rather happier errand than murder." He rocked himself ponderously upon his toes. "They wanted a quiet talk, you see — about Mr Lomax's offer for one of Mr Harris's daughters."

Dido remembered Catherine's words about Tom's debts, and also the purple colour that had lately been on Mr Harris's face, and she rather doubted whether such a talk would have been so very quiet.

"I see," she said. "And Mr Harris confirmed Mr Lomax's account?"

"Yes, he did."

128

So that had been Mr Harris's mission. Little wonder that he had been distressed, for he could not have liked owning to the conversation. Tom's audacity in even asking had been an insult. But, it seemed, he was a good, principled man and he had known it was his duty to lift the suspicion of murder — even from a man he disliked.

"So, you see, Miss Kent," continued Sir Edgar with great condescension, "there is another wedding in sight here at Belsfield. Now that is something pleasanter for you to be thinking about than murder, is it not?"

"A wedding!" Dido stared in disbelief. "Sir Edgar, am I to understand that Mr Harris *gave his consent?*"

"Oh yes. Both gentlemen were quite clear about that. They both spoke of an agreement having been made."

"No! No, it is quite impossible," said Catherine when she joined her aunt a few moments later in the hall and was told what had happened. "They are both lying. They must be. I could sooner believe that Mr Harris shot the woman himself than that he should give his consent for Tom Lomax to marry dear little Sophia or darling Amelia."

"Well, I mean to ask Mr Tom Lomax about it myself," said Dido with determination. "I do not care much for Mr Tom. It seems that wherever I turn there he is, smiling his foolish smile and looking altogether too pleased with himself."

Resolutely, she turned and made her way across the hall to the gloomy billiard room.

Tom was alone at the big green table, working away diligently with his cue and still smiling contentedly to himself in between whistling snatches of a coarse popular song.

"I understand," said Dido, stepping into the male atmosphere of old cigar smoke and brandy, "that congratulations are the order of the day, Mr Lomax."

Tom's cue scraped the table and he cursed as balls clattered about in all directions. "I beg your pardon?" He turned, cue in hand, looking wary.

"Oh, I am sorry!" cried Dido clapping her hand to her mouth in mock innocence. "Is it meant to be a secret? But Sir Edgar just mentioned to me the subject of your talk with Mr Harris, and I was so delighted! Another wedding! I do so love to hear of weddings, and marriage does seem to be quite the fashion at Belsfield just now. So lovely!"

"Well . . ." Tom ran a finger round his cravat. "We have not yet made the engagement public. So, perhaps if you would not mind, well . . . not mentioning it for a little while . . . I am sure you understand how it is, Miss . . . er . . . Kent."

"Oh! A secret engagement! How delightful!" Dido clasped her hands together — and began to wonder whether she might not be overplaying the part of silly spinster. But Tom seemed to suspect nothing.

He made a great effort to be gallant. He laid down his billiard cue, took Dido's hand and bowed over it. "It shall be our secret for now, shall it, Miss Kent? I am sure I can rely upon you not to betray us."

130

"Oh yes, of course," simpered Dido. "I shall not breathe a word." She started for the door and then turned back. Tom was rubbing chalk onto the end of his cue and frowning at the confusion on the table. "There is just one question I cannot help asking, Mr Lomax. I am sure you will not mind."

"Yes?" he said with an effort at patience.

"Which of the Misses Harris is it that you are in love with?"

"Well, as to that ... I mean I cannot, at the moment ..." He faltered to a standstill as he saw that the smile spreading on Dido's face was neither silly nor vague.

"It is rather strange, is it not," she said, "to be unsure of the name of the lady to whom you are engaged?"

... Well, Eliza, I have made an enemy, I do not doubt. But I dislike Tom Lomax too much to care whether or not I have his good opinion. I am quite sure now that he was lying about his reason for being in the shrubbery. But if he was lying, then so was Mr Harris — which seems altogether much more surprising. Unlikely as such an idea seems, I cannot escape the conclusion that Tom and Mr Harris are confederates in some mystery. But how does it relate to the death of Miss Wallis? Or is there more than one mystery carrying on in this house? I begin to think that there must be and that I am surrounded by a great confusion of guilt and deceit.

Oh, Eliza! It is the little things that trouble me most. Things like the hiding of the dog behind my chair when Sir Edgar came out of the library; the game of football which Mrs Potter's Kate saw carrying on at Tudor House; Catherine's account of Mr Montague's headaches. And out of all these little things is building a picture which I do not like to contemplate.

You see, I know, by Mrs Holmes' account, that Mr Montague is anxious to please his father. And I think she falls short of the truth. Despite her denial, Eliza, I believe that the poor young man does indeed fear him. Because Sir Edgar is a bully. I am sure that he is — for why else would his own dog flee from him? Why else is his young footman afraid to speak to him even when he has important information to give? Why do the villagers dislike him? Yes, I make no doubt that Sir Edgar is a bully, a bully who does not like his son. Why he should have taken such a dislike to him I cannot understand, unless he perceives him as being weak. But the question that torments me is this: under such disapproval at home, what might a young man be driven to do?

And that brings me to what Catherine said yesterday when she talked of Mr Montague being at Lyme. She said something which she had not mentioned before. She said, "When Richard goes away — <u>as he does when he feels unwell</u>." Eliza, do you see what this means? Mr Montague is in the habit of absenting himself from Belsfield. Indeed, now I think of it, her ladyship told me as much on my first evening here. She spoke of Mr Montague's marriage fixing him at Belsfield and preventing him from wandering off. As if that was something he was in the habit of doing.

And this brings me — as I am sure you have anticipated — to that game of football at Tudor House, which convinced the bobbing maid — and even the egregious Mrs Potter — that Mr Blacklock is only a temporary resident in Hopton

132

Cresswell. Well, where is Mr Blacklock when he is not at Tudor House? Or, more to the point: <u>who</u> is he?

Is he, in fact, Richard Montague?

A young man, driven from his own home, living as much as he can in retirement, might, perhaps, form an unsuitable attachment. And if that attachment was likely to be made known to the parent he feared . . .

Well, Eliza, you see, no doubt, where all this is leading.

And, in support of this account, there are the undeniable facts; that the murder must have occurred while the guns were out; that the gentlemen from the house all vouch for each other during that time; and that Mr Montague <u>might</u> have returned to Belsfield that morning and reached the shrubbery without being seen by anyone but Mrs Holmes — whose affection for him would, no doubt, lead her to lie in order to protect him from suspicion.

I am quite sure that, despite his brave resolution, Mr Montague did not tell the full truth to his father at the ball. He left something at least unsaid — perhaps he did not mention the expected child. This incomplete account left Sir Edgar willing to forgive; but his son knew that if — when — the full truth was revealed, disinheritance would surely follow. He was in a desperate situation, in danger of losing everything. Perhaps he went away hoping to reason with the young woman, but she resisted and came to Belsfield to tell all. And he followed her . . .

Eliza, am I allowing my imagination to run away with me? Such an end as murder to an amour seems so very unlikely. Surely a generous payment to the woman and a sharp reprimand from Sir Edgar to his son would be less like the plot of a horrid novel and more in keeping with the manners of the modern world.

However . . .

Dido broke off as she heard the door open behind her and pulled the blotter across her incomplete letter. She was writing in the morning room, where she had hoped to be undisturbed at this time of day, when most of the household were already above stairs dressing for dinner, and when the sun had moved from the windows on this side of the house, leaving the room gloomy and rather chill, with a single log smouldering on a heap of fine grey ash in the grate.

She looked round and was immediately glad that she had hidden her letter, for the intruder was Tom Lomax. She hoped that he was in pursuit of the young ladies and would go away when he saw only her; but, on the contrary, he gave a slow satisfied smile, as if he had been looking for her, and lounged into the room.

"I am always suspicious," he said as he sprawled in a chair beside her table, "when I see a lady hiding her correspondence. I cannot help thinking that she has been broadcasting information which she ought to keep to herself."

"Indeed? No doubt that is because of your conscience, which tells you there is information you wish to keep hidden."

Tom frowned and sat for several minutes watching her insolently. Dido, determined not to be disconcerted, returned the stare.

134

He had, as she had observed before, a rather handsome face, but there was something ridiculous about the dark shadows on the sides of his cheeks that showed where he was attempting to grow fashionable long side-whiskers and, by the look of things, not succeeding very well in his ambition. And his small mouth turned down sourly at the corners, as if the world, like his whiskers, was disappointing him. Which, she didn't doubt it was, since it was — so far — refusing to provide him with a living for which he did not have to exert himself.

At the moment there was impatience and contempt in his pale eyes and, though she would not have confessed it, Dido was hurt by it. She found herself calculating for how long young men had looked at her in that way. Six years? Seven? Certainly no more than that. Before that she had been young. Never quite beautiful, of course, but reckoned pretty by some and never rated as less than "a fine girl". Then young men looked at her differently, even when they were angry with her — as they quite often were. Then there might be irritation but never, never, contempt. A young well-looking woman always had a kind of respect.

A fragile, short-lived respect, she reminded herself. And one which all too easily prevented a girl from being honest, because she was too anxious for admiration. At least when the world had branded one a "spinster" there was a kind of freedom, a release from that overwhelming concern for others' good opinion.

"Have you something to say to me, Mr Lomax?" she demanded at last. "Or have you only come to stare me out of countenance?"

He frowned, disconcerted by her honesty. But in a moment he had placed a cushion behind his head and was smiling as if he was very much at ease. "I have come to give you a little advice."

"That is very kind of you."

"Yes. You see, Miss Kent, it won't do. All this poking about asking questions. It won't do at all."

"I was not aware that I was 'poking about', Mr Lomax. And as to questions — perhaps you can explain which questions of mine you dislike."

He shifted uncomfortably in his seat. "I know what you are about," he said. "You are trying to patch up things between Dick and Catherine."

Offended by his familiar use of Catherine's Christian name, Dido chose not to reply.

"And that won't do at all," he said. "Because that affair concerns matters you don't understand. Matters no woman can understand."

"What is it that you fear I do not understand?"

"That note," he said, surprising her greatly.

"Oh? And which note would that be, Mr Lomax?"

"The one Dick left for Catherine."

For a moment Dido was at a loss. Then she remembered Catherine telling her that Mr Montague's last note had been conveyed by Tom Lomax. She met his gaze with a level stare. "But," she said, "you can know very little about that note. It was, after all, addressed to my niece and, since I am sure she did not show it to you, your part was only to hand it over, and you can know nothing of its contents."

"As to that," he said with a wave of his hand, "if Dick had cared about me reading it, he would have sealed it."

"So, you read what was not addressed to you?"

"Yes, yes. The point is —"

"The point," said Dido, rising from her seat and taking up her letter, "is that I am not willing to discuss with you information which an honourable man would not possess." She crossed the room with what she hoped was dignity and he watched her scornfully.

"The point," he said mockingly, "is that that note is a complete lie. It's plain that Dick is tired of the engagement and wants to end it. So he has made up this story about being disinherited."

Dido opened the door and stood for a moment with the brass door-knob in her hand. Sunlight from the hall streamed into the gloomy room and with it came a lovely rippling melody from the pianoforte across in the drawing room. "Of that," she said coldly, "you can have no proof at all."

"Oh, I have proof! Proof that would be plain to any man. Only a woman could be blind enough to believe what was in that note."

Dido hesitated in the doorway. Her pride and her anger urged her to walk on and yet her curiosity was all for staying. To ask a question now would have all the appearance of inconsistency — and yet she could not prevent herself.

"What then," she said quietly, her back still turned to him, "is this proof?"

He did not answer. She turned back and saw him lounging still in the chair, his hands folded behind his head and his long legs stretched across the Turkey carpet. He smiled at her. "Dick can't be disinherited," he said. "The old man might want to do it, but he can't."

"I beg your pardon?" She took hold of the back of a chair to steady herself. "I do not understand you."

"No, women never do understand inheritance. But you don't need to believe me, Miss Kent. Ask any man in the house. Ask Harris. Or ask my father. They will all tell you the same. The whole of the Belsfield estate is entailed on the next male heir. It *must* pass to Dick when the old fellow dies. The terms of the settlement are quite clear. No one can stop him inheriting."

"But . . ." Dido struggled for both understanding and dignity. "If there was a serious disagreement between Mr Montague and Sir Edgar . . ."

"It would make no manner of difference. My dear Miss Kent, Dick could spit in the old man's face at dinner and he'd still inherit everything."

"Perhaps he would inherit on his father's death. But in the meantime, without his father's goodwill, he would be penniless."

"Again, you are arguing like a woman. A man with Dick's prospects is *never* penniless. He could borrow against his expectations and live very comfortably until the old man pops off."

For a moment confusion threatened to overwhelm her and it was nothing but her determination not to show weakness in front of him that kept her on her feet. He was watching her, cruelly eager for any sign of pain on her face.

"So you see," he said. "All this 'I have nothing to offer you and it is only right that I should release you from our engagement' is nothing but hog-wash. The truth is, he's tired of the girl and wants rid of her. In fact, I don't believe he was ever wholeheartedly in favour of the match at all. It's the old man that's got his heart set on it."

Hot blood ran to Dido's cheeks at the insult. "I wonder," she said, "what your motive can be, Mr Lomax, in telling me this?"

He rose slowly from his chair and bowed to her. "I merely wish to be of service to you, Miss Kent. I mean to put you on your guard. It is very unwise of you to keep asking questions which can only result in the truth coming out and dear Catherine being very badly hurt by it."

And with that he strode past her and crossed the hall to the billiard room, whistling as he went.

Left alone, Dido sank down into a chair as if the life-force had been drained out of her. It was impossible to know exactly what to think; but every possible thought was unpleasant and the clearest of them all was that if Tom had spoken the truth about the settlement of the estate, then it changed everything.

CHAPTER
TWELVE

Dido was miserable.

She had struggled for some time over Tom Lomax's assertion that the Belsfield estate was entailed, reasoning that it could not be true. She would not believe that Catherine could have been so deceived. Surely she had properly understood the expectations of the young man before the engagement was formed.

But she could not comfort herself with that thought for very long before honesty forced her to admit it as all too possible that Catherine's exaggerated notions of disinterested love had prevented her from even asking about such things.

However, she did continue to cherish a hope that Tom might be lying — for she had very little reason to suppose him honourable or truthful — until she made enquiries, in roundabout terms, of his father one evening as they were sitting together by the fire. And he confirmed Tom's account exactly.

Her disappointment must have shown on her face, for he immediately asked what was amiss. "I am sorry if I have said anything to make you uncomfortable."

"Oh no," she said quickly. "I am quite comfortable, thank you."

And, despite her worry over the entail, that was true. At that moment she was comfortable. She and William Lomax had by now fallen quite into the habit of conversing companionably by the hearth while the others played at cards. It had come to be Dido's favourite part of every day. He was a very pleasant companion: clever and full of information and yet always ready to listen in his turn, and so quick in understanding her strange comments and observations as to make her feel that she too was clever — which is always the greatest recommendation in a companion.

She felt quite resentful of Sir Edgar when business of his took Mr Lomax away to the library after tea and left her to spend her time reading — or rather sitting with a volume open before her while she stared blankly at the page and listened for the opening of the library door.

And then, on the very evening that he explained the entail to her, Mr Lomax informed her — with a very pleasing degree of regret — that he would be leaving early on business the next morning and expected to be away from Belsfield for several days.

Dido was very miserable. There was no one else in the house whose society afforded her so much pleasure. And her enquiries into Mr Montague's disappearance had, after a rather promising beginning, come to nothing and left her surrounded by questions which she could not answer.

And there was, in addition to all this, a suspicion that she was being excessively foolish; a suspicion that there were truths, not only staring her in the face, but actually crying out at her to notice them, shrieking at her — and laughing at her behind her back for her stupidity.

She was sitting in the gallery one morning, meditating upon all this and attempting to establish exactly what she knew and what she could surmise. The sum total was not very promising.

If Tom Lomax was to be believed then the scene in the ballroom was nothing but a pretence, a kind of elaborate charade enacted to deceive Catherine. But if that was so, she could not understand why the charade should have been played so badly. Pollard might only be a friend of Mr Montague's impressed into the scene, but why had he played his part so badly? Why had he not spoken? An appearance of conversation had been necessary to make the charade believable — and yet he said nothing.

No, even though she was forced to believe Tom about the entail, she could not believe the conclusion he had drawn. Mr Montague had not set out to deceive Catherine. It was, after all, a lie which could easily be detected, for it seemed everyone in the house knew about the settlement of the estate.

But that only left the possibility that Mr Montague had told the truth when he said that he was a poor man. And how could that be? Since even if Sir Edgar was a bully who had no affection for his son, he could not disinherit him.

It made no sense at all — or else she was too stupid to understand the sense that it made.

It was while she was in this state of despair that a letter was delivered to her. And its contents did nothing to raise her spirits. It was from her sister and had been written two days ago.

Dearest Dido,

I take up my pen with a heavy heart, for I know you will not like to read what I know I must write and I cannot remember when I have ever written to you before without being sure that you will welcome my letter.

Dearest, are you not being as blind as poor Catherine? You are so very tender-hearted, for all your pretence of being satirical, that I fear you are failing to see guilt where it is most obvious. It is quite natural that you should do so, of course, for it seems to me that the guilty man is particularly plausible and charming. And I do not mean to set up my opinion against yours, nor pretend to possess your quickness of mind, but it may be that some things are seen clearer at a distance.

To own the truth, I distrust your Mr Lomax. I mean Mr Lomax senior, not the son, who, by your own account, you do not trust, and very rightly I am sure. Though he is, of course, still very young and it is to be hoped that he may turn out well in the end. Oh dear, I am getting quite off the point, but one should always try to think the best of one's fellow creatures, which makes it all the harder to say what I am quite determined to say — even though you may be as angry with me in the end as Catherine is with you.

Dearest, have you considered the possibility of Mr Lomax's guilt? I know that it is very difficult to do so. But we have to believe that someone is guilty. Unless it is possible that the poor woman died through some terrible accident. Has that possibility been properly considered? I think that it should be.

But to return to Mr Lomax. If we have to think someone a killer, then why not him? We have reason to suppose him an adulterer. Now, maybe it is to Judor House that his carriage conveys her ladyship. Perhaps that is the purpose of that establishment. Perhaps Mr Blacklock is not Richard Montague, but William Lomax. After all, Mr Lomax is not always at Belsfield. Do you know where he resides when he is not in his employer's house?

Do you not see how likely all this is? I have been thinking about it a great deal. Mr Montague, you see, discovered what was carrying on. That was the family shame that he wrote of in his letter. The visitor to Judor House, Mr Pollard, who was probably, by some coincidence, a friend of Mr Montague's, informed him (I mean Mr Montague) of it at the ball and he immediately told his father about it.

Now, in order to preserve the honour of the family — for you tell me that nothing is of greater consequence with Sir Edgar than the honour of the family — he was all for smoothing matters over and covering up the business. But Mr Montague is moral and religious — for I cannot believe that dear Catherine, for all her little faults, would attach herself to a man who was not moral and religious — and he quarrelled with his father over this matter. Mr Montague left the house — perhaps he went with his friend to Judor House — yes, I think that he must have done, because that is how Miss Wallis — who was, of course, Mr Lomax's housekeeper — discovered that the lady who came regularly to visit her master was none other than Lady Montague. And so she pursued Mr Lomax to Belsfield, threatening, no doubt, to expose him unless he paid her a considerable sum.

144

And he killed her. Though I don't doubt that the poor man is very sorry for it now . . .

Dido dropped the letter into her lap and stared along the polished length of the gallery, momentarily overwhelmed by such a variety of emotions that she did not exactly know what she felt.

There was anger at her sister for suggesting such an unlikely course of events. But the anger was not lasting. Eliza was not the sort of woman one could be angry with for long and soon Dido was more inclined to smile over the sorry conflict that there was in the letter between natural good nature and a desire to try her hand at mystery solving. And then, when she reread the letter, she found that, fanciful though much of it was, there was a small kernel of sense in it.

It was, she realised with shame, very true that she had not considered properly the likelihood of Mr Lomax's guilt. She had not considered it because — and there was no escaping this horrible truth — because he was a very charming man and she was foolish, foolish in a way that she should have left behind her when she gave up curling her hair and began to sit out dances in the ballroom.

Well, she thought with determination, I shall consider the matter now. But still she found that she was strongly inclined to argue against the suggestion. She could not help it. To clear her mind she drew a pencil from her pocket and noted down on the cover of the letter her arguments against Eliza. They consisted of:

1. There is no appearance of affection between Mr Lomax and her ladyship. I have observed them closely and they do not exchange more than the simplest civilities with one another.
2. The other gentlemen swear that Mr Lomax did not leave the shooting party.
3. How did Mr Pollard convey the information of Mr Lomax's adultery without saying a word?

She read through what she had written and found it singularly unconvincing. Points two and three could, of course, be argued with equal force against the guilt of any other member of the household. Nor would point one stand up to examination, for the show of indifference between the couple was entirely consistent with a guilty, clandestine affection.

So she wrote down everything she could think of that supported Eliza's position.

1. Gossip about her ladyship.
2. Catherine's observation of her ladyship going out in Mr Lomax's carriage.
3. Her ladyship's medicine.
4. Mr Lomax has a post-chaise with yellow wheels — like the one which visits Judor House.

Well, she thought looking over the list, it is hardly enough to convict a man.

She sighed and passed a weary hand across her face. Relieved, in spite of herself, that she did not have to suspect Mr Lomax so very much.

The problem was that there was still a great deal that she did not understand. There seemed to be so much afoot — so much amiss — at Belsfield that one scarcely knew who to trust and who to suspect. As Annie Holmes had said, every family has its secrets. But there was no denying that the Montagues of Belsfield Hall seemed to have more secrets than most.

Dido stared along the ranks of old Sir Edgars and all the Annes and Elizabeths and Marys that they had married. The autumn sun, shining in through the window, was warm upon the nape of her neck; dust-motes floated in its light and a warm, pleasant scent of beeswax rose from the polished floor.

Somewhere here, if Annie Holmes was to be believed, there was a clue to one of those secrets. Somewhere among these paintings was the key to the trouble between father and son. She stood up and walked along the gallery, studying the pompous, painted faces as she had done many times before. None of them suggested any kind of solution to her.

The gallery ended in a wide staircase, which led down to the best bedrooms at the front of the house, and just to the left there was a dark, narrow passageway that led to the back stairs. As Dido reached this point she heard a voice raised on the landing below. She paused beside the banister.

"Ah, boy! D'you mind coming here, sir!" It was undoubtedly the colonel's voice; there was no mistaking the hearty, archaic tone of it. But it had a pleasant, far from ill-tempered sound — indeed, it sounded almost affectionate, which made it rather surprising that it should be followed by the sound of nimble, running feet.

A moment later Jack's black head came bobbing quickly up the stairs. Dido stepped aside and the boy ran past her, turned into the dark passage and was instantly lost to view.

She stood alone for a minute, reflecting that perhaps her notion of hide-and-seek had not been so very far from the truth after all. And then there was a sound of much heavier feet and the colonel's broad red face appeared.

"Ah, Miss er . . ." (Would it, Dido wondered, be only fair to inform him of her name, or was it allowable to leave him floundering with his *ahs* and *ers* for the rest of her visit?) "Ah yes, m'dear. Have you seen young Jack? Did he come by you?"

"No," she replied on an impulse. "He did not come this way."

"Ah, very well, very well. It's of no great consequence, y'know."

He bowed and retreated. Dido turned into the narrow passage, only to hear Jack's footsteps fading rapidly down the kitchen stairs.

She stood for a moment in the gloomy corridor, which smelt of dust and very old carpet, with just a suggestion of the roasting of long-forgotten joints from the kitchen. She shook her head. Before she came to Belfield she had thought she was rather partial to puzzles and mysteries. She had a great regard for the work of such authors as Ann Radcliffe and Charlotte

148

Smith, but lately she was beginning to suspect that her appetite for the unexplained was surfeiting.

She could not even begin upon the wildest surmise as to why a military gentleman of rather advanced years should be pursuing a young footman about the upper corridors of a house — nor why the said footman should be so determined upon escape. There was nothing in Dido's experience to suggest a solution to that particular mystery.

She started back towards the gallery, then came to a standstill.

There was another painting hanging here upon the wall of the little passage. Hanging where no one could see it. Even when she strained her eyes she received no more than a vague impression of a very large green and brown landscape in a heavy, ornate frame.

Was it perhaps a bad painting, put out of the way so that it did not spoil the effect of the gallery?

Dido was exceedingly fond of bad paintings; they appealed to that part of her that her sister called "satirical". After a little struggle, two broken fingernails and a bleeding thumb, she succeeded in unbolting and pushing back one of the heavy shutters that covered a window almost opposite to the picture.

Light fell in upon it.

It was most certainly not a bad painting. Dido was no connoisseur, but she was almost sure that it was better than anything else in the gallery. For a moment she forgot everything else and simply enjoyed looking at it.

It must have been painted a little more than twenty years ago and it showed the Belsfield estate in all its grandeur and prosperity: the gardens, the elegant sweep of parkland, and even, in the distance, cattle grazing and corn in its stooks. The sun of late summer shone on a perfect day and so skilled had been the painter's hand that there in that stuffy, cramped space she seemed almost to smell the ripening grain. It was a domain that any man would have been proud to possess. And Sir Edgar *was* proud; for there he was, pink-cheeked and proprietorial, in the shade of a fine large tree to the left of the foreground. There was no mistaking him for anything but the lord of this domain — with his confident stance and the marks of his status: his dog gazing up at him and his shotgun on his arm. His free hand rested on the back of an ornate iron bench upon which sat his lady, with young Richard, just a baby, in her lap.

The ruling character of the whole thing was pride, from the stance of the new father, to the magnificent scale and quality of the painting and the elaboration of curling scrolls and gilding on its frame.

And yet, here it was hidden away in this dark passageway. Why?

Dido frowned and chewed at the end of her pencil. It felt as if she was a little girl again and back in the school-room puzzling fruitlessly over long division. Her head hurt. Everything seemed dark and confusing.

Something in this picture had had to be hidden. But what? Not the landscape, nor the wife, surely. For all his tyranny, Sir Edgar was a conscientious landlord and

150

an attentive husband. Could it be Richard that he wanted to hide?

And then, with the suddenness of that stiff old shutter swinging open (and without so much as a split nail) light poured in upon her mind.

She understood.

She ran back into the gallery and turned about and about until she was dizzy. The cracked and grainy Edgars and Annes and Elizabeths stared down in contempt of her slowness.

It was so very obvious to her now that she had been looking at the wrong thing in this gallery of portraits. She should have looked, not at the pictures themselves, but at the names beneath them. There they were, the holders of this estate, ranked down through history: Edgar after Edgar after Edgar.

But the latest Sir Edgar, to whom the tradition of his family was as essential as the air that he breathed and the blood that ran in his veins, had not given his son the family name: he was Richard, not Edgar.

Why?

Dido spun round with her hand to her mouth. Was it because he had come to suspect that the boy was not his son?

And was that why he had hidden away that proud portrait of fatherhood and inheritance?

CHAPTER
THIRTEEN

. . . It is very shocking, Eliza. I am almost tempted to echo her ladyship and declare that one does not know what to think. But, truly, I think that it could be so. I cannot get it out of my head. That Sir Edgar and his lady should live with such a secret between them! And how wretched Mr Montague must be if he knows about it! I have passed a near sleepless night with thinking about it all — which I tell you, of course, on purpose that you may scold me and entreat me to have more care for my health.

It is a matter to which I must give a great deal more thought before I quite decide whether I believe or disbelieve it. However, it is not entirely without a brighter aspect. For I have at last succeeded in saying something which pleases Catherine. You see, of course the great advantage that there is to her in all this. The man she loves bears the stain of illegitimacy — though Catherine will naturally not allow that there is any stain and talks very stoutly of how he is not to be held accountable for the sins of others. But, since she does not expect her liberality to be shared by Francis and Margaret, she gleefully anticipates being soon relieved of the burden of their approval.

I, as you have probably guessed, am rather less happy, being a great deal less certain that if he is disinherited they can live on love alone. But this is not a serious worry for me because I do not believe that this discovery can explain anything beyond Sir Edgar's dislike of Mr Montague. For, no matter how certain he may be of the young man's fathering, he could never prove it, nor, I think, cut off the entail on such grounds. Catherine, however, is quite sure that this is the information Mr Montague received at the ball — the reason he describes himself as a poor man. She talks happily of cases she has read of in newspapers in which men have been able to deny fatherhood; but I think she is led astray by her strong desire to starve in the company of her beloved. Which starving, you must understand, will be accomplished in the most elegant manner possible and will never be accompanied by such unromantic expedients as old cloaks or the preservation of shoes with pattens.

Human nature is a very strange thing, is it not?

I make that highly original observation, not because I suppose that you need it to be pointed out to you, but purely for the purposes of composition, because the next thing which I particularly want to write about is a further illustration of its truth.

Colonel Walborough.

I apologise for running on so rapidly, but there is little time for writing and there are things which I must tell you about the colonel.

He sat beside me at dinner today. This is not, in itself, a strong proof of the strangeness of his nature, though I was extremely surprised to find that he had at last discovered my name. And, by the by, he left me in no doubt that he had discovered it, for he used it at every opportunity. But the style of his conversation was a great shock to me.

In short, the colonel has heard the account of my skill as a future-gazer, which Catherine has been spreading so assiduously. And it was about that that he wished to talk. Did I often foresee the future? he wanted to know. And had I known about my gift for long? And — most particularly — what did I see in <u>his</u> future?

And I wondered that such a sensible man and one so successful in his profession should attach so much importance to such nonsense. It is so very strange, is it not, that men can be very clever about some subjects and foolish about others? With women I believe it is different; we are either wholly sensible or wholly foolish.

Well, the colonel talked so through the soup and the fish, with a digression or two upon the different modes of fortune telling that have fallen within his observation in various parts of the world, and I began to hope that there would be no need for me to satisfy him with a fortune; but, just as the mutton was put upon the table, he began to press me for an answer.

"A man of action like yourself will make his own fortune," I said, meaning to be very clever and to flatter him into dropping the subject. "You can have no use for future-gazing."

But, unfortunately, that only took me deeper into the matter. He confessed that in his professional life he did indeed, as I so aptly put it, make his own fortune. No man more so. There he never had a doubt; had never yet had to ask for anyone's advice and sincerely hoped he would never need to. G– –! m'dear, he'd put a gun to his own head rather than ask for help. With men and weapons he always knew just what to do. But, he didn't quite know why it should be.

154

Never had understood it, don't y'know; but in matters of the heart — and here he cast a rather fearful look across the table at the Misses Harris — he had not quite the same d– – – –d certainty.

He was not, he confessed, always quite the thing in society. Didn't know what to say to the ladies. Indeed, sometimes he felt it necessary to quite shut himself away. Like a hermit of old — don't y'know.

And he talked on until I began to fear that all the hopes and accomplishments of the Misses Harris would come to nothing if I did not oblige him with a reassuring fortune.

So I have agreed that I will soon look into his palm to see what I may of his future — though I do not quite know when this will be achieved since the colonel is as anxious as I am that we have no audience for the performance and I do not know how we are to gain a tête-à-tête without arousing the jealousy of the Misses Harris. However, I am determined that when it does take place I shall use the opportunity to discover a little more about him. I most particularly wish to know why he has so recently broken his resolution against marriage — has something occurred in his private life to incline him towards matrimony — or perhaps to free him for an advantageous match?

For, you see, a very intriguing thought came to me when the colonel spoke of sometimes shutting himself away. Eliza, you write in your letter that Mr Blacklock might be Mr Lomax, and I have wondered whether he is Mr Montague. But could he not also be Colonel Walborough — or indeed Mr Harris, or Sir Edgar, or Tom? Gentlemen are so free to move about in the world; they are not fixed in one place as women are.

I have contrived to send a message to the bobbing maid by Jenny the housemaid, whose home, you will remember (if you have been paying my letters the very close attention which they deserve) is at Hopton Cresswell and who, I am glad to find, is due to take her monthly day off again very soon. I have asked whether it is possible to discover from Mrs Potter's Kate what Mr Blacklock's appearance may be.

Unfortunately, before I can hope to receive any reply to this enquiry, I must go to Lyme. It is all quite settled. We are to travel there tomorrow and spend the night at an inn in the town. It is, as Catherine says, to be a regular exploring party, comprising myself and Catherine and the Misses Harris, escorted by the colonel and Tom Lomax. Sir Edgar condescendingly hopes that a little excursion will cheer the ladies and take our minds off the unpleasantness of late events and regrets that his public duties prevent him from availing himself of the honour of accompanying us, etc etc. Her ladyship is not to be of the party; she is indisposed. (I very much fear that she has procured a replacement for the physic which I poured away.) Mrs Harris stays behind to bear her ladyship company, and Margaret remains here too — because she wishes that she had been the chosen companion and, no doubt, hopes to prove herself better suited to the office.

Catherine is quite wild to go. She is very certain that she will find Mr Montague at Lyme, upon which she plans to throw herself into his arms, declare that she cares not whether they have bread to eat or not, so long as they can be together, and so live out the rest of her days in blissful poverty.

Oh, Eliza, I wish I too could believe that it will all be so easily settled!

CHAPTER
FOURTEEN

Lyme was as beautiful as everyone had promised, and, afterwards, Dido very much regretted that she had not been in a state of mind to do justice to its views. The hours that she spent there were too crowded with incident and surprise to leave her memory with more than an indistinct impression of waves sparkling in autumn sunshine, a steep hill leading down to the curve of the bay, pretty little old houses tumbling almost into the sea and, of course, the great stone bulk of the famous Cobb, stretching out into the water like a sleeping monster.

She was enjoying this prospect about two hours after their arrival. She had walked out onto the Cobb, leaving her companions gathered around Miss Harris, who was attempting to capture the scene upon her easel. Dido rather doubted her success, for she seemed to have so poor a grasp of perspective that a lopsided sheep grazing upon the low cliffs looked almost large enough to devour the town; it was partly to conceal her laughter that she had separated herself.

It was exhilarating to be alone on the exposed stone walk with the wind driving the white-crested waves about her and snapping at her bonnet ribbons, and she was not pleased to see Colonel Walborough walking intently towards her, red-faced, head bowed against the wind, hands clasped behind his back.

"Ah, Miss Kent, I wondered whether this might be an opportunity . . ." he began and was then forced to pause from lack of breath. "My fortune, don't you know," he reminded her and held out a large, plump hand. "You were so kind as to say that you would read my palm."

"Oh yes." Dido looked down at the hand and wondered what she ought to do with it. The rage for palmistry had not yet arrived at Badleigh and she had never witnessed the science. But she bent her head over the proffered hand and endeavoured to look wise.

The sunlight showed up calluses on the palm — no doubt caused by weapons and the reigns of horses. The lines criss-crossing the hard skin were unremarkable. What struck her most forcibly was the childish shortness of the big, square nails, which were bitten down almost to the quick.

"Ah, yes," she said slowly with a shake of her head, which she hoped suggested profound musing. "I see that you are very worried about something, Colonel Walborough. Something is troubling you a great deal."

"You are right, m'dear. That is quite remarkable! Can you see *that* in my hand?"

"Oh yes," Dido assured him. "It is all here to be read in your hand." She smiled and held aside the unruly ribbons of her bonnet, which were flapping about her face. "Now, let me see," she said, thinking much more of how she might discover information than reveal it.

158

"There is something very strange here in these lines. Very strange indeed."

She looked up and saw his eyes fixed intently upon her and his broad cheeks glowing in the wind. She could almost fancy that he was holding his breath. "Colonel, I see that you have lately undergone a change of heart. That you have taken a decision to alter the course of your life."

"Miss Kent, you are quite remarkable!"

"Thank you, Colonel Walborough. You recognise what I am talking about?"

"Oh yes." He looked anxiously about him. Their companions were still gathered about the easel. Miss Sophia's earnest chatter was borne to them on the wind, followed by an extravagant laugh from Tom Lomax. "What I wish you would tell me, m'dear," he continued in a low, hurried voice, "is whether I am *right* in making that change. It is so damned hard to be sure. Will it answer? Will it bring me all that I hope it will? Don't you see? That's what I need to know."

Dido bent lower over the plump hand that was still held out expectantly and made a pretence of studying it. The waves slapped upon the wall of the Cobb; a seagull shrieked and laughed as it fought its way up the wind. The hand before her began to shake a little. She gave a long sigh. "I am sorry, Colonel, it is very difficult to decipher . . . Perhaps if you could explain a little to me about the nature of this change in your life — and why you have made it. Then I might be better able to understand . . ."

He took a step closer to her and lowered his voice to a whisper that was all but torn away on the breeze. "Well, the fact of the matter is, m'dear, that I've made up my mind to . . . enrol my name in the lists of Hymen, as they say. In short, I plan to marry, Miss Kent, and it ain't something I ever thought to do."

"Yes, indeed, I see," said Dido, nodding sagely over his palm. "Yes, that would explain this great change in your future, which is written so clearly here." She pondered again for the space of time that it took for three waves to break on the Cobb wall. "Mmm, I cannot quite make out still whether your decision will increase your happiness . . . Perhaps if I knew why you had decided to break through your resolution of not marrying . . ."

"Well, you see, Miss Kent," he whispered, "this is the way it is. And this is quite in confidence, don't y'know?"

"Oh yes, I will be very discreet."

"Well, this is the way it is. There's this uncle of mine; old fellow and pretty sick too, likely to pop off any day now. And he's got a monstrous big estate and I'm the only kin he has in this world. So, you see the way the land lies, don't you?"

"Oh quite! Naturally you look forward to inheriting and I am sure it is a great comfort to your uncle to know that his property will pass into such good hands."

"Ah, yes. But the devil of the business is, m'dear, that he ain't that comfortable about it. You see, he's heard rumours about me." He gave a spluttering cough. "Ill-natured gossip that I won't trouble a lady with . . .

160

But the old fellow has taken against me and he won't put his name to the will until I 'regularise my life', as he terms it."

"And that regularising must take the form of matrimony?"

The colonel nodded.

"I see."

So, thought Dido immediately, the colonel fears only respectable ladies. He is, in fact, a libertine and a womaniser. She was sure it must be so, despite what the other men said about him, for she could think of no other irregularity in a man's life for which marriage might be considered a cure . . .

She stood in thoughtful contemplation of the hand for several moments longer. His reply had presented her with a dilemma. Should she advise him to marry or not? The trick she had undertaken for her own ends had given her a power which she did not want.

His motives for marriage were selfish and his character, apparently, doubtful. But how eager to be married was Miss Harris? How acutely did she feel the approach of three and twenty? And, in a prudential light, it would be a fine match for her . . .

Well, these were questions which the lady must decide for herself.

"Ah! I understand now," she said raising her eyes to his red, anxious face. "This was why I found your hand so difficult to read. You see, Colonel, your future happiness depends entirely upon how you act now. It is written here that you will find true contentment only with a woman who exactly understands the demands of your uncle. You must explain to any lady you ask to marry you the reason why you have broken through your lifetime's resolution of remaining single."

"I think," said Catherine a little more than an hour later, "that Colonel Walborough will make an offer to Miss Harris before the day is over. I see that they are walking out together along the beach."

"Hmm," said Dido thoughtfully, "and that leaves Mr Tom Lomax to entertain her sister."

"Why do you look so ill-tempered? I did not know that you disapproved of love-making."

Dido made no reply, but it passed through her mind that she did most heartily disapprove when either one of the two gentlemen making love might fairly be suspected of murder. For, with them both so set upon matrimony for their own mercenary reasons, might not either one of them have destroyed a woman who stood in his way?

She sighed deeply and they walked on a little way in silence. They were now upon a rutted track and had left the town a little way behind them. The voices of visitors had faded and there was nothing about them but short, sheep-bitten grass; no sound but the rush of waves and the crying of gulls overhead.

Suddenly Catherine stopped, turned to her companion and surprised her greatly by saying very rapidly, "Aunt Dido, there is something I must tell you. Something about Richard. I did not like to tell you before. But now that you are going to meet him, I feel you should know it. If you don't you may ask questions that will pain

162

him. You have got to be such a great asker of questions lately."

"Have I?"

"Yes, you know that you have. It is all: How? And who? And where? with you now."

"My dear, you did ask me to discover things."

"Yes, but I did not mean . . ." She stopped helplessly and brushed away the strands of hair that the breeze was blowing across her cheek.

"What is it that you wish to tell me about Mr Montague?" asked Dido.

Catherine frowned and scuffed at the grass with the toe of her shoe. (She had always done that, Dido remembered, no matter what they had said to her about it injuring the leather.) "He is not . . . He is not quite what you would expect a man of his age and birth to be," she said. "He is not quite the man of the world."

"I see."

"He is . . . very diffident."

"I see."

"Surprisingly diffident. He has no confidence in himself at all. He has always been like that. Ever since he was a little boy. It is all Sir Edgar's fault. He was so unkind to Richard. He made him work so hard at his lessons and he was hardly allowed to leave Belsfield, you know. He had no friends except the servants' children."

Like Annie Holmes, thought Dido. And she wondered too whether this extreme diffidence and lack of confidence in his own abilities might be the reason behind the way the family talked of Richard; was it this which made them seem so unwilling to say anything which clearly delineated his character?

Catherine's sudden disclosure interested her in another way, too. For it suggested a deeper knowledge of the young man's character than had appeared before. In fact, this honest description of her lover accorded with other observations which Dido had lately made and, together with them, made her rather wonder whether there were other things about him which Catherine knew and was determined to conceal.

Out loud she said only, "Catherine, why do you feel that you must tell me this now?"

"Because . . ." She drew in a long breath. "Because I do not want you to distress him with a lot of questions when you meet him."

"If I meet him . . ."

"No, Aunt, it is a case of *when* you meet him. Because you are going to meet him now. We are on our way to Richard at this very moment. I made enquiries at the inn, you see, about the house. It is called the Old Grange. I remember him telling me that. And we will find it at the end of this track."

Dido looked doubtingly from the track which led off across the grass — turning now slightly uphill and away from the sea — to Catherine, who was smiling at it as if it were the very path to happiness. "My dear," she said cautiously, "we can by no means be sure that he will be at this house."

"But I know he will, Aunt. I know."

"You are very good at knowing exactly what you wish to know."

"You will see," said Catherine and without another word she hurried on along the path, setting a pace which left neither of them any breath to spare for conversation.

After about ten minutes they came to the top of the rise. Catherine stopped.

"There it is," she cried, breathless and triumphant.

Standing alone and fronting the sea, it was a solid, four-square house such as young children delight in drawing, with two clumps of tall chimneys and four large windows on either side of the front door, and a gravel sweep with iron gates before it.

"It is just as he described it," cried Catherine happily. "I know we will find him here."

She began to run towards the house, but Dido, following at a more sedate pace, could not share her certainty. The place had an unpromising appearance to her. There was no smoke issuing from the chimneys and the windows all looked dark. Her heart sank. Drawing closer, she discerned not a few weeds in the gravel of the drive, and when she came up to Catherine she found her staring in amazement at the gates, which were locked together with a great length of rusty chain.

"I don't understand," said Catherine wretchedly and she took hold of the gate and shook it, but all the good that did was to stain her gloves with rust.

"He is not here," said Dido gently. "It is plain that no one has lived here for many years."

Catherine continued to stare at the house. "I was so sure . . ." Tears gathered on her eyelashes and her lip trembled. "Aunt Dido, I was so sure he would be here."

165

"I know, my dear, but really there was no reason why he should be." She put an arm about the girl for she looked as if she might faint. They stood for some moments staring at the blank face of the house and the dark windows seemed to stare back at them. Dido shivered. "Come, there is no use us staying here in the wind. We had better walk back to the others."

But Catherine resisted and held her ground, stubbornly watching the house as if by willing it, she could *make* her lover be there.

"Is the young lady unwell? Can I be of assistance?"

Dido turned and saw an elderly gentleman hurrying anxiously along the track towards them with a pair of terrier puppies playing about his ankles. "No, thank you," she said, stepping forward to shield Catherine's distress. "We are just a little disappointed. We had hoped to find friends of ours living here."

"Here?" said the man. "Well now, there's been no one here at the Old Grange for many a year."

"Are you sure?" cried Catherine, almost pleading. She passed a hand across her face to wipe away the tears — and left a smear of rust on her cheek. "We are looking for a Mr Montague. Do you know him?"

"Montague?" the man repeated, and then was distracted by the puppies, who, now that he was standing still, were having a fine time worrying at his gaiters. He released himself by picking up a stone from the track and throwing it as hard as he could across the turf. The little dogs bounded happily after it. "Montague? No, it's a very long time since anyone of that name lived here. Not since that little boy was here with his tutor. And that would be, well now, let me see. Fifteen . . . no, it must be sixteen years ago because it was just after we first came here and before my dear wife died. I remember that because she used to feel so sorry for the poor little chap. Many's the time, after we'd seen him out here playing, she'd go home and weep, bless her tender heart!"

"Sorry for him?" asked Dido quickly and Catherine too gave the gentleman a look of some surprise.

But the puppies were back now and he had forgotten their conversation in the more pressing business of searching for another stone and keeping his bootlaces away from sharp little teeth. When they had again bounced off on a fruitless errand, Dido repeated her question. "Why did your wife feel sorry for the little boy, sir?"

The man rubbed at his chin. "Well now," he said. "Fine looking little chap he was and yet . . . well . . ."

Dido and Catherine looked at each other in puzzlement. "You mean he was sickly?" said Dido.

"Yes . . . sickly." The old fellow had gone red in the face and he shuffled his feet on the track as if he knew not what to say. "Sickly in the head, if you know what I mean," he added at last. "Well, the fact is, it was plain for all to see, he was weak in his wits."

"I see," said Dido as calmly as she could and put herself forward so that Catherine might be spared from speaking. "How very sad. And how could you tell that there was anything wrong with the boy?"

"Well now, you see, we'd see him out in the garden. Just between ourselves, I fancy the physicians had said the sea air would benefit his health. Though it was plain to me that nothing could be done for him. I have no great opinion of physicians, myself. Take your money and make all manner of promises . . ." He paused. "Well, yes, as I was saying, the boy would be out in the garden in all weathers, rain or shine, summer or winter, and my wife and I, we'd call out and say 'how do you do?' and he'd never say a word. Just wave his hands at us, he would, and make a kind of roaring sound. Very sad. Very sad."

Dido felt Catherine's grip tighten upon her arm and, indeed, she herself felt rather shaken by this strange account. But she was now becoming so accustomed to her role of discoverer of truth that it was natural for her to exert herself and to extract as much information as she could.

"And what of the tutor? Does he still live in Lyme?" she said. "Do you happen to remember the name of the man who was tutor to young Master Montague?"

The elderly gentleman rubbed thoughtfully at his chin again. "No, I am not sure I ever knew his name," he said. "But I would certainly know him again if I saw him. There'd be no mistaking him. Very tall fellow, he was, with flaming-red hair. I remember my dear wife used to say . . ." He stopped suddenly at the sound of frantic yelping in the distance. "Little devils are down a rabbit hole again!" he cried, and, with a hurried bow and an apology, he was off across the turf.

Dido and Catherine stood for several minutes staring at one another, hardly knowing what to think. Then, still in silence, they linked arms and started slowly back along the track towards the town. A little way off they could see the old gentleman on his knees bellowing furiously into a hole in the ground.

"Catherine, my dear . . ." Dido began after a little while.

But Catherine merely shook her head. Her heart — and, no doubt, her eyes — were too full for conversation to be attempted.

Dido held her arm in silent compassion and they walked on through the scent of salt and wild thyme with seabirds wheeling and calling over their heads.

She was not sorry to have time to reflect, for her own mind was overflowing with troubling thoughts. What exactly was Mr Montague's present state of health? How much was he recovered from the little boy who roared and waved his hands about? How severe were those fits of headache which caused him to leave his parents' home? And how might the sickness in his mind affect his actions?

Stealing a glance at Catherine's white, shocked face, she guessed that she had, so far, seen little to distress her in the behaviour of her lover. Well, she had not known him long . . .

And yet, there was something in the girl's manner which demanded Dido's respect, something which spoke of a deeper attachment, a love founded more in reality and less in romantic notions than she had previously suspected . . .

They walked on in silence towards the lights of the town.

CHAPTER
FIFTEEN

... This sickness in Mr Montague might explain so much. It provides a motive, not only for Sir Edgar's dislike, but also for his determination to marry the young man quickly to a girl who scarcely knows him — even though that girl has no great fortune and no family worthy of note.

Could this be the reason for the hidden picture and the withholding of the family name? No, it could not of course have been a reason for the naming, for the child's affliction would not have shown itself until he was a few years old. No, I think my first surmise is sound and Sir Edgar does indeed doubt his paternity. For there is still my lady's physic to be considered.

You have my thoughts just as they arise, Eliza, I do not know what I write — nor what I think. But it is a great relief to write to you and I sincerely hope that you will not be so very unreasonable as to expect sense from me.

One source of distress is that I believe I have misjudged Catherine. I think that her affection for Mr Montague goes a good deal deeper than I have thought. You see, she was so very upset by the old gentleman's words this afternoon, struck almost senseless by them, in fact. And, lately, Eliza, I have begun to wonder whether I might not have been too hasty in thinking her only slightly acquainted with Mr

Montague; for one might perhaps become rather well acquainted with a man in a short time — if there was a very remarkable coincidence of temperament and the time was passed in rational converse on subjects that were of interest to both, rather than in the idle chatter of the ballroom — or card table . . .

Well, that is all quite by the by; the material point is that Catherine is now suffering a good deal and I have persuaded her to go to her bed.

So now I have a little time for quiet reflection here in the inn parlour, for the gentlemen have gone about business of their own — in the tap room or stables, I suppose — and I am sitting here in very companionable silence with the Misses Harris. The candles have been lit and the shutters closed and the fire is roaring in the chimney with the wind that is blowing in from the sea, and altogether we are very cosy here — with the occasional sound of wheels and horses outside to remind us that other folk are still abroad and make us glad that we are at rest for the night. Miss Sophia and I are writing our letters while Miss Harris is engaged upon her drawing — which, by the by, is vastly improved. Despite her efforts to conceal it, I contrived a peep just now. The giant sheep is gone and the perspective is very good and, all in all — as well as one can judge of such an incomplete performance — it promises to be a very fine picture indeed. How very strange!

It seems that I must amend my opinion of her as an artist — though not as a companion. I cannot say that I find either of them winning upon my affections. In the absence of the gentlemen not even Miss Sophia has anything much to say. And I am beginning to suspect that they are both naturally of a rather taciturn disposition and that Miss Sophia only exerts herself into chattering emphasis because she mistakenly believes it is becoming. Why do young women think that they must put on such airs to catch husbands? Were we ever such fools, Eliza? Well, well, I suppose we were, and I am allowing myself to wander quite off the point.

Perhaps when Mr Montague absents himself from home it is not entirely a matter of free choice. Perhaps the establishment at Hopton Cresswell has been formed as a place of concealment when his behaviour is disturbed. Exiled from his family, cut off from equal society, might a lonely, impressionable young man not all too easily from an unsuitable attachment?

And Mr Pollard was once Mr Montague's tutor. Or so it would seem by the old gentleman's description. And that accords well with him being now "a university man", as the ostler described him. Catherine said that he looked like a professional man and his profession is no doubt the Church, for I am sure I remember Edward telling me once that only clergymen can hold posts at the university.

So what was his mission at the ball? I will not fall into the common modern cant of deriding all clergy; like the dutiful daughter of a clergyman that I am, I shall take it as an article of faith that a man so ordained must have had an honourable motive. Did he come to urge Mr Montague to confess his sins?

But why did he not speak? How could Mr Montague have guessed his meaning by a look? I keep coming back to that silence in the ballroom. I feel that if I could but understand that then I would have the key that unlocks all this mystery.

I am sorry for this rambling talk, Eliza. But I feel that there is an answer here in all this, and I am too stupid to find it.

172

I keep trying to remember everything that Charles and Edward used to tell us about the rules of argument and debate when they were at Cambridge and I heartily wish that my own education had had a little more logic in it and rather less playing of disastrously bad scales upon the spinet.

But then, to be fair upon our poor mother, I do not suppose that the solving of mysteries or the detection of murderers was much in her mind when she devised our schooling.

However, I may lay claim to one fairly rational thought today and that concerns Mr Harris and Tom Lomax — and their visit to the shrubbery. I am almost sure that they are both lying about it. Why are they lying? Well, Mr Harris is a member of the family and might easily be persuaded to hold his tongue about anything that he saw that day. And Tom? Well, might he not very easily be bribed into silence? Do you see my meaning? Perhaps the fortune which he looks forward to does not come from marriage.

Distasteful as any interview with Mr Tom Lomax must be, I rather think that I shall be forced to contrive another tête-à-tête with him and see what I may discover.

I am sorry, Eliza, I will have to break off my letter in a moment. The gentlemen have returned and . . . Now that is very strange indeed!

Eliza, I am sure I am not mistaken. When the door opened just now, Miss Harris changed the picture on her drawing board. I am sure she did it. She pulled out another paper from underneath and placed it over the drawing she was working on. I shall drop my sand shaker and try to steal a look at the drawing board as I retrieve it . . .

Yes! I was right. The monstrous sheep is back!

Now here is another mystery. Why should a woman who can draw very well pretend incompetence? And now I remember something else ... But I must stop now; Tom Lomax is moving this way ...

Dido was abroad the next morning before anyone else from the Belsfield party had stirred from their beds. She was able not only to take a long, thoughtful walk on the Cobb — where the beauty of white-capped waves dancing under the first narrow beams of sunlight did little to soothe her troubled mind — but also to take a little wander about the village and the church.

She turned back towards the inn, sunk even deeper in thought than when she left it and, a little way from its door, she met with Sophia Harris, who was also returning from a solitary walk. Miss Sophia had a remarkably serious look upon her face and she was lacking the fussy curls about her ears. Her hair was simply dressed in a tight, uncompromising knot at the back of her head. To Dido's mind, it improved her appearance considerably.

Together the two women made their way along the narrow street where yawning housemaids were washing doorsteps and clattering pails, and errand boys were hurrying past with baskets of bread and pitchers of milk.

They were engaged first in exclaiming upon the beauty of the morning and the place. And then Dido took the opportunity of adding, "I shall be pleased to see your sister's drawings of Lyme when they are finished. She draws extremely well."

174

"Does she?" said Sophia in some confusion. "That is . . . Yes, I think that she does. But I am her sister, so I don't doubt that I am prejudiced."

"I cannot but notice, however," said Dido cautiously, "that her performance is somewhat . . . variable. But perhaps it makes her nervous to be observed at her work?"

"Yes, yes I suppose that it does."

They walked on a little way. Dido tried to read her companion's feelings from her face — but could not make them out: her lips were tightly compressed and two little lines above her nose puckered her brow. "It is quite remarkable, is it not," continued Dido, "how the presence of another person can distract us? It can quite spoil the execution of a drawing — or a piece of music."

Sophia stopped and gave her a long look, then she turned and walked on. "Yes," she said. "Perhaps it can."

Dido was sure she had hit upon something. She hurried after her. "On the morning before yesterday," she said, "while I was in the hall at Belsfield, I heard someone playing in the drawing room so exquisitely that I wondered who it could be. Afterwards, when I came into the drawing room, I found that it was you who was sitting at the pianoforte. Miss Sophia, I hope you will forgive me for saying that you play much better when you are alone."

"Thank you, Miss Kent. It is no doubt, as you remarked, the distraction of being observed which sometimes injures my performance." And she walked on as quickly as she might to the inn door.

As they stepped into the smoky warmth of the inn's dark little hall, Sophia took off her bonnet hurriedly. "If you will excuse me now," she said, "I will return to my sister. She is a little distressed at present." She started up the stairs, but then she stopped. The morning sunlight coming in through a little landing window caught her face, which was tinged with colour from her walk. She looked lively and intelligent. "The fact is, Miss Kent, Colonel Walborough made a proposal of marriage to Amelia yesterday evening." She gave a little grimace. "It seems," she said, "that the colonel is more musical than he is artistic."

With that she ran away up the stairs, leaving Dido alone in the hall.

She took off her bonnet slowly and stood for several minutes running its ribbons thoughtfully through her fingers, but could find no way of accounting for Miss Sophia's last, strange remark. With a little shake of her head, she opened the door and went into the parlour. She had hoped to find the room empty and to be able to think in peace there until breakfast was ready, but she was disappointed. Tom Lomax was lounging upon a bench, reading a newspaper.

"Miss Kent," he cried as she entered. "I believe you never sleep! Now, what are you busy about so early in the day?"

Dido smiled serenely. "Why, I am just poking about," she replied. "In the way that I do, Mr Lomax."

"And what do you hope to discover here at Lyme?"

She sat herself down beside the newly lit fire and considered as she gazed into the flames, which were burning white and blue as they consumed the salty sticks of driftwood. No better opportunity to confront Mr Tom might appear and she decided to make the best of this chance meeting. "One thing I hope to discover, Mr Lomax," she began slowly, raising her eyes to his, "is why you were in the shrubbery on the day that young woman was killed."

Tom folded his newspaper and sat up, looking extremely wary. "You know the answer to that," he said.

"I know the answer which you gave to Sir Edgar." Tom said nothing. "But," she went on, "in your own inimitable words, that explanation 'will not do.' Come, Mr Lomax, we both know that it 'will not do at all.' "

"Sir Edgar was quite satisfied with it," said Tom sulkily, rubbing a finger across his bristling cheek.

"He was, but I cannot say that his satisfaction is a great credit to his understanding. For it is clear — clear even to a woman — that you are not engaged to either of the Misses Harris. Neither of the ladies seems to know anything of the business and, since you cannot even remember which of them has been so fortunate as to win your devotion . . .." Dido finished with a smile and a shrug.

"I do not think, Miss Kent, that it is any concern of yours whether I am engaged or not."

"But, you see, it is. I am very concerned that you seem to be lying. For when a life has been taken, I believe it is the duty of us all to ensure that justice is done."

Tom shifted on his bench and gave a strange smile — though whether it was intended to charm or to threaten she could not quite determine. "And have you decided that *I* killed that woman?"

Dido continued her level stare. "Did you?" she said.

"No!" His face was red. "I don't even know who she was."

"Then you will not mind telling me — or telling the magistrates — the real reason for your presence in the shrubbery that day."

He gave a kind of snort and kicked furiously at the leg of his bench. "You had better ask Harris about it," he said. "For what you don't understand is that there are a great many things beside murder which a gentleman might wish to conceal."

"I do not doubt it, Mr Lomax. But I think that to clear himself of the suspicion of murder a gentleman might own to most secrets."

"You really are the most insufferable, interfering woman I ever met!" cried Tom furiously. He jumped up from the bench, paced to the window then back to the fireside and stood before her on the hearth rug, talking vehemently. "But it is not me, it is Harris who most wants secrecy in this case. And though you do not seem to mind stirring up trouble for me, I think you might regret the embarrassment you will bring on John Harris — and on his womenfolk — with your infernal questions."

That made Dido hesitate. But it was only for a moment. "If you would but tell me the facts of the case, Mr Lomax."

"And if I do not then I suppose you will go running to the magistrates bleating about me not being engaged?"

"Yes, I will."

He strode back to the window, kicking the bench out of the way as he went. He leant upon the window sill and stared out into the yard.

"Mr Lomax, I believe it will not be long before our friends join us. And if I have not received some assurance from you before we return to Belsfield . . ." She left the broken sentence to hang in the air of the little parlour.

"Very well, I shall tell you what my business was in the shrubbery," he said violently. "And you will not like what you hear. But remember you pressed me to tell you. It is not me that chooses to relate such details to a respectable spinster." (There was a sneer in that.) "Harris and I went to the hermitage to talk. He was too afraid of being overheard to transact our business in the spinney. And I was not lying: we went to talk about me marrying one of the girls. And it is true that he and I came to an agreement."

"Indeed? I think it must have been a rather unusual agreement."

"Perhaps it was." He turned to face her, which put her at rather a disadvantage for the morning sun was behind him and, though he could watch her face, he was nothing to her but a tall dark figure against the brightness and she could make out nothing of his expressions. "The agreement was that he would not oppose me marrying either of his daughters. But I did

179

not fix on either of them. In fact," he added with a heavy attempt at humour, "I was gentleman enough to say that I would wait for Colonel Walborough to take his pick and pay my addresses to the one that was left."

"How very generous of you! But what interests me, Mr Lomax, is how you persuaded Mr Harris to this arrangement. What was he to get in return for his consent to the marriage of his daughter to a man so deep in debt that even the village apothecary is refusing his business?"

That hit home. The dark figure looming against the shining squares of the window started visibly and when he spoke again his voice was choking with fury. "He is to get my silence, Miss Kent. That is what he is to get — and very valuable it is to him."

"Yes?" said Dido calmly. "Your silence on what subject?"

"On the subject of his marriage."

"I see," said Dido, taking great care that neither her face nor her voice should betray the shock which he hoped to detect. "Now, I wonder what you have to tell on that subject. It is nothing to do, I am sure, with Mrs Harris's low origins, for all the world must know of those since she talks so freely of them herself."

"Ah," said Tom with relish. "All the world knows that John Harris's present lady was nurse to his first wife, but what no one else in England knows is that she was still no more than a nurse when Miss Amelia was born. And that was a month before her patient died. Now, what do you say to that?"

"One of your acquaintance in India has informed you of this, I suppose?"

"More than one, as it happens; bad news has a way of travelling. And there is nothing to be gained by trying to doubt my word, Miss Kent, for Harris has admitted to the business himself — or as good as done so, for he has not denied it."

Dido did not doubt its truth, nor could she doubt that Mr Harris would be anxious to keep it hidden — for the sake of his wife's reputation. She became aware that Tom was watching her closely and she did not doubt that he was smiling. Indeed, when he spoke again she could actually *hear* the smile in his words even though the sun was still dazzling her too much to see his face.

"So you see, Miss Kent, if you broadcast your suspicions about me, you would do no good at all and you would be the means of destroying the Harrises' respectability. Is that what you wish to do?"

He knew that it was not. He knew that she would not now speak out about her suspicions. In short, he was sure that he had got the better of her. He really was the most horrible, provoking man!

"No," she said, standing up. "That is not what I wish to do. All I wish to do is to find out who killed that woman, and to discover why Mr Montague has absented himself from his father's house." She walked to the door, but there she hesitated. "Though I believe I have just acquired a new purpose," she added thoughtfully. "I think I now also intend to put a stop to your selfish plans. Good morning, Mr Lomax."

CHAPTER
SIXTEEN

. . . And so, Eliza, here I am back at Belsfield, and I have just received a piece of news which I had hoped very much not to hear.

There was a note awaiting me when we returned this afternoon, brought by Jenny, the housemaid. Here is what it says:

Deer Madam,

Mary that is made at the crown aks me to rite My Kate sys Mr Blaglog is a torl yung genlman he has big brown eys and a vere plesunt smile

Yor servent Eliz. Potter (Mrs)

PS she is a vere trothful chile and wos 2 yers at Sunday Scol

Well, there is only one man at Belsfield who suits that description and that one man is Richard Montague. As I said, it is a piece of news which I would much rather not have received.

Oh, this really is a wretched business, Eliza! For everything seems to bring me back to those suspicions which are most dangerous to Catherine's happiness. I begin to wonder whether the time has come when I must talk very seriously with her. But still I do not know enough. I wish that I could find out more about this household; in particular about Mr Montague's absences from home and how long they last and whether there are ever arguments between him and his father.

I had hoped to make some discoveries from the servants and, to that end, have been questioning as many of them as I might since my return from Lyme; but their loyalty, or rather, I think, their fear of their master, has proved too strong for me and I can find out nothing. I think that I must somehow create a remarkable degree of goodwill in one or other of them before I can break down this reserve.

Have I not become very calculating since I turned into a solver of mysteries? But it cannot be helped for, as Charles often assures us, success in any enterprise is never achieved without a little deviousness. And I do believe that I have devised a way of gaining the goodwill of the young footman, Jack.

When he came to my room to bring some logs — for he still keeps me very well supplied — I noticed that his eyes were red and, all in all, though one does not like to suspect it of a young man, it seemed to me that he had been crying.

So I asked him what was the matter and, as you may imagine, he denied that he was upset and so we went on for a little while with fruitless questions; but the upshot of it all is that it is Colonel Walborough who is troubling him by sending for him at all hours to bring logs and wine and I know not what to his bedchamber. And the boy is very distressed by it for he seems to have taken quite an inordinate dislike to going to the colonel's room alone.

Well, I suppose servants are as entitled to have their vagaries as much as the rest of us! But the great advantage of this to me is that I have undertaken to relieve Jack of the gentleman's inopportune demands — though Jack shakes his head doubtfully and says that this is not something a "nice, kind lady" can do anything about. My plan is that, by so doing, I shall win his gratitude and, I hope, his willingness to talk about his master's business.

Well, I shall let you know how I go on . . .

Dido frowned so earnestly at Colonel Walborough as he drank his soup at dinner that evening, that he became nervous and began to suppose that she had had some terrible premonition concerning him.

Indeed, if the other people at the dining table had been as superstitious as the colonel, they might all have shared his apprehension. For, during the course of dinner, she considered them all; moving on from her contemplation of the colonel to meditate upon the changes in her knowledge of them all since she first sat at that table. She had discovered that there was hardly one of them who was not hiding a secret.

Here was Sir Edgar, smiling so beningly as he carved the fine goose; yet she knew now that there was stark tyranny behind his geniality. At his side sat Mrs Harris, cheerfully relating some tale which required her to fold her napkin about and about in explanation. In *her* past there were indiscretions which should make any woman blush.

Beside her was Mr William Lomax, returned at last from his business and looking more than usually grave. What did he have to hide? A guilty liaison? Or only the family secrets of his employer? Dido was some time

184

watching him and wondering what the reason might be for his excessive gravity this evening. A little while ago, in just crossing the hall to the drawing room, she had overheard Sir Edgar and Mr Lomax talking in the library. "I am determined to find the killer," the baronet had been saying. "I will do everything in my power . . ." But she had been unable to distinguish the words of Mr Lomax's reply. Had he been arguing for more zeal or for more caution in the investigation?

Then, further along the table, there were the Harris girls, whose pretended incompetence and rage for accomplishments hid very real talents — but why? And there was Tom (with his side-whiskers still no more than a shadow) sitting between the girls and rolling his eyes about in a great effort of gallantry. His charming smiles concealed a plan of utter selfishness. And a little higher up was Margaret, and next to her, Mr Harris, his hard, leathery face set now in lines of resignation, looking sometimes at Tom and sometimes, with a softening of his expression, at his wife. Dido found herself wondering whether there might be some truth in Charles's words about the insensible hardness of men with fortunes got from India. It certainly seemed that Mr Harris had only one point of weakness — his wife. And for her comfort he was willing to sacrifice even his daughters.

And then, sitting on the other side of Mr Harris, there was Catherine: even paler than usual, and rather silent, but with little else to show how many tears she had lately been shedding. Of Catherine, too, her opinion had changed in the last few days. Catherine's affection for Mr Montague was more firmly founded than Dido had at first supposed . . . And did that mean that she too had secrets to hide: confidences that had been exchanged between the lovers and which she was determined not to break? Dido was beginning to suspect that it might be so.

And then, at the head of the table, sat her ladyship. Dido paused, for here perhaps was the greatest mystery of the household. With her blank face and her fingers forever twisting at her rings, her insipid air and her flashes of sharp intelligence, her exquisite beauty and her costly fashionable clothes . . .

Dido stopped. She had noticed something that she should have noticed long ago. There was something wrong about the way my lady was dressed.

When the ladies were alone in the drawing room, Dido looked about her purposefully. She had a plan in her head for saving Jack from the colonel's constant demands and, in order to carry it out, she had need of a pack of cards.

At the pianoforte the candlelight shone on the bright little faces and the bobbing curls of the Misses Harris, and on the rouged cheeks of their mother. At the fireside, in another pool of candlelight, her ladyship was already spreading out the first Patience of the evening, her attention absorbed in the patterns she was making with the deft little movements of her hands. It was, thought Dido, a way of removing herself from the company around her. She moved towards her and took a seat, close enough for conversation but not so close as to be quite overwhelmed by the scent of rose water, which was mixing with the wood smoke. On the opposite side of the hearth, Margaret noticed the intrusion with pursed lips.

"May I have the use of these a little while?" asked Dido, picking up an unbroken pack of cards from the inlaid table.

Her ladyship nodded graciously and Dido began to rearrange the cards in the pack. As she did so, she covertly studied her companion's hands. They moved elegantly and precisely over the table, never fumbling or making a mistake. Delicate hands with long white fingers, looking very beautiful with the creamy lace of her sleeves falling half across them; but, Dido saw now for the first time, their beauty was sadly marred by my lady's habit of twisting her rings. The flesh around the rings was rubbed red and sore. It was as if the fine gold and diamonds and rubies were nothing more than the chafing bonds of a prisoner.

Dido set down her cards, and reached across the table. Making some pleasant remark about its loveliness, she just lifted the edge of lace at the lady's wrist.

Instantly the hand was withdrawn and all the cards my lady was holding cascaded onto the floor.

There was a loud "hmph" of disapproval from Margaret.

"I beg your pardon," said Dido bending quickly to retrieve the cards.

"It was nothing, Miss Kent. You merely startled me." Her face was impassive; but her eyes were cold and angry.

Dido was glad that the appearance of the gentlemen and Sir Edgar's approach to his lady with his usual questions about her health and her medicine gave her an excuse to move away to the other side of the room. There was no staying within range of those furious eyes.

She walked away very thoughtfully and took up her post on a distant sofa. She laid the pack of cards down on a table at her side — and she waited.

She did not doubt that the colonel would walk into her trap.

. . . And I was right. He soon came. My looks in the dining room had of course alerted him to the terrible peril that I had foreseen for him.

And I had foreseen a _terrible_ peril for him, Eliza. I did not attempt to conceal it from him. Though, I confessed, I might have withheld the awful knowledge from a lesser man. A lesser man might have been too much frightened. But to a military hero like himself I was willing to own that I had received the most direful presage of doom.

What kind of doom? he asked immediately.

Well, to own the truth, the society of someone within this house was of the greatest danger to him. There was someone within this house who he should sedulously avoid. I did not, of course, know who it might be that was so dangerous to him.

Could I not discover the identity of this individual?

No, no, I did not think I could. It would be too great a test of my abilities.

Was there no way of discovering more?

Well, sometimes a careful reading of the cards might . . .

And then, since we discovered that, quite by chance, there was a pack of cards on the table beside us, and since he pressed me so very urgently, I reluctantly consented to try what might be done. I was not pleased, however, with my own performance and regretted very much that it seemed to help him not at all. For twice when I dealt the cards there appeared — quite unaccountably — in the very centre of my pattern, a black jack. Which could only suggest to me a dark-haired fellow in a lowly walk of life — and how such a person could be an associate of the colonel I was quite at a loss to understand . . .

He, however, much to my surprise, nodded vigorously and thanked me again and again for my warning.

How strange!

It is as well, I think, that I am not inclined to turn spy, Eliza. For it would, no doubt, be of the utmost advantage to the French to know that they might lay aside their muskets and cannons because the doughty leaders of our armies can be routed with a mere pack of cards.

It is late now and I am in my chamber celebrating my victory with a very wonderful luxury indeed — a delicious hot jug of chocolate. Jack has just brought it to me with a great many smiles and thanks. So it seems that he is already enjoying the good effects of my warning. How he came by the stuff I do not know. In all probability he raided Sir Edgar's private store. But I find myself liking Sir Edgar less and less so I do not care about stealing from him; and, besides, I learnt long ago that in these great houses it is as well to accept such kindnesses gratefully and hold one's tongue.

I am becoming quite accustomed to Belsfield's luxurious manner of living and you will; no doubt, find me completely spoilt when I come home.

I must go to bed now, for tomorrow I shall be very busy. I intend to put some of those questions to Jack which I was too weary to begin upon tonight. And, emboldened by my success this evening, I have determined that tomorrow I will set about defeating Mr Tom Lomax. You see, Eliza, I have concocted a plan. It is made partly from the things that he said to me once when he found me writing to you, and partly from that extraordinary conversation which I had with Lady Montague in the gallery. It is a bold scheme and I hardly think that you will approve it, but I think that it might just succeed . . .

CHAPTER
SEVENTEEN

"Thank you." Sophia Harris put a shaking hand to her throat as if talking was a very great effort. "Thank you, Miss Kent, for telling me this."

"I hope," said Dido rather fearfully, "that I have done right in speaking to you. Mr Tom Lomax did not expect me to take such a measure, I am sure. And if I could have thought of any other means of defeating him, I should have spared you the pain of hearing his plans — and his accusations."

"Please," said Sophia exerting herself to sound calm. "Do not distress yourself on that account. I was already acquainted with the circumstances of my sister's birth — and of all the cruel things that could be said about Mama were they known. Once or twice over these last days I have wondered whether Mr Lomax meant mischief by the things he was saying — those remarks about his wide circle of friends in India. My father, too, I know has been uneasy about it almost since we came to Belsfield, and I am sure it is only my mother's good nature which has allowed her to remain ignorant of the danger."

She paused, her face burning red in the cold, gloomy afternoon and her gloved hands pounding together in evidence of her inward agitation. They had walked out into the gardens for privacy and were now seated upon a wooden bench against a high, clipped yew hedge that formed a kind of alcove in which was placed a statue of a plump little boy that was so worn and moss-grown that it was impossible to determine whether he was pagan cupid or Christian cherub.

Sophia had listened to the news just as Dido had hoped she would: with strong emotion — but with good sense too. She was pleased to find that her assessment of the girl had been sound. The silly manner was, after all, not an essential part of her character. There was no trace of it to be seen now. There was instead a strange self-possession and, certainly, no lack of intelligence.

"Something must be done about this," Miss Sophia was saying now. A strand of hair, damp from the misty air, fell down across her face and she pushed it back impatiently. She tapped a finger against her lip. "But what can we do?" She shook her head. "Tell me, Miss Kent, what do you know of Mr Tom Lomax?"

"Very little — but I know that there are few young men that I like less. His father seems to be a very respectable man."

"Yes. I wonder whether an appeal to Mr William Lomax might help us."

"I think not. I considered it; for I am sure he would be mortified by the way his son is behaving. But, from what Catherine tells me, I collect that Mr Tom is quite in the habit of defying his father."

"I have heard he has very heavy debts," said Sophia with a sigh.

"Yes, his circumstances are, I believe, becoming desperate. He is holding his creditors off with promises and I think he is determined to make his fortune by marrying well, for he is too indolent to take up any profession."

"Ah! And that must make matters worse. For I do believe, from everything I have read, Miss Kent, that there are few things more dangerous than a desperate man."

"Quite so," said Dido. "And yet, perhaps we may be able to use his desperation — and his own plans — against him."

"You have an idea?"

"Maybe — yes, I think I do."

"What is it?"

Dido hesitated. She could not quite say that in return for her help she wished to have her curiosity satisfied. Though that was the truth of the matter. "I wonder," she began cautiously, "whether, before I explain myself to you, you might explain yourself to me."

Sophia folded her hands in her lap and stared down at the gravel. "I am sure I don't know what you mean, Miss Kent," she said stubbornly.

There was silence between them for several minutes and the little sounds of the garden crept into their alcove: a little desultory birdsong; the rattle and scrape of a gardener's rake working somewhere in the gravel; the splashing of the great fountain on the lower terrace.

"I hope," said Dido quietly at last, "that Miss Harris is feeling better today?"

"Yes. I thank you," said Sophia gravely. She was silent for several more minutes, then she sighed and gave her companion a sidelong look. "The proposal was unexpected," she explained reluctantly, "and Amelia was a little shaken by it. It will, of course, be refused — politely, regretfully. And the business will soon be forgotten."

"Forgive me," said Dido cautiously, "but I cannot help enquiring: was it her intention that the proposal should never be made?"

"Of course it was!" Sophia sighed again, more loudly, recognising that she would only hear Dido's idea after she had explained herself. "If you are going to help us, Miss Kent, then I suppose it is only fair that I should be candid with you. We have never talked of our scheme to anyone before, but I think . . . Yes, I am sure, that in these circumstances my sister would agree with me that disclosure is justified." She said all this with such solemnity that Dido wondered what could possibly follow. "It is," she intoned with great dignity and weight, "our intention that *no* proposals of marriage should *ever* be made."

Dido stared. "That is a rather singular aim for two young women!"

"I have a notion," said Miss Sophia, primming up her mouth, "that it is more common than one might suppose, though most women do not perhaps go to quite the lengths that Amelia and I have adopted. But, you see, we were very young when we decided against marriage and had several years in which to perfect our scheme before we were in serious danger."

Dido studied her companion carefully, for, despite what she had observed over the last three days, she could not quite judge how serious she was in this. But it seemed that Miss Sophia was serious in everything. She certainly showed no propensity to laugh at herself. "You intrigue me," said Dido. "May I ask why you came to such a decision?"

Sophia folded her hands and shrugged up her plump shoulders a little. "I suppose," she said, "that it was because of my dear mother's attempts to make us marriageable. You look puzzled, Miss Kent! I had better explain. Mama, never having had the advantage of an extensive education herself, was quite determined that Amelia and I should be as accomplished as possible; that our minds should be improved and all our talents encouraged."

"I see."

"Well, we were provided with the very best masters and given every opportunity to learn. And, either because of the excellence of our education, or because of some natural taste in us, the undertaking was very successful; more successful, I suspect, than such programmes of study generally are. Too successful, I might almost say. For, by the time Amelia was fifteen years old and I was fourteen — when everyone expected, of course, that we should start to neglect our books for invitations and visits and hair curling — well, by then, we were both so devoted to our studies, so accustomed to finding pleasure in the serious business of books and drawing and music — that even a ball seemed an unwelcome intrusion upon our time."

"That is very singular!"

"Is it?"

"I do not think I have ever heard before of a young lady of fifteen who would not be happy to abandon her studies for a ball."

"Yet I see no reason," said Miss Sophia severely, "why there should not be as much variety of temperament among young women as among young men — and among young men we are not surprised to find examples of the serious as well as the trivial."

"Well, I suppose you are right," said Dido. "It may be that I am prejudiced by my memories of my own talentless struggles upon my mother's old spinet and my wretchedness over drawing houses that would, despite my best efforts, look like mountains and chickens that looked like trees. There was only one thing which I hated more and that was arithmetic. I certainly had no more cause to love the visits of the drawing master and the music teacher than they had, poor fellows."

"But you are a clever woman, Miss Kent, and I think that you must have loved your books."

"Oh yes!" cried Dido. "I was excessively fond of books. Provided, of course, that they came from a circulating library and had a great many handsome villains and horrid mysteries in them and were quite free from any serious moralising or instruction."

196

"Now," said Sophia, rather offended, "I am sure that you are mocking me and, furthermore, doing yourself a grave injustice."

"You are too kind! And I shall say no more upon the subject on purpose that I may pass for an educated — but modest — woman. But I interrupted your very interesting account just now. I believe you were going to tell me that you and your sister decided that the most unwelcome intrusion upon your time — the very worst disturber of your studies — would be marriage."

"We did. For have you ever met a married woman who practises upon her instrument or touches her crayons?"

"No, on that we would certainly agree. The demands of a husband, a household and a family prevent even the most talented woman from pursuing any endeavour which does not relate directly to them."

"Quite so, Miss Kent. Marriage is so very final. It changes everything."

Dido gave a little start. For some reason those words touched something deep inside her. It was almost as if they answered a question she had been asking herself, but just at the moment she could not remember what the question had been. It was something which she must think of later. For now Miss Sophia, quite blind to anything but her own concerns, was continuing with her strange tale.

". . . and so, you see, we laid our plan. We knew that to declare our intention of never marrying would do us no good at all: we would only be laughed at and disbelieved. So we set ourselves parts to play. Amelia's

197

quieter character made her prefer to adopt a repelling silence; while I chose — well, I need not explain. You have seen my behaviour in company. We aim to disgust sensible men with our silly manners and devotion to accomplishments in which our performance is less than mediocre."

"And what," asked Dido with a smile, "of men who are not sensible?"

"They," said Sophia solemnly, "do not generally present a problem. Our parents do not expect — or wish — us to marry foolish husbands."

"I cannot fault your plan, Miss Sophia," said Dido after a few moments' thought. "And yet I wonder whether it is entirely necessary. For I have a great idea that real accomplishments, education and intelligence might frighten away lovers — even sensible lovers — more surely than any amount of silliness and incompetence."

Sophia's face clouded. She clasped her kid gloves in her lap and frowned down at them. "You may be right, Miss Kent," she said at last. "It is a subject which Amelia and I sometimes talk about. And yet, there is this to consider: whatever means we use to escape marriage, we will be mocked for it. That cannot be helped. It is the way of the world."

"Yes," said Dido with a pang, "an unmarried woman will always be a target of laughter."

"Exactly so," said Miss Harris, quite insensible of the pain she was causing. "And I believe, Miss Kent, that there is not a woman born who would not rather suffer ridicule for what she knows to be a pretence — a part she has acted — than for the very thing that she most wishes to be true — the ideal to which she aspires."

"You are right, of course," said Dido politely. "I am sure you have found the best way of arranging things."

Sophia breathed a heavy sigh and shook her head. "Except, of course," she said, "that our scheme is powerless against Mr Tom Lomax. This is quite a different sort of danger."

"Yes, your plan cannot protect you against such a suitor."

"I don't doubt," said Sophia slowly, "that if we both refuse him . . ." She broke off and her fists curled in her lap. "Amelia and I care little for what the world thinks of us, and the shame would only protect us more certainly from marriage."

Dido rather doubted that she could be as insensible to disgrace as she declared — but she let the matter pass.

"But poor Mama," Sophia continued, "her greatest pleasure lies in society and I will not . . ." One fist struck the palm of the other hand. "I will not allow him to be the means of destroying her happiness."

Dido, who had been finding the girl's self-satisfied manner rather repulsive, was touched by this concern for her mother. It strengthened her resolution of helping.

"Listen," she said, "I have a plan. We shall confront Mr Tom Lomax after dinner. But, first, this is what I would like you and your sister to do . . ."

★ ★ ★

After Miss Sophia had left her, Dido sat for a quarter of an hour in the gloomy arbour, struggling with the ideas which those words about the finality of marriage had suggested. And when, at the end of that time, the contemplation of clipped hedges and crumbling cupid had done nothing to relieve her mind, she set off across the park to try what exercise might do.

So occupied was she with her own thoughts that, for some time, she hardly knew where she was walking and was rather surprised to find herself approaching the yew-shaded path that led to the family chapel. However, the little old building with its one squat tower and its windows winking in the last feeble light of the day had a rather reassuring appearance. She turned into the path and paused on flagstones which were stained red with fallen berries from the yew trees. She was surprised to see that the heavy door of the chapel was standing ajar.

She stepped forward and peered around it, but could make out nothing in the gloom. She slipped silently through the door and looked about. The air was stale and dead and cold; the stone arches rose up into darkness, the white marble of family monuments loomed in a side aisle and the only patch of light, tinted blue and green from the coloured window, fell upon the white cloth that covered the altar. The place seemed to be deserted. She advanced several steps, then her eyes became accustomed to the poor light and a slight movement caught her attention. There was a figure — a man's figure — kneeling in prayer close to the altar rail.

Her first impulse was to withdraw politely before she was detected; but then — as it so often did — her curiosity got the better of her manners. She took a few more cautious steps and peered through the dusk. The kneeling figure was Mr William Lomax. His head was bowed on his clasped hands and his shoulders were shaking with the violence of his supplication.

As she stared, she began to make out the faint sound of the familiar words he was repeating. "Lead us not into temptation, but deliver us from evil . . . Lead us not into temptation, but deliver us from evil . . ." The whispered words echoed faintly in the holy chill of the chapel.

Dido turned and hurried out into the daylight, not pausing even to draw breath until she gained the knoll and the green bench in the park. What, she wondered as she sat herself down, was the evil from which Mr Lomax so ardently wished to be delivered? And what was the temptation into which he dreaded being led?

She sighed and shook her head. Of course it had been quite unpardonable to listen to a man's private devotions. It would be very wrong to suspect him on such evidence, would it not . . .?

It was six o'clock before Dido returned to the house and the outcome of her many troubling reflections was such that left her face, in Catherine's opinion, looking "sour and old-maidish".

However, since they were divided by almost the full length of the table at dinner, it was not possible for her niece to get at her with this pleasant remark until after the ladies removed into the drawing room. Then, finding her upon the distant sofa with a piece of work lying untouched upon her lap, Catherine demanded to know why she must sit all alone and talking to no one. "It is a sure sign of encroaching age, you know," she said.

"Then you had better leave me alone to doze quietly. That is the privilege of dotage, is it not?"

"But you are not dozing," Catherine pointed out. "You are merely sitting in this corner watching everybody with that sharp, satirical eye of yours. I wish you would not do it; you make me quite ashamed."

"Oh dear! And I had hoped that since I am now a clever future-gazer and since I am at this moment wearing neither pattens nor pelisse, I could not embarrass you before your friends."

"Well, you can," said Catherine ungraciously and Dido had to remind herself of the poor girl's misery in order to keep in charity with her. "Who is it that you are watching so intently?"

"As you said, I am watching everyone. I cannot help it. It is on account of having a sharp and satirical eye."

"You are in a very ill mood this evening."

"And you are all sweetness, I suppose?"

Catherine linked her arm through Dido's. "You know that I only insult you because I am fond of you."

"And if you disliked me I suppose you would be full of compliments?"

"Yes, I probably should."

"Well, well, you always were a contrary child."

Dido patted her hand and studied her pale unhappy face with great affection and an irresistible memory of the little girl who used to cling to her every morning as she asked, "Has Mama returned?" Very little had changed; Dido still longed to protect her and make her happy.

But it was impossible. She could no more restore Catherine to her happy engagement than she could reply to her all those years ago, "Yes, all is well, your mama is here in the house."

The reflections of the afternoon had left her more troubled than ever. There was, stronger than ever, a feeling that she was being foolish; that there were answers which she ought to see and yet was blind to.

And there were also some very difficult things which must be said.

"My dear," she began cautiously, "there is something I must talk to you about. And I had better say it now while I have leisure, because I expect to be occupied shortly with a little scheme I have promised to help the Misses Harris with."

"Indeed? I did not know that you were intimate with the Harris girls."

"I am not particularly intimate with them — but, in fact, it was something Miss Sophia said this afternoon which made me think . . ."

"Made you think what?"

"Oh," said Dido, trying to speak lightly, "it just made me think that I should talk to you about . . . about one or two observations that I have made."

"Observations?"

"Yes. Just little things." Dido picked up her work and began to stab in stitches rather randomly. "There is, for example, Annie Holmes' great regard for Mr Montague." Catherine's head jerked; her lips moved, but no sound came out of them. "And," continued Dido earnestly stitching away, "there is the very comfortable parlour at the lodge house, and little Susan's costly doll . . . and her large brown eyes. Things like that. But, most of all, my dear, there is your very great dislike of Mrs Holmes; the way you cannot bear to look at her or hear her spoken of."

"Aunt Dido," cried Catherine suspiciously. "What have you been about with your endless questions?"

"There is no need to worry, my dear; no one has told me anything. No confidences have been broken. I have only made use of my senses and my brain to see what is before me."

"And what do you see? Or, rather, what do you think that you see?"

Dido stopped sewing and instead began to turn her work around as if intent upon studying the pattern she was making. "I see that when he was a very young man, Mr Montague was fond of Annie Holmes — and that little Susan is his natural daughter. I see that Sir Edgar knows of the business and the woman and her child have been provided for. I also see that Mr Montague has confessed to you his youthful mistake. Asked your forgiveness perhaps . . ." There was a gasp from Catherine and Dido stopped. "Please, don't be uneasy about me knowing this, my dear," she said, taking her hands. "Because it has helped me to understand you;

helped me to understand how well founded your love seems to be — if he could be so honest with you. This is why you have been so determined to trust him, is it not?"

Catherine gulped and nodded. "I have good reason to trust him," she said. "I know he could not have broken with his father over a lover. Why should he? Why should there be a 'rupture', as you so elegantly put it, over this woman when there had not been over the last one? Aunt Dido, I tried to make you understand that that could not be the trouble, but without betraying Mr Montague's confidence, I could not convince you."

"Yes, I understand. And I am very sorry that, at first, I thought so lightly of your attachment. That was very wrong of me, my love. But I was convinced in the end — convinced that you must have some good reason to place so much trust in Mr Montague. And then I knew that there must be more at stake here than a youthful mistake — or a natural child." She sighed. "It all goes much deeper than that."

CHAPTER
EIGHTEEN

It wanted but half an hour until tea was brought in when Miss Harris and Miss Sophia caught Dido's eye and beckoned her out of the drawing room into the hall, where a good fire was burning and the spaniel was pursuing dream-woodcock.

Sophia said, "We are going to the morning room. We will wait for Mr Tom Lomax there. We thought it would be the best place to carry out your plan."

"The place will suit our purposes very well," said Dido. "But how do you know that Mr Lomax will follow you there?"

"He will," said Amelia.

"My sister means that when he does not find me in the drawing room, he is sure to come in search of me. It would hardly be attentive of him not to, would it?"

Dido smiled. "You are Mr Lomax's sole object now, are you?"

"Yes. As you suggested, Amelia has given him to understand that she has accepted the colonel's offer."

"That should make our plan work more smoothly."

The three women paused a moment and listened to the sound of voices from the dining room, where the gentlemen were still sitting over their port wine.

"They will be finished soon," said Amelia abruptly.

Sophia nodded and again explained her sister's remark. "You can judge by the sound of their voices, Miss Kent. They always talk louder just before they leave the table."

And then, as if to prove her point, there came the unmistakable sound of a chair scraping back across the floor. Sir Edgar's loud voice was heard proposing that they "join the dear ladies". The dog woke and hid herself behind the hooded chair. Dido and her companions hurried away into the morning room.

"We will not have long to talk to him," said Amelia as she took a seat beside the low fire.

"No, Mama will come to look for us when tea is served." Sophia hesitated and looked about. It was a large room with heavy, old-fashioned furniture; there was a great deal of very dark wood and velvet upholstery which had once been red but which had faded over the years to the colour of cold chocolate. At the moment the room was full of shadows because the only light came from the fire and from one stand of candles on the writing table by the window. After considering for a moment, Sophia took a seat upon a couch close beside the table and Dido noted that she had chosen her position very well; the colonel himself, commanding his troops, could not have made a wiser decision. When Tom came into the room and sat beside her — as he surely would — she would be able to turn her back to the candles; but the light would be full in his face.

Dido placed herself opposite Amelia by the hearth and put two fresh logs into the grate. The fire was little more than a heap of grey ash and red embers, but the logs — like everything else at Belsfield — were of the very best and little flames were soon licking around them and giving up a faint smell of applewood. Their crackle and the ticking of a clock upon the mantelshelf were the only sounds in the room. Amelia and Sophia exchanged looks — anxious, but determined too.

It was a quiet domestic scene: two young women in muslin and shawls and patent slippers sitting after dinner in a comfortable old room in gentle candle- and firelight. But Dido felt that she had been right to think of the colonel and his army; for there was a battle to be enacted here. There might be no cannon and no swords — no blood to be shed — and yet the girls were here to fight for everything that was dear to them. She only hoped that the weapons she had put into their hands would be strong enough to gain them a victory.

She had prepared them as best she could. There was little that she could do now except watch and hope that they could carry off the attack.

There came the unmistakable sound of the drawing room door opening. They all looked at one another. Something like panic crossed Sophia's face, but she mastered it and drew in a long breath. Footsteps — a man's footsteps — crossed the hall. Tom's voice called out a hearty greeting to the dog. Dido picked up a book and pretended to read.

Tom appeared in the doorway.

"Miss Sophia!" He hesitated as he noticed Dido and Amelia. "Miss Harris, Miss Kent." He made a small bow in their direction before returning his attention to Sophia with a little smirk which was, no doubt, intended to suggest the extreme tenderness of his regard. "Will you not come into the drawing room and play for us, Miss Sophia?"

"No." Sophia's voice was badly distorted, and for one anxious moment Dido thought it would fail her completely, but she made a valiant effort to control it and continued in a tolerable imitation of her usual manner. "Thank you, Mr Lomax. You are *very, very* kind. But I do not intend to play today."

He crossed the room and took the seat beside her. Dido thought of an enemy force moving into the trap which has been laid for it.

"You are very cruel," he declared dramatically. "I do believe that my evening will be a blank unless I hear you play, Miss Sophia." The light shone into his face, revealing that the last few days had done nothing to improve his dark, ragged sidewhiskers. He stretched his long legs across the rug and placed one arm along the back of the sofa so that his thick fingers almost touched the pretty ruching on her short white sleeve. "Come, will you not relent?"

Sophia looked down at her hands and shook her curls. "I am *so* sorry, Mr Lomax, but *really* I fear that to play *anything* would be *quite* beyond my powers this evening."

"I hope you are not unwell," he cried with exaggerated alarm and formed his bristling cheeks into an expression of doleful concern.

"Thank you," she said, sinking her voice. "I am just a little *tired*. That is all."

"Her hands are tired." This rather surprising remark came from Amelia and Tom had to turn about in his seat to look at her — which rather spoilt the nonchalant pose that he had struck.

"I beg your pardon, Miss Harris?"

"Her hands are tired on account of the letters, Mr Lomax."

Tom looked confused — as well he might. Dido had hoped for confusion at this point.

"My sister and I have been *very busy*, you see," said Sophia. He turned back to her. "We have been writing letters all *morning*. Why, we have written *seven* each, you know! That is a great many letters, is it not?"

"It is quite remarkable!"

Hardly knowing what she was doing, Dido lowered her book into her lap. Now, she thought, keep him confused. Keep him off his guard.

"You must," Tom continued gaily, "be enjoying your stay at Belsfield very much if you wish to tell so many of your friends about it."

Dido saw the sisters exchange meaningful looks — the army was signalling that the moment had come to close in for the attack.

Sophia raised her eyes to his and gave a shy smile. "Oh yes," she simpered. "We like Belsfield *very much*, very much *indeed*."

Encouraged by the smile, Tom leant closer and, like a good chaperone, Dido watched and listened carefully. "I hope," he said in a low voice, "I hope, Miss Sophia, that *I* may have played some small part in making your stay enjoyable."

Sophia looked down at her hands and, though she did not quite blush, she contrived to look so very, very conscious that one might almost have believed that she did. Dido would have been surprised that a gently reared young lady could give a performance that must rival anything achieved by Drury Lane's most hardened actress — if she had not known that this particular young lady had been playing a part for many years. Her character was certainly more than enough to deceive Tom, predisposed as he was to believe in his own charms.

"Tell me," he whispered, "please tell me, or I shall be miserable. Did I figure just a little bit in any of those letters? Did you mention my name to your friends?"

Sophia did not raise her eyes, but the curls about her ears trembled in a modest little nod. Oh, it was an excellent performance!

The workings of Tom's face betrayed strong emotion — as well they might, for at that moment, twenty thousand pounds and an easy life seemed to be within his grasp.

"And what did you say about me?" he whispered.

"I said . . ." Sophia continued to avoid his eye. "I said that you had been very . . . attentive. And that you seemed to value my society very highly."

"And you were quite right to say it."

"I said, in fact, that you enjoyed my society so much you were prepared to go to quite remarkable lengths to secure it."

"I am sorry." He was still leaning over her, in the attitude of a lover, but his face was troubled. "I am sorry, Miss Sophia, I am not sure I quite understand you."

"Do you not?" She raised her eyes at last. Her voice lost all its silliness; her manner became businesslike. "But it is quite simple, Mr Lomax. I referred of course to the remarkable conversation that took place between you and Papa." She met his eyes fearlessly.

Tom started back from her. For the moment he was beyond speech, but the look that he threw in Dido's direction suggested that he was not beyond calculating who was to blame for this sudden turn of events.

Amelia left her seat and went to stand behind him. "It is in all the letters," she said quietly.

"All fourteen of them," said Sophia.

"All about your agreement with Papa," said Amelia.

"And the horrible threat that you have made."

"We have told all our friends about it."

"All our unmarried friends."

"All our unmarried, *wealthy* friends."

"And if you attempt to expose Mama," Sophia continued gravely, "we shall take those letters to the post office."

Tom's face was burning red. He looked from one to the other of them in confusion. "You mean you would broadcast the matter yourselves?" he said in bewilderment.

"What would we have to lose?" said Amelia.

"If you had already spoken out against her, it would do our mother no more harm. And you see, Mr Lomax, we would not wish any of our friends to be deceived by your attentions — deceived into thinking you a gentleman."

He stared at her — too dull-witted to comprehend that a woman could be threatening *him*.

"And there is something else which I ought to mention," Sophia said, calmly rising from her seat. "Each one of our letters contains a request that the reader send seven similar letters to her friends — particularly her wealthy friends — with a request that each of those friends send another seven to *her* friends. And so on. I am no mathematician, Mr Lomax, but I am sure you would agree with me that within a very short time indeed there would be a great many letters circulating and I doubt very much whether you would find an unmarried lady of fortune in the country who had not heard of your deception — and was disgusted by it."

Dido smiled her approval. They had carried out her plan to perfection. And there was certainly no doubting that, if they were sent, those letters would be copied and sent out again and again. There was hardly a young lady born who would not delight in being part of such a scheme. From the look on his face she judged that Tom certainly did not doubt it.

Sophia and Amelia linked arms and walked to the door — just as the sound of tea processing across the hall to the drawing room began to be heard. At the door they turned.

"Remember, Mr Lomax," said Sophia, "if you breathe one ill-natured word about Mama, it is most unlikely that you will ever be able to make your fortune by marriage."

CHAPTER
NINETEEN

It was almost four and twenty hours since Dido's triumph over Tom Lomax and the glow of success had faded sufficiently from her mind to allow her to recall that her real purpose at Belsfield was still not accomplished — nor, indeed, very near to being accomplished.

She still had no proper answers to give Catherine about Mr Montague's behaviour, nor any explanations of the murder which might satisfy herself. Failure seemed to stare her in the face wherever she looked. And still she was haunted by the feeling that there was something which she was not seeing, something which perhaps she was not wanting to see because it would somehow involve her in very painful considerations . . .

So it was in a rather desponding state of mind that she set out across the park, an hour or two before the usual dinner time, to try yet again what air and exercise might do for the stimulation of her brain. It was a pleasant, mild evening with a red sky and a smell of burning leaves from the gardeners' bonfire. Skeins of geese honked across the sky and, far out in the park, sheep bleated occasionally to one another.

She walked again towards the chapel, for it was a pleasant direction to take ... and, though she would not of course eavesdrop, it would be very interesting to just know whether Mr Lomax had gone to pray again this evening. She would perhaps just look around the chapel door ... She would certainly not be so dishonourable as to listen ...

The little church presented the same tranquil appearance; a dove was roosting on a ledge above the porch, adding its soothing, bubbling song to the air of calm and retirement. The door was again standing slightly open.

She peered in; but the afternoon was brighter than the one before and by contrast the darkness in the chapel was impenetrable. She took a few cautious steps into the building.

"Good evening, Miss Kent. You are walking late." It was the voice of William Lomax.

Dido gasped, stepped back and squinted into the gloom. She could just make out his figure — standing close beside her.

"Yes," she stammered, feeling very foolish. "It is a beautiful evening and ... and I have not visited the chapel before."

"I am sorry that I startled you," he said. "But please come in and look around. The place is well worth looking at." His manner was as smooth and well bred as usual — or perhaps a little more so, as if he was trying just a little too hard to act in his accustomed way.

"Yes, it is pretty, is it not," she said, trying valiantly to match his calmness. She took a few steps along the aisle and, as her eyes adjusted themselves to the darkness, began to make out the family monuments upon the walls with their blackly written eulogies.

"The chapel is Elizabethan," Mr Lomax continued smoothly, coming to stand beside her. "About the same age as the house." She took a sidelong look at him and now she was able to distinguish his features — and to see that there was a gleam of damp upon his brow. And there was something else that disquieted her. If it had not been indelicate to notice such things, Dido might have thought that there was a smell of fear about him — as if he was rather heated in spite of the chapel's coldness.

But she made an effort to appear as if she had noticed nothing unusual and did her best to meet him in conversation. "I had not known that the house was so old," she said.

"Ah, that is because of the new façade that was built after the Great Storm. I daresay, Miss Kent, you have heard of the storm that did so much damage here in 1780. The park lost many of its finest trees and several chimneys were blown down from the house. Sir Edgar had the front of the house rebuilt. The style is Palladian — as I am sure you know . . ." And he talked on very pleasantly, until, fearing that she was becoming chilled with standing still for so long, he offered her his arm back to the house.

Dido was flattered by his attention and, as usual, enjoyed his discourse very much, for the conversation of a sensible, well-informed man was a pleasure she tasted but rarely. Yet she could still not quite forget what she had seen and heard yesterday, nor cease to wonder. Why had he come here today? To pray again for a deliverance from evil and temptation?

As they left the chapel, he seemed to become more at ease. "It is a great pleasure for me to have such an attentive audience, Miss Kent. I hope I have not wearied you with my little lecture."

"Certainly not. You know a great deal about the family history; I think you must have been acquainted with the Montagues for a long time."

"I grew up here on the estate. My grandfather managed the affairs of Sir Edgar's father. It seems sometimes as if the family is a part of me — or I am a part — a small, humble part — of it. Perhaps it would be more proper to put it that way."

"You are too modest, Mr Lomax. I am sure Sir Edgar relies upon you a great deal."

"You are very kind."

They walked on a little while in silence across the park and Dido took the opportunity of studying her companion's face. The low light of the sun was making him narrow his eyes, rather emphasising the deep lines at their corners. She was suddenly struck by the inconsequential thought that, though lines upon a woman's face always marred her beauty, they could merely lend interest to the features of an intelligent, handsome man. And yet, for all that, she thought, he looks tired and worried. A great deal more tired and worried than before he went away.

"You are very quiet, Mr Lomax. Is anything troubling you?"

218

"It was impossible!" The words seemed to burst from him.

"I beg your pardon?"

He stopped and gazed towards the knoll and the spinney where the lowering sun was glinting through the trees and throwing long shadows from their trunks across the park. "It was impossible," he said more calmly, but still with great feeling. "The murder. I see no way in which it could possibly have taken place."

His vehemence surprised her. "It does indeed seem impossible that any of the gentlemen left . . ."

"Ah, but it goes deeper than that," he said, shaking his head.

"Does it?"

"Oh yes. Much deeper. Miss Kent, when I had the pleasure of talking with you the other evening, you very eloquently represented the difficulties that a stranger would have in walking armed with a shotgun into Sir Edgar's grounds without being observed."

"And did I convince you, Mr Lomax?"

"I believe you did."

"I am delighted to find my arguments so persuasive!"

He smiled. "Your reasoning is undoubtedly excellent, Miss Kent, but I must confess that on this occasion it was not unaided by my own recollections. You see I was not shooting that day — which, of course, gave me a great deal of opportunity for looking about me. And," he said with another nod towards the sunny little hill, "from the knoll there is an excellent view of the park. I am certain that I saw no one cross to the shrubbery.

Neither the murderer, nor — and this is a point to be considered — the young woman."

"I see." She said thoughtfully. "Then you believe that they both entered through the gardens?"

"But that, too, is, we know, impossible. For the gardeners are quite certain that they saw no one."

They had come now to the bench beside the stump of the old walnut tree and, at his suggestion, they sat down. He sighed and gazed out across the park. "I like this spot," he said. "I believe it commands the best view on the estate."

Dido studied his face and tried to understand his mood. He looked so very troubled. It was true of course that the murder did present a puzzle; but baffled curiosity alone could not explain his agitation. She remembered the great urgency of his prayers in the chapel.

"Mr Lomax," she began cautiously. "May I ask? I hope you do not think I presume too much; but why are you so troubled by these questions now?"

He made no reply, but there was no sign of anger or displeasure at her enquiry. She waited. A sheep called and was answered by one of its companions. In the distance she watched a farmer at work with his plough, turning a field of grey stubble into rich, chocolate-brown furrows. A cloud of gulls wheeled about him and, so still was the evening, their cries reached her faintly on the smoke-laden air.

Mr Lomax rested his arm on the back of the bench and leant his head upon his hand. His suffering troubled her.

"When we last spoke of the murder," she said, "you seemed only to wish to put my mind at rest and you were kind enough to do all that you could towards that end. Today, if I may say so, it is your own mind which seems to be sadly in need of repose."

He merely shook his head.

"I should be very glad to return the favour and ease your mind."

"You are very kind."

"You know — I am sure you know — Mr Lomax, that you may trust me with any confidence."

"Yes," he said simply. "I know that."

She tried again. "I believe something has happened to make the business of this murder more troubling to you."

"Well, well," he said. "It is perhaps nothing. But you must understand, Miss Kent, that from the very outset I have been concerned — very concerned — for the embarrassment, the public notoriety, which this unfortunate incident has caused Sir Edgar's family."

"Your loyalty does you great credit, I am sure, Mr Lomax."

"But," he replied with some vehemence, "it would be no credit to me — nor to my employer — if I were to neglect the pursuit of justice in such a cause."

"No, it would not." She hesitated, half afraid to go on, yet unwilling to give up the interesting subject. "Would I be right," she ventured at last, "to guess that you have lately discovered something which would — if publicly known — increase Sir Edgar's embarrassment?"

He nodded heavily and then, after a moment's hesitation, said, "The truth is, Miss Kent, that, in the course of my recent business, I have discovered that a Miss Wallis — a young woman in the employ of Sir Edgar — has gone missing from her home."

Dido started and it flashed through her mind that his business had taken him to Hopton Cresswell. Nor was she insensible to the idea that Miss Wallis had been employed by Sir Edgar. But she found — rather to her surprise — that her chief concern was for the man before her — and his evident suffering.

"And you think that it was this Miss Wallis who met her death here?" she asked.

He nodded. "She left her place of employment on the day of the murder saying that she was travelling to Dorchester to visit her family, and she has not been heard of since. I have made enquiries and I have discovered that she never arrived at her mother's house, nor has any message been received from her. I think that it is all too likely that it was she who . . . No, it is saying too much to say it is likely. But it is, at least, possible."

"And you wish to make this possibility public?"

"Sir Edgar is, naturally, very reluctant to agree. He believes that it will raise a great many unpleasant conjectures without materially advancing the cause of justice. But I think that maybe it is my duty to speak to Mr Fallows about it."

She remembered their conversation as they left the chapel and comprehended how difficult such a step would be for him. It would be acting counter to a lifetime of promoting and safeguarding the Montague name and credit.

He gave a long sigh. "But, since the whole business is so perplexing, Miss Kent, and bearing in mind that I have no definite proof of my suspicion, would I be justified in going against Sir Edgar's wishes in this?"

"I doubt," said Dido carefully, "that the perplexity of the business can be a sound argument for not throwing a little light upon it."

"Except that it might not be light that was thrown — but only more darkness and confusion. The disappearance of this young woman might be nothing but a remarkable coincidence." He sat in silence for some minutes and his eyes seemed to be drawn back to the spinney. "It is impossible, Miss Kent. It cannot have been done by anyone connected with this family."

"And yet," she pointed out gently, "by your own reasoning, Mr Lomax, it cannot have been done by an outsider either."

"That is true."

"But we know that it was done. We have the body of the woman as proof that it was done."

"Your logic is without fault, Miss Kent. And," he added with rather a sad smile, "without mercy too. You will allow me no escape."

"Because I do not believe that such an honourable man can find lasting peace in an escape which denies the truth."

He gave her a very penetrating look. "Thank you for your good opinion. And, of course, you are right to apply cool reason to the matter. If only we knew *how* it was done, then I might be able to decide . . ." He stopped and shook his head. "I see no way to come at it."

"Well, I am no great reasoner, Mr Lomax. My education had too much playing of scales and too little logic in it, you see. But my brother Edward — who once won a medal for debating at Cambridge — used to tell me that in an argument, all possibilities, however unlikely, must be weighed and either proved or disproved."

"It is an excellent rule. But how do you mean to employ it in this case?"

"Let me see." She considered a while. "You say that you believe it is impossible that the woman was killed between ten and one as we have all been supposing, because the gentlemen did not leave the spinney and no strangers entered the shrubbery?"

He nodded.

"Well, if she was not killed then, she must have died either before that time or after it."

"Yes," he said rather doubtingly.

"And, since Mr Harris and your son visited the shrubbery and the hermitage at five and twenty past twelve, and saw nothing remarkable there, then we know that the murder cannot have taken place *before* the guns went out."

"You argue remarkably well, Miss Kent, for . . ."

"For a woman?"

"No. I meant to say that you argue remarkably well for someone who spent her childhood playing scales."

"Thank you, Mr Lomax, but I think you would be even more surprised if you were to hear my shocking performance upon the pianoforte."

He smiled. "But," he said, "this leaves us only with the possibility that she died after one o'clock."

"Yes." It was Dido's turn to be doubting now.

"And that, you must agree, presents us with the difficulty of how a shot so close to the house as the shrubbery could go unheard. You know the ways of Belsfield well enough by now, I am sure, to understand just how quiet our afternoons are. Would it go unremarked if our peace and our quiet conversations were shattered by so loud a noise?" He stopped. "My dear Miss Kent! Are you unwell? Have I said something amiss?"

Dido was holding her hands to her mouth now and was looking exceedingly pale.

"I see," she whispered. "Oh, Mr Lomax, I see now how it was done."

CHAPTER
TWENTY

. . . My dear Eliza, it is a simple matter of putting Swisserland in the correct place.

And from that profound statement you should, of course, understand everything and I ought to have no need to wear out my genius with tiresome explanations. But, since I would wish to be celebrated as much for my compassion as my cleverness, I shall explain a little more.

Do you remember our schoolroom and the map of Europe which must be put together in our geography lessons? Do you recall how Swisserland was always the key and once that was in place, France and Saxony and the Austrian Monarchy and all the others fitted in around it?

Well, in the park today, when Mr Lomax spoke of a loud noise disturbing our conversations, it was as if he had put that one piece of the map in the right place for me. And all the other pieces began to fit in around it.

You see, I remembered how, when I was walking along the drive with Mrs Harris, our conversation was indeed broken in upon by a very loud noise. But one which the household is so accustomed to hearing that it passes without comment.

The servants' dinner bell!

And then I saw how — and when — the murder must have been done. At three o'clock on any day at Belsfield there is such a noise for a full half-minute that a gunshot would certainly pass unheard.

So you see, Eliza, Miss Wallis was not, as we supposed, killed while the gentlemen were shooting in the spinney, but at precisely three o'clock — a full two hours after they returned.

I have said nothing, as yet, to Mr Lomax about all this. I needed some time to collect my thoughts. But, no sooner was I sure of the time of the shot, than other things began to suggest themselves. For to have been so exact about the timing the killer must surely have planned the terrible deed with great care — and must have known, too, where to find the victim.

So then I fell to thinking of the difficulty which Mr Lomax has suggested and which I have not properly considered before. How and why did Miss Wallis come to be in the shrubbery?

Oh dear! How stupid of me not to think of this before! You see she cannot have walked through the gardens because the gardeners were there. I have spoken to them again, and two of them were on the lawns raking leaves from midday until their dinner bell sounded. (And when the bell sounded the poor woman was, of course, already in the shrubbery being murdered.)

So, she must have walked across the park from the side gate. Which she might have done with ease after one o'clock, when Mr Lomax was no longer watching from the knoll. But, Eliza, she would not have crossed the ha-ha with ease!

This is a difficulty which Mr Lomax has not reckoned with because I suppose that he has never worn a gown. But it would require a great deal of determination to negotiate that obstacle in a skirt and petticoat and I cannot but think that Miss Wallis was resolved on being unseen. Why else would she go to such trouble instead of walking along the drive and across the lawn? And that means that she never planned to go farther than the shrubbery, for she would certainly have been seen as soon as she stepped out of it into the rose garden.

Now, Eliza, I must ask you this: why did Miss Wallis travel nine miles from Tudor House and scramble through a ditch and over a fence in order to visit Sir Edgar Montague's shrubbery?

I am quite certain that it was not to admire the beauty of his laurels.

In short, I can think of no other reason than that she went there to meet someone. Secretly. At about three o'clock.

Well now, that is France and Spain securely in their places — and now for that awkward little Bavarian Republic.

There is only one person who is regularly to be found in the shrubbery at three o'clock. Lady Montague. Everyone knows that she takes her walks there at that hour. And I doubt very much that anyone else in the house would have arranged to meet Miss Wallis by the hermitage at a time when her ladyship might be expected to be there.

Of course, we are told that my lady did not walk out that day. But is this correct? Jack assured me that she was in her dressing room until the men returned. But maybe afterwards she contrived to go out.

Oh, Eliza! What nonsense this is! Is it likely that Lady Montague should somehow procure a shotgun and boldly stride out across the gardens to commit a murder — and do it, furthermore, quite unobserved?

And yet . . .

Well, I shall talk to Jack about it again and I am sure he will give me all the help that he can — he really does seem to be so very delighted to be relieved of the colonel's demands! Though he has not been able to answer many of my questions about Mr Montague and his father on account of only having been in the employ of Belsfield for a matter of weeks. But I make no doubt that he will, if I ask him, tell me all that he can about the day of the murder.

And then there is something else which I would dearly love to know. I must ask Catherine just when it was that my lady became so unfashionable as to put long sleeves to her evening dress.

I must look about me and make my enquiries quickly, for I have promised to meet Mr Lomax in the morning room within this hour. The dear man has such a very high opinion of my abilities that I would not wish to spoil it by presenting him with an incomplete proof.

"I am sorry, Miss Kent, I am afraid I have not quite the pleasure of understanding you. If you could perhaps speak a little more slowly."

Dido drew a long breath and endeavoured to calm herself. But the agitation into which the last hour had thrown her was so great, it almost took from her the power of rational speech.

It was late in the evening and the rest of the company were occupied at the card tables. In the half-light of the morning room, the clock ticked solemnly upon the mantelshelf and flames fluttered round a log in the hearth. The little spaniel had found her way in from the hall and was resting her head trustingly against Mr

Lomax's leg. He ran one of her long silky ears gently through his fingers as he watched Dido with grave concern.

"I understand all that you say about the dinner bell and about the young woman's arrival in the shrubbery," he said. "And it is all admirably reasoned. But this matter of her ladyship's sleeves: I am afraid I cannot comprehend why you should consider such a trifle so important."

"I am sorry. I was forgetting you are a man."

This was not quite true. In fact, she was rather keenly aware of him being a man. His reassuring, manly solidity, gathered into the chair across the hearth, was a great comfort to her. She was at that moment very glad to have such a confidant and it was very important to her that he should understand everything that was in her mind.

"Lady Montague is a very fashionable, well-dressed woman," she began.

"Yes, I suppose that she is. Though I am no great judge of these matters; my late wife frequently complained that I could not tell one of her gowns from another."

"Then you have perhaps not noticed that lately there has been something very unfashionable about my lady's appearance?"

"No, I have not."

"Her sleeves are long. She is the only lady in the house who dresses so."

"Ah," he said frowning. Then, after thinking for a moment, he added, "But, Miss Kent, I believe that when I met you in the chapel, you had on long sleeves."

"Oh dear, Mr Lomax! You must have been a sore trial to your poor wife! Do you not even notice the difference between day and evening fashions?"

He gave a helpless shrug of his shoulders.

"*In the evening*, none of the other ladies in the house wear long sleeves. Only Lady Montague."

"I must believe you since you are clearly much better informed on these subjects than I am. But I still do not see why you should consider it so very important."

Dido jumped to her feet and walked to the table where the candles stood. "It is important," she said, keeping her back turned to him, and staring into the candles' light until her eyes were dazzled, "because Catherine informs me that it was on the very day of the murder that my lady changed her way of dressing. And because . . ." She hesitated, but it had to be said. "And because I know why the change has been necessary. Mr Lomax, the other evening I was impertinent enough to turn back the lace of her ladyship's sleeve — and I saw how badly bruised her arm is." There was a sound from the gentleman somewhere between a gasp and a word of protest. She closed her eyes and saw in her mind again a vivid picture of that wrist; the ugly old yellow and purple bruises showing clearly the imprint of strong, rough fingers.

She turned at last to look at him. He was sitting with his hand resting on the dog's head, watching her anxiously.

"You do believe me?" she said.

"Of course I do," he said gently. "Your distress is more than proof enough for me. Now, come and sit quietly by the fire and tell me everything else that is in your mind. There is something else, is there not?"

"Yes, there are the things that Jack told me."

"Jack?"

"He is the youngest of Sir Edgar's footmen."

"And what is it that Jack told you?"

He had told her a great deal more than she had expected.

Cheerful now, with the white smile fixed permanently on his face rather than flashing nervously, he had seemed to feel it incumbent upon him to show his gratitude by answering every question she asked as fully as he possibly could.

"Well, now, let me see," he said in response to her query about his visits to my lady's dressing room on the day of the murder. "It was the logs first, miss. I took them up — well, I suppose that'd be just after the gentlemen went out."

"About ten o'clock, then?"

"Yes, that'd be about right. She wasn't up from her bed then. I only saw Mrs Pugh — that's her maid."

"And the next time you went up?"

"That was with fruits and cold meat. That's always about midday. She was there in the dressing room then. And then I went up with a glass of wine for her to take her medicine with. Then it was more logs. Then it was a screen from the drawing room because the fire'd got too hot for her. Then the next time, that was the chocolate. And then I'd only just got back down when Mr Carter gave me the letter to take up. That's how it always is, miss, days her ladyship spends in her dressing room, I'm up and down stairs all day."

"So this last visit you made, it would have been about one o'clock?"

"No, miss, that was later — after two, I'd say. It was certainly after the gentlemen came back from their shooting. I know that, you see, because Sir Edgar was there in the dressing room when I took the letter up. He was sitting with her, talking the way he does sometimes about how she should look after herself and take her medicine and all that."

"Sir Edgar was there? Are you sure of that?"

"Oh yes, miss, quite sure! Because I remember him making a fuss about the letter."

Dido's interest sharpened. "What kind of a fuss, Jack?"

"Well, I didn't mean to spy. I wouldn't want you to think that of me, miss. But I had to wait, you see, because that's what I'm supposed to do. Wait to see if there's an answer to be taken."

"Yes, of course, I quite understand. Under those circumstances you would not be able to help seeing what happened, though I am sure you did not wish to intrude."

"Yes, that's just how it was! Well, I was standing there by the door, waiting while the lady read her letter. And I couldn't help noticing — though I didn't mean to, of course — that she was a bit shocked by what she read."

"I see."

"Well then, miss, Sir Edgar asked her what it was and she sort of . . . well, she dropped the letter down into her lap as if she didn't want him to see it. But he reached over and pulled her hand up and took the letter from her."

"Did he do that roughly?"

"It's not my place to notice, miss. But since you ask, I must say, yes, it was rather rough . . . very rough. Because she tried to hold on to the letter to stop him seeing it."

"I see." She looked at the boy, who was smiling very earnestly under his fringe of black hair. "Naturally, you would have tried not to notice too much about that letter. But I wonder — after all, you had to carry it quite a long way. It would not have been very surprising if you had just happened to see what kind of paper it was written on perhaps — or what the handwriting of the direction was like . . .?"

"I didn't notice very much, miss, and, of course, I wouldn't talk about it to anyone else. But since it's you that's asking, I did see it was rather fine striped paper it was written on."

"And the handwriting? Was it a lady's writing?"

"No, miss, I don't think so." His brow puckered up in thought and eventually he said, "No, it wasn't a *lady's* writing. It might have been a woman's writing, miss, but it wasn't a lady's."

"And why do you say that?"

"Well, you see, miss, I could read it. And I can't read gentlefolk's handwriting — it's too clever for me — all loops and slopes and there's no making sense of it. But this was clear and round and I could read 'To Lady Montague' very well. Not that I tried to read it, but it just seemed to happen that I did — as I was walking up the stairs."

"Yes, of course. It is quite one of the misfortunes of being able to read, is it not? Sometimes we just happen to read things without hardly knowing that we are doing it."

"Yes, miss. That's just how it is!"

"So, I wonder whether you happened to notice if there was a direction as well as a name? The name of the house? The village? The county?"

"Oh yes, miss. That was all there."

"I see. Then it must have been brought with the letters from the post office, not handed in at the door."

"Maybe, miss. I didn't ask how it came."

"This is all very interesting. It is very kind of you to answer my questions so patiently, Jack. There is just one more point. Do you think that Sir Edgar read that letter?"

"I think he did, miss. He had it in his hand, but I can't be quite certain, you see, because just then Mrs Pugh came in with her ladyship's outdoor things and Sir Edgar looked up and he saw me and told me there was no answer to wait for and I could go . . ." He stopped and stared at her. "Miss? Have I said something wrong?"

"I am sorry," said Mr Lomax as she finished her account of the interview, "But, my dear Miss Kent, I am as much at a loss as poor Jack to understand why you should be surprised to hear that Sir Edgar sent the boy away. The rest, I grant you, is very interesting indeed and requires a great deal of thought."

"No, no. You are quite mistaken. I was not shocked to hear what Sir Edgar said. The shock was rather that the maid should have brought in Lady Montague's outdoor clothes. For we have been told that she did not take her walk that day."

"Perhaps she changed her mind at the last moment. Perhaps she had meant to walk out and so her maid brought her things, but then she found that she did not feel equal to the exercise."

"Perhaps she did, Mr Lomax," said Dido leaning forward eagerly in her chair. "But if that is the case, then Sir Edgar was the only one of the company who knew she was not going out. There can have been no talk in the house of her changing her usual routine if she did not decide upon that change until the last moment."

"Yes?" He looked at her earnestly. "Miss Kent, what exactly do you mean to say?"

"I am convinced that there are only two people who could have gone to the shrubbery at three o'clock. Indeed, there are only two people who could have killed the young woman. It was either her ladyship herself, or else it was Sir Edgar. Though how either of them could have walked out armed with a gun, without anyone remarking upon it, I am still at a loss to explain."

"You believe that the letter was sent by Miss Wallis?"

"Yes. She wished to meet with her ladyship. But Sir Edgar read that letter. And there is no knowing whether he prevented his wife from keeping the appointment —

236

and went himself instead — or whether the lady did go after all."

Mr Lomax looked very troubled. "But," he said slowly, "it is possible that neither of them went. It is possible that the letter had nothing to do with the murder."

"But how could that be?" she argued, aware that her words must be painful to him, but knowing she must speak them. "Everyone at Belsfield knows that Lady Montague walks in the shrubbery at three o'clock. And there was no reason to suppose that this day was different from any other. Who would be foolhardy enough to commit murder thinking that there was a witness close by?"

He passed his hand across his brow and tried again. "If the killing was a rash act of the moment. A flash of temper, perhaps. Then the killer might not have considered such things — and it was merely a matter of luck that her ladyship had chosen to take no exercise that day."

"But it was no impulse of the moment, Mr Lomax. It cannot have been. It was carefully planned to coincide with the ringing of the dinner bell."

He sighed deeply. "Your reasoning, as I have observed before, is very astute — and quite without mercy."

"I am very sorry."

"No, there is no need . . ." he began with a heavy sigh, and then stopped and sat for several minutes staring into the fire. "And why," he asked at last, "do you believe Miss Wallis wished to meet her ladyship?"

237

"I think we both know the answer to that, Mr Lomax. Miss Wallis was housekeeper in an establishment set up for Mr Montague at Hopton Cresswell, was she not?"

His head jerked up sharply. His eyes were bright and his narrow cheeks slightly red with the heat of the fire. He watched her rather fearfully, as if trying to gauge how much she knew.

"I am right, am I not?" she said.

"Yes," he said quietly at last, "you are right. She was housekeeper to Mr Montague at Tudor House near Hopton Cresswell."

"And, forgive me for asking, but one of your duties has been to oversee that establishment, has it not?"

He nodded.

"But there is something about Miss Wallis which I think perhaps you do not know, Mr Lomax." Dido avoided his eyes and looked down at her own hands folded in her lap. "She was expecting a child."

"How do you know that?"

Dido explained about the kitchen maid and the blue gown while he held one hand to his head and gazed at her in bewilderment.

"Again I shall have to believe you," he said with a weak smile, "for we seem to have strayed once more into the difficult area of women's dress."

"I am telling the truth, I assure you. And I am sure you will agree that it explains a great deal."

There was a long silence. The clock on the mantelshelf ticked ponderously. The little dog sighed and stretched herself across the hearth. Lomax sat with

238

his hands shading his eyes, almost as if he wished to hide his thoughts from his companion.

"And you believe," he said at last, without raising his head or looking at her. "You believe that Richard Montague was the father of her child?"

"Yes, I do."

He sighed more deeply and passed his hand across his face again, almost as if her answer was a relief to him.

"I believe that this liaison was the cause of Mr Montague leaving Belsfield," continued Dido. "And I believe that the young woman came here to plead her cause with her ladyship. Perhaps she intended to confide in her about the expected child."

There was another long silence in which faint laughter from the drawing room could be heard. Eventually, Lomax raised his head and looked very earnestly at her. He opened his mouth to speak then seemed to think better of it.

"There is something you wish to say?" she asked.

"No," he said uncomfortably. "It is nothing. Nothing that ought to be said."

"But I think it should be said. Pardon me, Mr Lomax, but I believe you were going to object that a natural child is no cause for murder."

He hesitated. "Well, of course it is very shocking," he said, "but . . ."

"But?"

"But, Miss Kent, we are not inhabiting the pages of a novel . . ." He smiled and shrugged.

"No, of course we are not," she said briskly. "And I quite agree with you that a sharp reprimand from Sir Edgar to his son, and a generous settlement on the woman would be more in keeping with the manners of the modern world."

"You are a remarkable woman!" he said with a much broader smile.

"Thank you for the compliment, Mr Lomax. But I do not think I am unusual in understanding the ways of the world rather better than men expect me to." She sighed. "But, you see, in this case, worldly wisdom has been confusing me. From the very beginning I have been blinded by it!"

"I do not think I understand you now."

"All along I have thought myself too clever to be taken in by such a simple explanation of the killing — or of Mr Montague's sudden disappearance. There must be more to it, I have reasoned; there must be a great deal which I was overlooking. And then yesterday, Miss Sophia said something to me which made me understand that one small detail could change everything." She stopped and shook her head in an effort to make her thoughts — and her words — more lucid. "I should have understood. You see I have suspected from the very beginning that Mr Pollard is a clergyman."

"I am sorry. What are you talking about?"

"Marriage, Mr Lomax. Marriage. Yesterday Miss Sophia said, 'Marriage is so very final. It changes everything.' And then I saw that if Mr Montague had been persuaded into a secret marriage with his lover; if

240

the child she was expecting was, in fact, legitimate — the future heir of Belsfield — then that would indeed change everything. And provide a motive for murder . . ."

She stopped. Mr Lomax was holding up his hand and looking down at the dog, who had raised her head with a little whine and was now padding towards the door. Beyond the clicking of her claws on the floorboards, they heard footsteps hurrying away across the hall.

Lomax leapt up and covered the distance to the door in two long strides. He threw it open, but the hall beyond was empty.

"Do you suppose that we were overheard?" asked Dido anxiously.

"I sincerely hope not," he said.

CHAPTER
TWENTY-ONE

... Well, like a heroine in a horrid novel, I have taken the precaution of pushing a linen chest against my door tonight. Except that I had to remove it just now when Jack came to bring my chocolate — which is a difficulty that I do not recall any young lady in a novel ever having.

It seems such a very foolish measure to take and even as I was pushing and tugging it across the carpet I was half laughing at myself. And yet the fact remains, Eliza, that someone in this house would seem to be a murderer — and that someone may have overheard my suspicions.

Oh, Eliza, I hardly know what to do next. Though one thing I am quite determined upon. Tomorrow I must persuade Catherine to break her engagement and leave Belsfield. It must be done and reluctant though I am to tell Catherine what I have discovered, I am yet determined to tell her as much as is necessary to make her abandon all connection with the family of Montague. So look for us at Badleigh within these next few days.

Though I confess that, for myself, I shall be extremely sorry to leave the place with so many questions still unanswered.

Was it Sir Edgar or his wife who went to that fateful appointment in the shrubbery? Will it ever be possible to discover exactly what happened?

And then there are two points on which I most particularly wish to be satisfied. Firstly: how could the murderer have walked armed across the grounds of Belsfield without anyone remarking upon the fact? And secondly: how did Mr Dollard contrive to convey his message at the ball without speaking a word?

Dido laid down her pen with a sigh, rubbed at her weary eyes, and blew out her candle.

It distressed her that she must leave Belsfield with these questions unanswered. And that, of course, must be the reason why she found that she was so very reluctant to go. There could be no other cause. She could safely resign the pursuit of justice to Mr Lomax and, even if there were no positive danger in remaining, there would certainly be very unpleasant scenes enacted here soon, scenes which she had no wish to take part in. She ought to be glad to go . . .

Of course she would miss her conversations with Mr Lomax; he was a very pleasant companion. And it was unfortunate that once Catherine's engagement was broken there was little chance of her ever meeting with him again. But it was foolish to waste time sighing over that . . .

No, she told herself stoutly, if only she could answer those few lingering questions, then she would be very happy to return to Badleigh. Very happy indeed.

The little room was full of shadows, and the dark bed-hangings and the little old witch shape of her cloak and bonnet on the door reminded her of her first night at Belsfield, when she had sat here beside her fire, dreading what the next day's investigations might produce.

It was about two hours after midnight and she was tired, worn out with the agitation and shocks of the day. She could not summon the strength, or the determination, to get herself into bed. She watched the firelight slide across the threadbare rug, her writing desk, the tray with her silver chocolate jug and the cup with its dark dregs, and she turned the two questions over in her mind. She could find no answers — and yet she was sure that they were there, somewhere within her reach.

The fire burnt low. She was on the very edge of sleep now and the questions began to form a kind of rhythm in her head until they seemed almost like a litany repeated in church. How can a gun be carried without it being seen? How can a man speak without opening his mouth? How can a gun . . .

The scene about her was growing indistinct, the shadows of the curtains seeming to swallow up the writing desk as her eyes flickered and closed . . .

She was sitting on the green bench in the park, looking across the long shadows of trees to the ploughman and his wheeling cloud of gulls.

"I like this spot," said a voice beside her. "I believe it commands the best view on the estate."

She turned towards the speaker and saw, not Mr Lomax as she had expected, but Sir Edgar Montague. He was standing, feet planted well apart on the short grass, under the broad canopy of a great tree. There was a half smile on his face and he was gazing out over the park with all the pride of ownership; completely in control of everything he saw. And he had the symbols of his status with him — the servile dog and, carried negligently under his arm, the gun . . .

Dido woke. She sat for some time staring into the grey ash and red glow of her fire; her mind was suddenly wide awake and working very hard.

Yes, of course. The picture. The answers were all there in the picture. How stupid she had been! But she had not wanted to look for the answers because they would involve her in calculations which were particularly distasteful to her.

But now she must face those calculations. There was no escaping from them. And the first thing to be done was to look again at the painting.

Without allowing herself time to think further about it, she took a taper from the box on the mantelshelf and relit her candle from the fire. Then she pushed the chest away from the door, turned the lock and stepped out of her room.

The passage was narrow and very dark. She stood still for a moment, hardly daring to breathe and listening hard. There was an occasional creaking sound, either from beds, or else from settling floorboards; and somewhere not far away, someone was snoring loudly. Beyond the little circle of light that her candle threw upon the plaster walls and old, uneven floorboards, there was utter blackness. Her courage almost failed her and she very nearly turned back. But that would be foolish. There was nothing to be afraid of in a dark house, she told herself firmly. And she crept along the passage, one hand holding her candle high and the other just brushing the wall.

This passage took her down the side of the East wing to a little lobby and three steps which connected it with the Great Gallery at the front of the house, and, as she tiptoed down the steps, she saw that there was more light in the gallery. The big windows at the end admitted long rectangles of moonlight, which fell over the window seat and the highly polished, honey-coloured floor and onto one wall, cutting across the face of a dark, cracked Sir Edgar with a wheel ruff and a pointed chin.

As she passed, she could not but think that his eyes had turned to follow her, and, as the candle's light fell on each of his companions in turn, she felt that they, too, were watching her progress with interest. The boards creaked alarmingly beneath her feet and she expected at any moment to be confronted by the butler in his nightshirt, armed with a cudgel and intent upon defending his master's property from burglary.

Her heart was beating so hard when she reached the end of the gallery that the light in her hand was shaking. She stopped and listened at the head of the stairs. And very faintly, from one of the best chambers on the landing below, she heard the sound of hurried footsteps. Carefully setting her own candle down upon the floor, she leant over the banister, but she could discern no light below her. She stood for several moments with the cold polished rail beneath her hands, listening so intently that she scarcely dared to draw breath. There was the sound of a door opening, the faint gleam of a candle's light flickered across the white wall of the stairwell, then there were more footsteps. A second door opened and the light was gone.

All was quiet again in the big old house. There was nothing now but the faint creaking of ancient floors and, very faint and distant, the same spluttering snore. Satisfied that she had not been detected, Dido took up her candle and turned into the dark passage in which was hidden the painting of Sir Edgar and his domain.

By candlelight it seemed larger than ever and it was not easy to study. The candle would light only a fragment of it at a time and the unsteady beam shimmered distractingly over the surface of the oil-paint. But there was Sir Edgar, just as she had recalled him in her dream: proud and self-important with his dog and his wife . . . And with his gun slung easily and negligently upon his arm as if it were a natural part of him.

She understood now.

How can a gun be carried without being seen?

The answer was plain. A gun could be carried by the master of the estate without anyone remarking upon it. They were so used to seeing it there upon his arm as he strode about the place that they would not think it worth mentioning. It was simply a mark of his status. A kind of symbol of that power of life and death that he had over every creature within his domain.

No one had thought to say that they had seen Sir Edgar walking about at three o'clock in the afternoon with a gun, *because they were so used to seeing it.*

And that was how the murder had been accomplished!

But this picture held other, much more disturbing, secrets.

Very slowly she raised her candle, fearing to see what she knew she must. There was no escaping it. There was the great tree spreading its shade over Sir Edgar and his lady — and she saw now that it had the unmistakable narrow leaves and spreading crown of a walnut tree. She moved the candle; there, stretched out below the green bench was the very view that she had looked upon as she spoke with Mr Lomax — the only difference being that here were the colours of summer rather than autumn and the ploughed furrows in the distance were replaced by stooks of harvested corn.

It was no wonder that the picture had been hidden away!

She moved her candle back and took one last look at the man, woman and child grouped beneath the tree. Then she crept along the gallery of watching eyes to the window seat and sat herself down to think.

The distasteful calculations must be made. It was, in fact, all a matter of arithmetic. As if she were once more back in the schoolroom, Dido applied herself to the hated subject and, with difficulty and rather more use of her fingers than should have been necessary, she worked out the sums.

And the sums showed her that, although almost everything she had so far concluded might be right, there was a great deal that she had missed. She had a sudden vivid memory of Mr Lomax sitting by the fire in the morning room and passing his hand across his face, sighing as if he was relieved at the answers she had given to his questions.

Of course he had been relieved. He had, for a moment, feared that she had uncovered the real secret of the Montagues.

She turned to the window and gazed out across the silent moonlit lawns that were striped black with the shadows of yew bushes, and she reckoned up the figures again.

This was the all important calculation: 1805 take away 23, equals 1782.

If Richard Montague was indeed twenty-three years old — as she had been told — then he must have been born in 1782. But the walnut tree in the park had been felled in the Great Storm of 1780.

It was as if Swisserland had been moved and she must begin to put her map together all over again.

CHAPTER
TWENTY-TWO

Dido was abroad very early the next morning, reminding herself of another of Shakespeare's characters (whose name and play, as usual, escaped her memory) who said "not to be abed before midnight is to be up betimes". For the truth was that she had not succeeded in closing her eyes all night.

Her first visit was to Catherine's bedchamber, where, sitting upon the edge of the bed, she asked, "Catherine, my dear, do you love Richard Montague very much?"

Catherine sat up blinking, shocked and still stupid with sleep. "Of course I do."

"If," said Dido, "if it could be shown that his honour was not compromised by what has happened here — that he has, in fact, acted with integrity throughout — would you wish to stand by him, no matter what difficulties and embarrassments he may have to face when the truth is revealed? Would you wish to fulfil your engagement?"

"Yes," said Catherine, still blinking and clearly bewildered by the early visit and the sudden questions. "You know I would."

"Yes," said Dido, patting her hand. "I think I do."

"Aunt Dido, what is this all about?"

"Nothing for you to worry about, my dear," she said, getting up. "Go back to sleep now." But, at the door, she stopped. "Oh, there is just one more question. Are you quite sure that when Mr Pollard came to Mr Montague at the ball, he did not show him anything? A letter perhaps?"

"No, I am sure he did not."

"Why are you so certain that he did not?"

"Well, because I saw his hands. When Mr Montague stepped back, I saw Mr Pollard's hands very clearly, and they were empty."

"You are quite sure that you saw his hands?"

"Yes. Quite sure."

"I see."

"Aunt, why must you wake me up to ask these questions?"

"Because, my dear, I believe hands are a very important part of this mystery . . . And the rats, of course," she added, half to herself. "I am beginning to understand now just how important the rats are."

And then she left before Catherine could say anything more.

Her next visit was to Annie Holmes, who was coddling an egg for her daughter's breakfast and who was clearly alarmed by the sight of such an early caller — and even more alarmed by the questions that she asked.

From the lodge cottage she walked across the park to the chapel and spent some time in looking at its monuments. Then, deep in thought, she started back towards the house.

The dawn had been grey and damp, but now the sun was beginning to break through the mist, turning the trees of the park into long black shadows and the drops of moisture that clung to every blade of grass into sparkling jewels. In spite of her pattens, the dew penetrated her shoes and chilled her feet, but she did not hurry. Indeed, as she approached the house, her steps became slower and slower, for she was reluctant to arrive before she had decided how she should behave when she was there. How — and to whom — should she reveal what she had discovered?

As she left the park and came into the gardens — where the sun was turning the great fountain into a shower of light and striping the gravel with the shadows of the yews — the bell in the stable tower began to toll slowly and mournfully, clanging out a terrible, unnamed dread into the bright morning air.

The sound made her afraid, though she hardly knew of what, and she began to run up the steps of the terrace before the house. She had just gained the lower terrace and was standing to rest beside the fountain, her hand on its damp stone lip and the rush and splash of it mixing with the solemn tone of the bell, when she saw Mr William Lomax coming down from the front door to meet her.

And the shocked look upon his face told her that something of great moment had happened.

252

CHAPTER
TWENTY-THREE

Belsfield Hall. Wednesday, 9th October 1805

My dear Eliza,

Do you remember how Edward used to tell us that we should beware of believing something simply because it was written in a book? Well, I daresay that these last few days have been very useful to you in extending that lesson and I expect that you now know not to believe a thing simply because it is written in a letter.

For it cannot have escaped the attention of such a clever woman that, quite contrary to the information in my last note, neither Catherine nor I have arrived at Badleigh. We are, in point of fact, still here in the lap of luxury at Belsfield and expect to remain here a while.

You see, everything has changed here. And the greatest change is one that I ought, properly, to write of with great sorrow. But the truth is that I feel no sorrow at all and can aspire to nothing more than shock — though the shock is profound.

For, the long and the short of it is, Eliza, that Sir Edgar Montague is dead.

It is true. He was found dead in his bed two days ago and Mr Bartley, who has been in attendance, declares that he was taken with a seizure in the night and died quickly and painlessly. That last I am sure is merely a comfort for his widow, for I cannot believe that Mr Bartley — or anyone else — can judge the exact nature of a seizure by only looking at the mortal remains. However, he talks very wisely of bile and a weakness of the heart and a sudden crisis and I know not what, and we all listen and pretend that we are as wise as he appears to be. But, like the old gentleman at Lyme, I have no great faith in physicians.

Nor, I find, does Mr William Lomax. At least, not in this case. For neither he nor I can forget that someone was listening to our conversation in the morning room. Mr Lomax is of the opinion that Sir Edgar, knowing that his crime had been discovered, took his own life by drinking laudanum — to preserve his family from the shame of a trial. It is a belief which puts the best possible light upon the event and, since Mr Lomax finds comfort in it, I do not speak against it.

He has had enough trouble these last two days in attempting to bring some order to this shocked household, for all the business of the death has fallen upon him. Her ladyship has kept to her room with a sleeping draught of Mr Bartley's. Mr Harris — who might, from his position in the family, have been fairly expected to assist him — has done little but "support the spirits of his poor wife" — which support has consisted chiefly of listening to her foolish prosings — and the rest of the household seems to be beyond anything but staring at one another and gossiping. Margaret, it is true, has been so kind as to send an express to Francis, and takes every opportunity of assuring Mr Lomax that he will be of inestimable use, when he arrives. He bears her assurances with great patience and meanwhile proceeds with the all the correspondence and arrangements that are necessary at such a time.

As you may imagine, I have been very unwilling to add to his difficulties, but I had to talk very seriously with him — my duty to Catherine demanded it . . .

She had, in fact, lain in wait for him some time in the hooded chair in the hall, and, upon him just crossing from the stairs to the library, she had delayed him with, "Mr Lomax, may I ask a favour of you?"

He stopped, his broad shoulders slightly stooping with weariness, his brow furrowed, and one finger tapping restlessly upon the bundle of papers that he carried; but with his head courteously inclined towards her. "Of course you may, Miss Kent. I shall be very happy to oblige you."

"Oh dear, I rather doubt that. You see . . ." She glanced quickly about the hall to be sure that they were not overheard. But all the company, except her ladyship, seemed now to be gathered in the drawing room. She continued in a lower voice. "You see, Mr Lomax, I am afraid I must ask you to break a promise which I am sure you have given. In short, I do not wish you to allow the late Sir Edgar's secrets to survive him."

The effect upon the gentleman was striking. His face became pale and his eyes wary. He too looked about him to be sure that they were alone. "We had better talk about this in the library," he said abruptly and, stepping to the door, he held it open for her. She walked in and he closed the door behind them. "Now," he said, "can you explain what you mean by this extraordinary request?"

It was some time before she could collect her thoughts. She took a seat beside the curtained window and looked about the gloomy candlelit room. Between the high, shadowy shelves of leather-bound books was a large table strewn with documents and writing materials where he had been working. Like every other part of the house, the room seemed heavy with a sense of mourning and that shocked confusion which always follows sudden death.

Among the many sensations crowding in upon her was a great reluctance to speak and a fear of losing his regard. And, which was perhaps worse, there was a fear, too, that, when this interview was done, she would no longer be able to respect him. Her eyes strayed to the pile of correspondence on the table: some letters lay open for their ink to dry, some were already folded and sealed; there was a scattering of sand still lying on some of the papers and a candle and a block of red sealing-wax were beside them; there was a faint smell of hot wax mixing with the dusty scent of old books.

"You have written to Mr Richard Montague?" she asked.

He nodded. "I believe him to be in town — at Mr Pollard's lodgings. I have sent to him there."

"You have asked him to come home and take his place as head of this household?"

He stood for several moments watching her levelly; then he sat himself down beside the table, pressed the tips of his fingers together and rested his chin thoughtfully upon them. He said nothing.

She forced herself to press the point. "Have you, Mr Lomax?" The silence stretched between them. "Have you asked him to take what is not his?"

She waited. Outside on the lawns a peacock screeched harshly but there was no other sound; just that blanketing silence of mourning which is made of the absence of music and laughter and loud voices.

"Richard Montague," he said at last, "will act as he sees fit."

"Richard Montague is a very young man; he is inexperienced and I rather think that he will be guided by your advice." She paused. "What advice will you give him, Mr Lomax? Will you tell him to follow his conscience, or will you suggest that he should fall in with his dead father's wishes and take the fortune to which he has no rightful claim?"

"No claim?" His eyes narrowed a little. "Now, why do you say that he has no claim?"

"Why indeed? Mr Lomax," she said, meeting his eye. "How can a young man — an heir to a great estate — lose, in the course of a few minutes, all his prospects of inheritance?"

He passed one hand across his face and gave her a faint smile. "Is this a riddle, Miss Kent?" he asked.

"If it is, it is a very dull one, for we both know the answer to it."

"Nevertheless, I think you had better explain it to me."

"Very well, I shall. It is really very simple, though I confess that I was for some time unable to see it. Because Mr Montague did indeed lose his fortune in those few moments in the ballroom, did he not? He is not the heir to Belsfield. It is not he who should now be coming home to take his father's place."

He did not confirm, or deny, he merely continued to regard her over his fingers.

"He lost his fortune that night and he did not lose it through the uncovering of some misdemeanour that cost him his father's favour. He could not. Because, as your son was at pains to point out to me, the Belsfield inheritance is not dependent upon anyone's goodwill. It is entailed."

His face remained impassive. "Very well then, Miss Kent, what is the answer to your riddle? How can a young man so quickly lose his prospects of inheritance?"

"There is only one way, Mr Lomax — by discovering that another man has a better claim."

"And you believe that that is what happened to Mr Richard Montague?"

"Yes, I do."

"And may I ask who this man is who has a better claim to the Belsfield estate?"

"Richard Montague's older brother, Edgar. The son who was born two years before him. The heir with whom Sir Edgar was painted under the walnut tree. The child who was afflicted and so was banished from this house."

Lomax stood up suddenly and paced to the hearth. Placing one hand upon the mantel and one foot on the fender he stared down into the fire as if anxious to avoid her eyes. "You seem to know a great deal, Miss Kent. May I ask how you know it?"

"Oh, chiefly by piecing together a great many little things. There is the painting of course — and Annie Holmes gave me some hints about why young Richard was so fearful of his father's displeasure. He, of course, dreaded that he shared his brother's infirmity and would, like him, be rejected. And then there was the gentleman we spoke to at Lyme. He remembered a little boy of the name of Montague staying at the Old Grange, and Catherine and I both believed it to be Richard — who recuperated from scarlet fever there. But afterwards I saw that it could not have been him. For the man said that the child played out in all weathers — *summer and winter.* Yet Richard Montague never spent a winter at Lyme. He was there for one summer only . . ."

"Upon my word, Miss Kent, you are remarkably observant!"

"Thank you."

"It quite frightens me to think that you have been scrutinising us all these last few days."

She smiled. "You need have no fears for yourself, Mr Lomax. Your only weakness is your courtesy. It is only that which gives away your secrets."

"Indeed?"

"Yes, for although Sir Edgar persuaded you into conniving at the lie that he had only one son, your sense of propriety is always unconsciously betraying you."

"Is it?"

"Oh yes. I noticed that, unlike everyone else, you never speak of 'Mr Montague'; you must always give him his Christian name and call him 'Mr Richard Montague' — as is correct for a younger son."

He shook his head and stirred a log upon the grate with the toe of his boot. "You are, as I have said before, a truly remarkable woman." He watched the sparks from the disturbed fire fly up the chimney. "But, my dear Miss Kent, since you know so much, you must know . . ." He stopped, seemed to collect himself and began again. "I don't doubt that you have heard from someone the conclusion of young Edgar's story."

"Yes. It was not easy to discover, for Sir Edgar has made it very plain that his eldest son is not a subject he wishes to be talked about. But Annie Holmes has — reluctantly — informed me that the boy remained at Lyme — and is supposed to have died there of a putrid fever when he was sixteen."

"And yet you do not believe this?"

"Mr Lomax, I have visited the church at Lyme and the chapel here at Belsfield and I know that this particular Edgar Montague has not a grave or a memorial in either place."

Dido wished that he would look at her. She longed to know how he was feeling — and how he intended to behave. But his back remained turned and his face bowed over the fire. There was nothing for it but to carry on with her tale. When it was done, then was the

260

time for him to reveal his intentions — and his true character. He was, at heart, she did not doubt, an honest man, but how much had he been corrupted by long loyalty to an unworthy master?

"I am sure, though, that nearly everyone at Belsfield believed him dead," she continued. "You have always known the truth, of course, for you formed the household at Hopton Cresswell and established the young man there under the name of Blacklock. Her ladyship knows that her son is alive, though such was Sir Edgar's unkindness to her that she would have been entirely cut off from him, had you not sometimes taken her to him in your carriage." She paused, but still he did not turn. "I suppose," she went on, "that it was the only conveyance he would consent to since he wanted none of his own servants to know about Tudor House."

Still he did not stir.

"Of course, the material point is that Edgar's brother, Richard, believed him dead — until that moment at the ball . . ."

"Ah!" He turned at last, his face flushed from the heat of the fire and raised one long finger. "The scene at the ball! I shall be very glad to hear what you have to say about that, Miss Kent. You believe that Mr Pollard told Richard that his brother was still alive?"

"Oh yes. Most certainly. That is the only thing which can have made him behave as he did. Consider the matter, Mr Lomax. Here was a young man very much in love. And he was, most sincerely in love — the level of trust and confidence he had placed in my niece certainly proves that. What other motive can he have had for abandoning his lady other than the conviction that he was acting in the interests of her happiness? His conscience would not allow him to continue to usurp his brother's place, but he knew that the most painful scandal would ensue if he exposed his father's lie. He behaved in the only way possible for a loving and honourable man to behave."

Lomax paced back to the table, threw himself down in his chair in an attitude not unlike his son's, and studied her face. "Miss Kent! I do believe that despite your love of reason and logic, you are a romantic at heart! But this will not do. Last night you told me that the young man had betrayed your niece and was secretly married to another woman."

"Last night I was mistaken. And," she added more quietly, "last night you allowed me to continue in my mistake, Mr Lomax. That was not fair of you."

The colour deepened on his face. "Are you suggesting that I lied to you?" he demanded.

"Oh no, you were very careful not to lie. But you allowed me to believe what you knew was not true." She was surprised at her own anger. She felt it heating her face and making her grip the arms of her chair. She had not known until that moment how badly his behaviour had hurt her.

They regarded one another warily. The library suddenly seemed very airless. Dido did not trust herself to speak, lest she should say something hasty which she would regret — and his looks suggested that he was fighting the same battle between temper and propriety. But it was eventually he who broke the silence.

262

"There is, of course, a flaw in your reasoning," he said coolly. "You say that Mr Pollard told Mr Richard Montague that his brother was alive. And yet, Miss Kent, both you and I know that Mr Pollard said nothing at the ball."

"Yes," she said slowly, "that is the strangest part of this mystery." But inwardly she was contemplating the mystery of the man before her. Lounging as he was in the chair, he reminded her irresistibly of his son. Was corruption, after all, a family trait? Or was William Lomax truly the honourable man she had always taken him for?

Catherine's future happiness depended upon his integrity, for unless he agreed to disclosure, the truth of what had happened here at Belsfield could never be made public. And that of course was why her head was aching with anxiety now. There could be no other reason why his character should matter so much to her . . .

She leant forward earnestly. "If I can explain to you this last mystery — if I tell you how a man can say so much in a moment of silence — will you agree to break your promise to Sir Edgar and make his secret known to the world?"

"You are very sure, Miss Kent, that I have made such a promise."

"Oh, I know that you have. You are almost twenty years his junior; he must have expected that you would survive him and I cannot believe that he did not make plans for what would happen after his death. You have promised him that you will continue to hide Edgar

Montague; but now justice and humanity demand that you break your promise. If you do not, you will be parting two young people who love each other dearly."

He frowned and shook his head, but said, "Well then, I shall admit it. Yes, I have indeed promised Sir Edgar that I will not reveal the true heir of Belsfield."

"And will you now agree to break that promise?"

He stirred his long limbs uncomfortably in his chair, rearranged the pens in their rack, drew his finger through the grains of sand on a letter. "You have not yet kept your side of the bargain, Miss Kent," he said, pushing the sand grains into a tiny pile. "Explain the mystery to me. Then we shall consider my promise and the demands of humanity and justice."

"Very well then. That is our last riddle: how does a man speak without saying anything? And once it is answered, everything that has been happening here at Belsfield becomes plain. It is all a matter of hands, Mr Lomax. Hands — and rats — and a game of football."

She jumped up restlessly and went to the window, pulled the curtain aside a little and peered out. The sun was drying the dew on the lawns, and the trees of the park burnt in glorious golds and reds and russets. She was shocked by the brightness and the ordinariness of the day, almost as if she had expected to see the trees and the rose urns draped in black and the peacocks all sombre-eyed with mourning.

"The hands puzzled me from the very beginning," she said, with her back still turned upon him and her eyes fixed on the glowing foliage of the park. "You see, I heard only two reports of Mr Pollard. One from

Catherine and one from the ostler at the Feathers. But it was remarkable that both reports mentioned his hands. That is strange, don't you think, Mr Lomax? Why should hands be so very memorable? Catherine is sure that when she saw Mr Pollard, his hands were empty. Why? Why was she so certain? It seemed to me that he must have been holding his hands up in some way. And the ostler said that he had fine white hands — which is a strange thing to remember. Faces, yes, we all remember faces, but hands? It seemed to me that Mr Pollard's hands must be particularly prominent. He holds them out in such a way that draws attention to them."

She turned and caught a small smile on Lomax's haggard face, but he immediately became solemn. She hurried on with her story, feeling that it was safest now to get it all told quickly.

"And then there was the football," she said. "Not much was known of the household at Tudor Cottage — except that sometimes the servants indulged themselves in a noisy game upon the drive. The girl who told me of it believed that the master must be absent from the house because, even though he did not see the game, she reasoned, he would have *heard* it."

Lomax folded his arms, shook his head a little and watched her as if she were something rare and rather remarkable. "And what of the rats?" he said.

"Ah, yes, the rats. It took me a long time to understand the rats. You see, soon after I came to Belsfield, Miss Sophia Harris told me about a rat hunt that had taken place here. Richard Montague had failed to let the dogs go when his friends gave the signal. Miss Sophia thought he was overcome with compassion for the rats, but I doubted that. Such tenderness would have been quite remarkable in a young man who had grown up at Belsfield, surrounded always by shooting and hunting, and would certainly have drawn attention on other occasions. But it was clear that something distressed Mr Montague that day."

Dido left the window and took a seat at the table; leaning across the clutter of pens and letters, she continued with a flush creeping up her cheeks. "In fact, it all happened just as he said, Mr Lomax. There was no great excess of pity. He simply failed to hear the signal that his companions gave. And, although for anyone else that might have been nothing, for Richard Montague it was a terrible moment. Because you see, Richard has always feared that he might go deaf — that he might come to share his brother's affliction."

There was a long silence in the library, broken only by the occasional crack of sparks on the hearth. Lomax showed no inclination to speak and, after waiting a while, Dido decided that it would perhaps be better, after all, to finish her tale before she lost her courage.

"Edgar Montague is only deaf," she said. "There is nothing wrong with his wits. He does not hear, and naturally he cannot speak since he has never heard speech. But in everything else he is a healthy young man. He is simply deaf. This makes sense not only of the way in which his servants knew they could play upon the drive with impunity, it also explains why the household at Hopton Cresswell did not in any way sound like one formed for the restraint of a lunatic and why Richard remembered the summer he spent in Lyme with such pleasure: his brother had been an agreeable companion." She hesitated a moment, but it must all be said. She pressed on. "It also explains the marriage. That was just as I said. A young man living a retired life fell in love with the woman who shared his home and married her secretly. But that young man was Edgar Montague, not Richard. The father's outrage was perhaps even greater than I imagined. For the expected child was not only the heir to Belsfield and the son of a common woman, but it might also share its father's infirmity."

"And why do you think the woman came here that day?"

"To tell her ladyship of her marriage — and her condition. It is impossible to understand her reason exactly because I know nothing of her character. But I think that it was hearing of her brother-in-law's engagement that prompted her to action. Motherhood — even expected motherhood — can change a woman. Many women are ambitious for their children even though they are content to live in obscurity themselves."

She stopped at last, short of both breath and courage. The look on Lomax's face was strange. His brow was still lined with anxiety but beneath it there was a new light in his grey eyes. He watched her for several moments — until she became too conscious of his look and lowered her eyes. Hot blood swept up her cheeks. The silence roared in her ears.

But when he spoke, his voice was calm and he sounded like nothing so much as a schoolmaster prompting a pupil who has given a promising but incomplete answer. "Very well, Miss Kent, and what pray is the answer to our riddle? How does a man speak without saying anything?"

"The answer, of course, is with his hands. A great deal may be said with the hands if they are used in one of those systems of signing that are taught to the deaf." She paused but he said nothing; he only continued to watch her while his long fingers played with the spilt sand. "Mr Pollard," she continued, "taught such a system to Edgar when he was a child. And Richard, no doubt, learnt it during that happy summer which he spent with his brother at Lyme. And, by the by, I believe that this was also the reason why Mr Pollard was asked to come to Hopton Cresswell. To a conscientious young man it would be very important that the clergyman conducting the marriage ceremony should be able to understand the language in which he made his vows.

"But once Mr Pollard knew of the deception that Sir Edgar was practising, he felt it was his duty to tell Richard Montague of the matter. He came to Belsfield and found the engagement celebrations in progress. And then," she paused and shrugged. "Well, what better way was there for him to convey a private message in a crowded ballroom than with his hands — using a system of communication which no one else but Richard would understand?" She stopped again, but again he remained silent. "Well?" she cried impatiently. "Am I right?"

"Yes," he said, withdrawing his hand from the table and folding his arms. "You are right."

"Very well then," she said eagerly, leaning across the table. "Edgar Montague is only deaf, he is not astray in his wits?"

"That is correct."

"Then you have no good cause to rob him of his inheritance. He is capable of enjoying his estate and of administering his own affairs."

"Indeed, he is probably more capable than most. He is a very able young man."

Her hands clenched into fists on the table. She was willing him with her whole being to relent and prove himself just and honourable. "Then you will make his existence known to the world?"

But he shook his head. "I have made a promise, Miss Kent. I have given my word . . ."

"To a man who was not worthy of your loyalty!" she cried, unable to contain herself any longer. "You have given your word to a tyrant and a murderer, Mr Lomax. His behaviour dissolves all ties and duties . . ."

Suddenly she was overwhelmed. Worn down as she was by sleepless nights and days of restless activity; shocked by the death of Sir Edgar and by her own discoveries; worried for Catherine and more disappointed than she dared own in the man before her, she found that she was quite unable to hold back tears. They rose up, scalding her eyes and choking her words.

For a moment she was blind and deaf to everything but misery.

Then she became aware of a strong warm hand laid over her clenched fists and an anxious voice speaking at her side. "My dear Miss Kent, please do not distress yourself. I shall do everything I can to help you." She looked up and saw him bending over her with great concern. He was looking at her clearly and directly. "I am not quite the scoundrel you take me for . . ." he began fervently and then seemed to recollect himself. He took away his hand and sat down at the table. "You must understand that when I spoke just now of making a promise to Sir Edgar, I did not refer to the man who is dead — I spoke of the *present* Sir Edgar — the young man who, of course, inherited that title the moment his father died."

Dido stared at him.

"It is his own wish to remain hidden from the world. When, at just sixteen, he agreed to his father's proposal of seclusion, I thought that he would perhaps change his mind as he grew older. And, if he had given the word, I was prepared to support him in exerting his claims. But he never has changed his mind. He is a very quiet, scholarly young man and he has no wish to expose himself to the curiosity of the world. He wants no other life than the one he lives at present. It is his expressed wish that the deception should continue."

"But," said Dido wretchedly, "unless Richard Montague can tell Catherine the truth, he and she can never be reconciled."

270

"I know," he said. "My only hope is that I can persuade the new Sir Edgar to a partial disclosure. It will not be easy. He is a very stubborn man and, as I am sure you will understand, it is a difficult time to persuade him to anything now, when he is mourning the loss of his wife."

"You have told him everything?" asked Dido fearfully.

"Yes and he bears it as well as any man could, but it has been a heavy blow. Until I wrote my account I believe he had no idea but that his wife was safe in Dorchester with her mother and feared rather that she had abandoned him than that she had come to harm. His first wish now is to be left alone to grieve in peace. To gain his consent to such a disclosure of the truth will be an uphill task. But . . ." He hesitated and looked down as if he was suddenly interested in one of the letters on the table. "But if your happiness depends upon it, Miss Kent, then it must be done."

CHAPTER
TWENTY-FOUR

... Well, Eliza, the outcome of Mr Lomax's persuasion is a very happy one for Catherine. The partial disclosure which he has achieved has extended not only to her, but, very properly, to Francis and Margaret too. And now she has gained the first desire of her heart and she will be able to marry the man she loves without being burdened with parental approval.

It all hung in the balance for a while. And it almost seemed that Francis and Margaret would give the union their blessing in spite of everything, for, by Mr Lomax's careful management, Richard is to have all the appearance of inheritance. However, after due consideration, Margaret has declared that a younger son is, after all, a younger son and, as she observes, everything depends upon the goodwill of his brother. And then there is the matter of Edgar's affliction — or the "bad blood", as she insists upon styling it. And the end of it all is that she has urged Catherine to give up Richard in the strongest possible terms. Consequently, Catherine has been able to take offence at the insult offered to her beloved, in the best romantic tradition, and Francis and Margaret left Belsfield this morning promising not to attend the wedding.

Which is all highly satisfactory.

Of course, Catherine has not achieved that abject poverty to which she aspired; but, though she will not confess it, I think she has recollected that some of the consequences of poverty — such as old pelisses and pattens — are not conducive to happiness. She certainly bears the prospect of riches with remarkable fortitude.

She is very happy indeed and, though it is quite impossible that she should remain for ever in her present state of bliss, I see no reason why she should not enjoy a very contented life here at Belsfield. I have at last met Richard Montague, and I like him. He has not a shining intellect, but he seems to have remarkably good principles for the son of such a father. He defers rather too much to Catherine's judgement, but he also has a great respect for the opinion of Mr Lomax and I hope that that will prove a steadying influence in their future life.

They plan to marry as soon as the period of deep mourning is completed and for Catherine the greatest difficulty lies in maintaining an outward show of proper sadness. Though she is not alone in that.

Her ladyship looks remarkably <u>well</u>. She <u>almost</u> smiles. Catherine expects that she will marry her mysterious lover as soon as decency permits. But I do not anticipate it, for I do not believe that any such gentleman exists. I say nothing of this to Catherine, because, Eliza, I am beginning to fear that the truth behind the rumours of adultery is even more shocking than it appears. I have been considering the matter carefully and I cannot help but think that the reports all originate with Mr Bartley, who has, more than once, supplied her with that terrible medicine. And I am inclined to believe that that is not concerned with any misdemeanour of hers.

You see, I keep remembering how her husband used to sit beside her, seeming so solicitous and always asking if she had taken her medicine. And how wretched the question made her

— how she would look away and twist her rings about. Was it, I wonder, that patent stuff that he was urging her to take?

A few days ago I would not have believed such a thing possible among civilised Christians. But now, Eliza, I know the terrible lengths he was prepared to go to in order to conceal his son's affliction. To what extremes of infamy was he prepared to go to ensure that another child was not born with the same infirmity? That he did not take the course of a gentleman and exercise restraint upon himself is all of a piece with his tyranny and selfishness . . .

Well, I doubt not that you think I am talking wildly now. But I cannot help but observe that my lady seems not only vastly content, but that she is also growing plump; and that she has given over twisting her rings and that she now sews instead. Nor can I help noticing that the article she is working upon looks remarkably like a christening gown . . .

Dido stopped, feeling, as she often did, that her pen was behaving like a runaway horse and taking her to places that she had not intended to go. She had certainly not meant to mention this matter in her letter.

There was a kind of forbidding reserve about Lady Montague, even now, which made such speculation seem a liberty. She had suffered during her marriage, certainly; but the extent of that suffering would probably never be known to anyone but herself. Of all the people at Belsfield, Dido felt that she was the one she understood least; wrapped as she was in silence and invalidish dignity, it was impossible to get at exactly what she thought or felt — or to understand what she might be capable of doing . . .

274

She hurriedly put her pen into the rack in order to put out of reach the temptation of writing down her thoughts. The time had come, she told herself, to stop asking questions and to put a curb upon her curiosity. There was nothing else useful for her to do here at Belsfield. There was nothing to be gained by wondering about such things as the footsteps she had heard, the light she had seen moving about on the landing, on the night that Sir Edgar died; or in remembering that it was her ladyship who kept a large supply of laudanum.

Sir Edgar had died by his own hand. He had overheard Dido and Lomax talking and he had known that he was discovered. That is how it had happened. There was no point in wondering whether someone else had heard of his guilt and taken upon themselves the role of executioner ... Nor in remembering the behaviour of the dog.

But it was strange ... It was very strange that the dog, sensing someone at the door, had gone towards that someone ... Because the dog always ran away and hid when Sir Edgar was close by ...

There was nothing else useful for Dido to do at Belsfield, but she would have gladly stayed with Catherine until the wedding could be celebrated. However, that was not to be, for unmarried women must not expect to remain where they cannot be useful. Within a week of Sir Edgar's death a letter arrived from her brother George which forced her to change her plans.

George was a captain in the Regulars and his regiment had been ordered away from home just as his very nervous young wife was approaching her first confinement. Dido must go into Hampshire without delay to bear her company.

"I am very sorry to hear that you are going," said Mr Lomax as he and Dido sat companionably beside the hall fire on her last day.

The house was quiet for it was empty now of its visitors. The Harrises were gone home and Tom Lomax was off to some horse races. And Colonel Walborough had hurried away to visit an old army acquaintance who was living near Bristol in very straitened circumstances — with four unmarried daughters.

This morning Richard and Catherine were walking in the grounds and her ladyship was in her chamber. In the hall the great clock was ticking steadily and the spaniel was dozing and whining in her sleep. For some time Dido's work had been lying forgotten in her lap as she watched Mr Lomax's face watching the flames. She had been thinking: this is how I will remember him when I am gone from here.

"I have enjoyed your company very much indeed," he began again, and then stopped and fell to stirring up the logs on the grate, though his attentions seemed to injure the blaze rather than improve it. "Indeed," he said with his face very red with exertion, or heat — or something else, "in fact, you are perhaps aware, Miss Kent . . ." He stopped again, set the poker down upon the hearth and held his hands to the dull fire he had made.

Dido waited, suddenly finding that it was very hard for her to breathe and staring down at her bright needle with its long scarlet silk as if she had never seen such things before.

"In point of fact, Miss Kent," he continued, "you have reminded me of what I am afraid I had forgotten. You have reminded me of the great . . . the very great pleasure that there is to be found in the companionship of a charming and intelligent woman."

She tucked the needle into the material in her lap; her hand had become too hot to hold it securely. She looked earnestly at him, but he was determined to keep his face turned from her.

"It is my misfortune," he continued heavily, "that I should rediscover such enjoyment at the very time . . ." she saw his throat move as he swallowed hard, "at the very time when I find I am quite unable to secure the blessing of such companionship for myself." He sighed deeply and raised his head. "Unfortunately, my present circumstances make it impossible for me to ask any lady to share my life. I have nothing to offer but poverty and dependence."

Dido exerted herself to speak calmly, struggling to sound as if her only concern was that of a friend. "I am sorry to hear that you find yourself in such difficult circumstances, Mr Lomax."

"It cannot be helped," he said resolutely. "My son has debts. Miss Kent, I do not approve of the life my son leads, but I am sure you will understand the feelings of a father. I cannot stand by and see him imprisoned by his creditors. I have pledged myself to pay what he owes. And I fear it will be many years before I have cleared the debt."

"I am very sorry to hear it, Mr Lomax," she said calmly, and she continued to pull the scarlet silk through the white linen.

Inside her head her thoughts were raging. To know that she had his regard was a source of intense delight. Her heart glowed with pleasure even as she grieved over his present situation.

Yet she found that she could not regret the steps that she herself had taken to obstruct Tom's plans, nor could she be so inhuman as to regret that the Misses Harris had escaped him. She would have liked to condemn the kindness of the father, but she found that that comfort was also denied to her. For that kindness was an essential part of the man she had come to esteem so highly over these last weeks.

And it all ended at last in her deciding that her best chance of happiness now lay in somehow finding a woman who was rich enough — and foolish enough — to be tolerably happy as Mrs Tom Lomax. It would be a task ten times more difficult than anything she had yet achieved at Belsfield. But somehow she would accomplish it. At that moment, secure in the knowledge of his affection, she felt equal to anything . . .

Also available in ISIS Large Print:

Death in Hellfire

Deryn Lake

When John Rawlings is asked to investigate a secret club and some shady goings-on, he is intrigued. The disreputable Sir Francis Dashwood is believed to be involved, as well as some illustrious members of the British aristocracy.

In disguise, and accompanied by the ungainly Samuel Swann, John befriends Sir Dashwood and gains access to his home and family, including someone from John's past, someone whose exceptional beauty still hypnotises him.

However, evil lurks in hidden corners of Sir Dashwood's opulent home and there seems to be a sinister element behind the infamous Hellfire Club's debaucheries. Is John putting himself and Sam in danger by trying to find out the truth?

ISBN 978-0-7531-8054-9 (hb)
ISBN 978-0-7531-8055-6 (pb)

Special Assignments

Boris Akunin

A Jack of Spades and his fragrant accomplice; an eager young deputy and a fugitive countess; a game of cat and mouse and a series of savage murders: the dashing, inimitable Erast Fandorin finds himself juggling them all . . .

His first adversary is a wickedly mischievous swindler and master of disguise, whose outrageous con tricks and machinations are sending ripples through the carefully maintained calm of late 19th-century Moscow. His calling card is the Jack of Spades.

The other is a brutal serial killer — nicknamed "The Decorator" — driven by an insane, maniacal obsession, who strikes terror into the heart of the city's slums, and who may have more in common with London's Jack the Ripper than just a taste for women of easy virtue . . .

With twists and turns around every corner, Fandorin's powers of detection are tested to the limit.

ISBN 978-0-7531-7996-3 (hb)
ISBN 978-0-7531-7997-0 (pb)

The Lost Luggage Porter

Andrew Martin

Winter, 1906. After his adventures as an amateur sleuth, Jim Stringer is now an official railway detective, working from York Station for the mighty North Eastern Railway Company. As the rain falls incessantly on the city's ancient, neglected streets, the local paper carries a highly unusual story: two brothers have been shot to death.

Meanwhile, on the station platforms, Jim Stringer meets the Lost Luggage Porter, humblest among the employees of the North Eastern Railway Company. He tells Jim a tale which leads him to the roughest part of town, hot on the trail of pickpockets, "station loungers" and other small fry of the York underworld.

But then in a tiny, one-room pub with a badly smoking fire he enters the orbit of a dangerous villain who is playing for much higher stakes.

ISBN 978-0-7531-7904-8 (hb)
ISBN 978-0-7531-7905-5 (pb)

Jam and Jeopardy

Doris Davidson

Was it the raspberry jam that finally killed her?

Revenge, lust, hatred and murder envelop a small Aberdeenshire village in Doris Davidson's latest novel.

Wealthy 87-year-old spinster Janet Souter takes pleasure in raking up scandal, old and new, about her neighbours. She also relishes refusing her two nephews the money they desperately need to bolster their struggling businesses. So when she acquires some arsenic to deal with rats in her garden, she decides to test them: whichever attempts to kill her will be her sole beneficiary; if both do, they will each get a half share of her substantial savings. Naturally she takes precautions to ensure that her life will be in no real danger, but news of her newly acquired poison spreads round the village, sowing the seeds of murderous intent in several people. And one of them will succeed in silencing her vicious tongue forever . . .

ISBN 978-0-7531-7848-5 (hb)
ISBN 978-0-7531-7849-2 (pb)